*"Do not run, Juliana," he said softly, reassuringly. "You have nothing to fear from me. You never did."*

It wasn't that easy, of course. She couldn't just turn off the panic at a word from him. Especially since his words didn't stop there.

"When I make love to you," he said, his eyes suddenly blazing, his deep voice curling inside her, making her knees weak, "you will come to me of your own free will. You will come to me because you want me the same way I want you."

A memory flashed into her mind, a memory she'd resolutely suppressed until now. And suddenly she was seeing Andre as she'd seen him all those years ago, his green eyes in a shaft of moonlight glowing with what she'd fooled herself into believing was love.

She was hearing his voice, that deep, throbbing voice she still heard in her dreams whispering in Zakharan, "Now it begins."

"Never," she whispered from a throat gone suddenly dry, fighting the sensual web he was weaving. Fighting herself. "Never again."

\* \* \*

Be sure to check out the next books
in Amelia Autin's exciting miniseries:
Man on a Mission—These heroes, working at home and
overseas, will do anything for justice, honor...and love.

\* \* \*

If you're on Twitter, tell us what you think of
Harlequin Romantic Suspense! #harlequinromsuspense

Dear Reader,

When I wrote *McKinnon's Royal Mission*, part of my Man on a Mission miniseries, two characters kept popping up, assuming more and more importance— my heroine's brother, King Andre Alexei IV of Zakhar, and her one-time best friend, the achingly beautiful Juliana Richardson, now an internationally famous movie star. Naturally, when I finished *McKinnon's Royal Mission* I had no choice but to let those two characters take me where they wanted to lead me. And what a story *King's Ransom* turned out to be! Royal intrigue, lovers reunited against all odds, the reenactment of a centuries-old love story and a villain who won't balk at murder to get what he wants.

I think every romance author falls a little bit in love with every hero she creates, and I'm no exception. While far from perfect, Andre embodies the best of what most of us look for in a hero—strong, faithful and true.

And my heroine, Juliana? She's the perfect foil for my hero. She's strong and just as determined as he is in her own way. She knows what she wants and goes after it without hesitation. She won't settle for second best, not in herself, and not in the man she loves. Juliana represents the best of who I would like to be...in another life.

I love hearing from my readers. Please email me at AmeliaAutin@aol.com and let me know what you think.

*Amelia Autin*

# KING'S RANSOM

## Amelia Autin

**HARLEQUIN**® ROMANTIC SUSPENSE

Recycling programs
for this product may
not exist in your area.

ISBN-13: 978-0-373-27924-1

King's Ransom

Copyright © 2015 by Amelia Autin Lam

**Printed in U.S.A.**

™ www.Harlequin.com

**Amelia Autin** is a voracious reader who can't bear to put a good book down...or part with it. Her bookshelves are crammed with books her husband periodically threatens to donate to a good cause, but he always relents...eventually.

Amelia returned to her first love, romance writing, after a long hiatus, during which she wrote numerous technical manuals and how-to guides, as well as designed and taught classes on a variety of subjects, including technical writing. She is a long-time member of Romance Writers of America (RWA), and served three years as its treasurer.

Amelia currently resides with her PhD engineer husband in quiet Vail, Arizona, where they can see the stars at night and have a "million-dollar view" of the Rincon Mountains from their backyard.

### Books by Amelia Autin

#### HARLEQUIN ROMANTIC SUSPENSE

#### SILHOUETTE INTIMATE MOMENTS

Visit the Author Profile page at Harlequin.com for more titles.

For my nephew, John Michael Autin, who gently goaded me into writing fiction again after many years...and probably doesn't even remember how he did it! How happy I am he met and married his true love, Kristy Len—he deserves the best, and he found it in Kristy. And for Vincent...always.

# Prologue

"*Absolutely* not!" Juliana Richardson told her lawyer agent with fierce determination.

Marty Devens stared at her in surprise. "But Juliana, you're already under contract—" he began before she cut him off.

"Break it." Her voice was implacable.

"I can't do that, and you know it. Not unless you have a damned good reason." His voice ended the sentence on an up note, turning the statement into a question.

Juliana had a damned good reason, but she couldn't tell Marty. Couldn't tell anyone.

"Besides," Marty coaxed, "you're the actress who always wants to film on location. You're the one who says nothing lends realism to historical movies like filming where the actual events occurred. I thought you'd be thrilled they received permission to film *King's Ran-*

*som* on location in Zakhar, and even within the royal palace itself."

Juliana walked to Marty's office window and gazed out at the sprawling city of Los Angeles below her. But she wasn't really seeing the city through the haze that hung over it like a sepia tint even on good days. She was seeing a lush green valley nestled between towering mountains, air fresh and clean, and Drago, the capital city of Zakhar, looking like a fairy-tale city from the sixteenth century dropped Brigadoon-like into the twenty-first century. She was seeing the royal palace there and the castle walls surrounding it as she'd seen it when she was fourteen, excited and thrilled to be attending her first reception in a real palace with her ambassador father.

*I can't go back to Zakhar,* she told herself, feeling suddenly eighteen again and oh so vulnerable. So defenseless. *I can't. I can't see Andre again. I'd rather die.*

Then she laughed bitterly as the mature twenty-nine-year-old she was now took over. *Don't be melodramatic, you baby. You've had eleven years to get over him. You're not eighteen anymore, and he can't break your heart again. Been there, done that. Where's your pride? You're an actress, damn it! A good one. Three months on location—how tough can it be to play a role for three months?*

"Juliana?" Marty's voice broke into her thoughts.

"What?" Her voice was husky with repressed emotion.

"Is it really that important to you? Not doing this movie?" He cleared his throat. "I'm your lawyer. Your agent. And your friend. The agent and the lawyer say hell no, we already signed the contract, but the friend says—"

"It's okay, Marty." Juliana swung around and pasted a smile on her face she knew didn't fool him one bit. She was going to have to work on that. If she couldn't fool Marty, there wasn't a snowball's chance she could fool *him* into thinking she no longer cared. "It's just that…well, never mind. It's a great part—almost as if it were written for me. And working with Dirk again on something with strong Oscar potential—how lucky can I be? Most actresses would kill for this opportunity."

*Most actresses,* she told herself as she turned away and stared out the window again. *But not me.* She blinked hard to hold back the real tears she hadn't shed for eleven years. Tears she'd sworn she'd never shed again over a man who wasn't worth a single tear.

# Chapter 1

King Andre Alexei IV of Zakhar, heir to a long line of imperious kings, absolute monarch in a world where absolute monarchs were extremely few, was royally pissed. He fixed his steely gaze on the master of the household and said in a soft voice that didn't fool anyone who heard it, "I thought I made myself perfectly clear with regard to the arrangements."

"Yes, Sire, you did," the man acknowledged stiffly. "But—"

"But what?"

"But the state apartments have always been reserved for immediate family or for visiting royalty." There was just a hint of outrage in his voice. "Since your mother's death, Your Majesty, no one has occupied the Queen's Suite except the Queen of England when she was here for your coronation three years ago. I had the maids prepare the suite formerly occupied by Princess Mara for Miss Richardson instead. It will be familiar to her, and I am sure she will be very happy th—"

"If the Queen's Suite is not ready to be occupied when Miss Richardson arrives, I will know the reason why." Andre's voice was even softer, and the elderly man in front of him quaked at the veiled threat in face and voice. The king was a gentleman as a general rule—kind, courteous and a wonderful employer to work for. Reasonable, too. But there was no doubt who ruled Zakhar—or this household. When he gave a direct order he expected it to be obeyed. Instantly. Not even forty years of faithful service would count when he looked and sounded this way.

Suddenly the king smiled. "Vladimir, old friend," he coaxed. "You have known me all my life. I learned court protocol at your knee. And many times you shielded Mara from my father's wrath—do you think I could forget that?" His smile faded. "But this is important to me. You cannot know how important. I realize it is a breach of state protocol, but do not fail me in this, old friend. Miss Richardson will be portraying Queen Eleonora in the film. I wish her to be treated as such, and not just in this way. In *every* way. She *will* be housed in the Queen's Suite."

Andre turned sharply and strode away before he betrayed himself any further. He'd worked tirelessly for this day for almost three years, ever since he ascended the throne. Now he would risk his future on one roll of the dice. But he wanted everything perfect beforehand. Everything that could be done to set the stage would be done. Then…if he lost…if he failed…he would have no one to blame except himself.

He'd been up since dawn, unable to sleep, knowing that in mere hours she would be here. Knowing that somewhere in the skies over the Atlantic Ocean, then over Europe, his men were closely guarding—albeit without her knowledge—the one woman for whom this entire endeavor had been undertaken. The woman for whom he'd paid the modern-day equivalent of a king's ransom to ensure she would finally return to Zakhar.

Juliana.

Even her name had the power to move him in ways he'd fought for years. Her memory burned white hot in his mind and his body. How many times had he cursed himself that he couldn't change his constant nature? How many times had he wished he was not a Marianescu? And how many times had he argued in his mind with the first Andre Alexei, only to hear the inevitable answer he did not want to hear, the same answer his namesake had implacably given to the church, to his Privy Council, to his subjects—*it is her...or no one.*

Forever and a day.

Most of the cast and crew of *King's Ransom* were already here and had been for several weeks: shooting exterior shots, scoping out the palace—especially the older wings—planning camera angles, testing lighting schemes and doing all the thousand and one things that went into making a blockbuster feature film. But the leads, the actor and actress who would portray the first King Andre Alexei and his beloved Queen Eleonora—Dirk DeWinter and Juliana Richardson—were arriving later this morning. And the grand, formal reception for the entire cast and crew was set for tonight in the Great Hall.

Restless energy pulsed through his body, and Andre

strode into the impressive Great Hall, with its massive mahogany pillars, three-story arched ceiling festooned with a grandiose display of gold inlay, and thick red-and-gold rug so immense it covered nearly the entire expanse of the floor.

Maids, footmen and equerries were hard at work preparing the room for the guests who would be there tonight. Banks of flowers and potted trees were being installed around the room, not just from the royal gardens but from professional nurseries in Drago and beyond, bringing the sweet freshness of the outdoors inside. The dust covers swathing the chandeliers had been removed, and in the morning light each prism sparkled and glittered, casting rainbow hues around the room. Tonight they would be even more dazzling.

Satisfied at the progress, Andre passed through the Great Hall to the Grand Staircase that led into it. He ignored the gilded, ornate railing and took the wide marble stairs to the second floor of the palace two at a time, his feet making no sound on the crimson carpet runner. Damon, Andre's personal bodyguard on duty today, followed him, scrambling to keep up.

His father had chosen his bodyguards when he was the Crown Prince. But once he ascended the throne he'd recruited his cousin Zax to head up the security force protecting him and had handpicked his bodyguards himself, men from his own unit in the Zakharian National Forces, men he'd trained with. Men he could trust with his life, who were also discreet.

Captains Damon Kostya and Lukas Branko were two of those men detached from the military to serve in the contingent guarding him. Damon was on duty today and Lukas would be on duty tonight during the reception. They were nearly fanatical in their devotion to him, to keeping him alive, sworn to protect him at all costs. As were all the men on his bodyguard detail. And they'd done a damned fine job so far through two assassination attempts in the past three years.

Normally Andre was considerate of his bodyguards, careful to make no sudden, unexpected moves that would take whomever was on duty by surprise. It wasn't his habit to make things more difficult for the men guarding him. But not today. He burst through the door to his suite of rooms, then turned abruptly. "Wait outside, Damon."

"But, Sire…" Damon obviously didn't like the idea of leaving his king unprotected, even in these relatively safe confines, but he acquiesced under the imperious expression on the face Andre turned on him. "Yes, Sire." Even though Damon had agreed, the king knew he would station himself right outside the door, within earshot. And he would fume and fret the entire time Andre was out of his sight.

Andre's elderly English valet was in the dressing room, humming to himself as he hung up on a stand the white gold-braided dress uniform the king would wear at the reception tonight. Brushing away a fleck of lint. Testing each button for a loose thread. Inspecting the belt, gold-handled sword and scabbard, ensuring the leather was polished to a high gloss and that there wasn't a spot of tarnish or a finger smudge on the steel. Checking everything twice so the king would be no less than perfect when he left his valet's hands. Normally Andre was amused at the way Sinclair fussed over his clothes, although he never let the other man fuss over him. But today wasn't a normal day, and Andre craved solitude.

"Later, Sinclair," he told his valet. "Come back later."

Alone finally, Andre glanced once at the large, intricately woven tapestry on one wall of the bedroom before he tore his thoughts away from it. Then he paced, reviewing every detail in his mind. As if by focusing on the minutiae he could push thoughts of Juliana to the background. As if he could quiet the eager pounding of his heart as it anticipated her arrival. Useless.

*"Propinquity is not love,"* Andre's father had reminded him repeatedly through the years, as he paraded one potential bride after another in front of his son's disinterested gaze. Refusing to believe what he didn't want to believe, despite knowing—as all Zakhar knew—that Marianescus mated for life. That they loved once…then never again. Refusing to believe his son's heart had been irrevocably given at such an early age.

*Not propinquity,* Andre told himself now. His father had been as wrong about that as he'd been wrong about everything regarding his children—especially his only son. Andre's love for Juliana had never had its roots in their close proximity, in their frequent encounters when they were younger. Eleven years without her would eventually have eradicated his love if that had been the case, but it had not. She was the other half of his soul—something he'd long since accepted, but that his father had always denied. And since Andre had despised his father for his treatment of Mara, father and son had rarely spoken except in confrontation. He'd never confided in his father that his love for Juliana burned like an eternal flame and always would—forever and a day.

He impatiently pushed open the French doors and strode out onto his private balcony. The balcony was another thing Andre's bodyguards didn't like. But the risk was slight. The royal palace stood on a hill above Drago, surrounded by a high castle wall patrolled by armed guards. No buildings were in gunshot range outside the wall, and there was very little that would give any would-be assassin cover as he lay in wait. Nevertheless, to a man Andre's bodyguards begged him to have a care how often he exposed himself on the balcony without them to protect him.

Andre wasn't thinking about that. He had something much more important on his mind right now, and he needed the escape the balcony brought him.

Usually the sight of Drago in the early-morning light, nestled in its green valley and ringed by towering mountains, calmed him. But not today. Now he clenched his fists against the stone railing, his eyes scanning the empty skies for the plane he knew would not arrive for some time. "Come to me, Juliana," he whispered, the words he had dreamed for years but had never dared to utter aloud. Until today. "Come to me."

The man picked up the newspaper, unfolded it and shook it out…then cursed. The headline blared what he'd known for weeks, so it wasn't the headline or the accompanying story that made him angry. It was the reminder that something he'd long ago thought he'd taken care of for good was coming back to haunt him, and the radiant pictures beneath the headline only added fuel to the fire of anger that surged within him.

"Damn you," he whispered to the photos.

He knew the ostensible reason why Juliana Richardson was returning to Zakhar after all these years. But he couldn't trust that secrets long buried wouldn't somehow resurface while she was here. Couldn't trust that the truth wouldn't somehow be revealed, destroying him and everything he'd plotted and planned for the past three years.

If he believed in God—which he didn't—he would almost have said God held the king in the palm of his hand, foiling the two covert attempts he'd made to remove the king from his path to greatness. But although he didn't believe in God, he did believe in the devil. And his two previous failures had recently prompted him to cut a deal with the devil himself—Aleksandrov Vishenko. The head of a particularly vicious branch of the *Bratva*—the Russian Mafia.

But now that Juliana Richardson was returning to Zakhar, it was no longer just the king he had to worry about. Unless he could find some way to keep Juliana away from Andre, or keep Andre away from Juliana, Juliana—sweet, beautiful Juliana—would have to die. There was really no other option.

Juliana put away the script she'd been studying and buckled her seat belt at the flight attendant's announcement. She glanced at Maddie Treister, her administrative assistant, sleeping peacefully in the first-class seat next to her, but since her seat belt was already fastened Juliana didn't feel the need to waken her yet. Her gaze slid across the aisle and she saw Dirk DeWinter buckling up. He'd already let his hair grow out into the shaggy length worn by men in the sixteenth century, and he'd dyed it several shades lighter than his usual brown pelt to match the paintings of the man he'd be playing in *King's Ransom*.

He wasn't wearing the green-tinted contact lenses yet, but she knew he would. He was a stickler for authenticity, just as she was, and he would have worn them even if they hadn't been required because it would help make him "feel the part." Like him, she would wear colored contact lenses, in her case to change her eye color from violet to pale blue, but at least she hadn't had to dye her hair—the two paintings of Queen Eleonora that had survived through the years showed her with long raven tresses similar to Juliana's own.

She smiled at Dirk and got his brilliant smile in return, the heart-stopping smile that had won him millions of female fans the world over. But Dirk was a man's man, too, despite his movie star looks. His appeal was universal. Men wanted to be like him on the silver screen—brave, strong, heroic and utterly irresistible to women. Women just wanted him. But at thirty-four, five years Juliana's senior, he was quietly, steadfastly faithful to his wife of twelve years, Sabrina, the lovely blonde who sat in the window seat next to him, gazing down with interested eyes at her first glimpse of Zakhar.

Dirk was one of Juliana's few male friends in Hollywood. He was also one among the tiny handful of men who'd never tried to seduce her. Probably the only man who really saw the vulnerable woman behind the glamorous facade. Dirk and Sabrina were the only people besides Marty who knew Juliana was dreading the return to Zakhar. But even they didn't know why. There were secrets in Zakhar she wanted to keep, even from her best friends.

"Did you sleep at all?" Dirk asked her, his knowing gaze sweeping over the faint shadows beneath her eyes.

"Not much." She'd finally dozed off shortly after dawn, but then she'd woken with a start, her heart pounding, hearing words she'd heard in her head many times over the years. *Come to me, Juliana. Come to me.* Loving words. Lying words.

"Didn't think so. And that's not you. You can usually sleep anywhere. Remember when we were on location in Death Valley two years ago? No one else could sleep in that searing oven…except you."

*Dirk knows me too well,* she told herself. Which wasn't surprising. She'd starred opposite him three times before in the past ten years, the last being the action-adventure flick set in Death Valley, San Francisco and Hong Kong—another hit for both of them. Such a resounding commercial success the studio was begging for a sequel, although so far Dirk had refused. *"No way,"* he'd told Juliana in private. *"There's nothing new that can be revealed about those characters."* And on his sage advice Juliana had refused, too.

Dirk had never steered her wrong. He'd been responsible for her big break in Hollywood right from the beginning, convincing the producers of her first movie to take a chance on an unknown. He'd already been a major star then—the marquee name that could sell a movie all on his own, so the producers had acceded to his wishes. Dirk had seen Juliana's screen test, had seen something in her that he knew would click with him onscreen, and after they'd talked in person he'd picked her over already established stars to play the heartbreakingly fragile Tessa opposite his Terry O'Dare in the movie adaptation of the runaway bestseller *Jetsam*.

Dirk's instincts hadn't played him false. They had sizzled on the screen for a variety of reasons, not the least of which was Juliana's petite stature next to his robust frame, which emphasized her fragile femininity and his uncompromising masculinity.

Now they were being paired up again for *King's Ransom*, and she knew why the producer had wanted both of them. Their on-screen chemistry ranked right up there with Tracy and Hepburn, Bogart and Bacall. Only more intense. And since movies had become more explicit since the heyday of those couples, even more sizzling.

Juliana had been excited by the script for *King's Ransom* when the part of Eleonora had been offered to her, and eager to work with Dirk again. Costume dramas in this day and age were always a risk for a movie studio. But the *King's Ransom* script contained thrilling battle scenes, not to mention incredibly romantic love scenes, and—as far as Juliana could tell—was almost religiously accurate in all the major details.

Great script, great director, a supporting cast she respected and Dirk DeWinter to star opposite her. Not to mention a studio willing to give the film the financial backing it needed. What more could an actress ask for? She *had* been excited about the role of Eleonora, as excited as Dirk still was about playing the first king of Zakhar…until she'd learned the movie was being shot on location. In Zakhar. In Drago. In and around the royal palace. Where—inevitably—she would encounter Andre again.

Juliana shut down that train of thought ruthlessly. *You will* not *remember,* she ordered herself forcefully, but she knew it was in vain. The memories already haunted her. They'd haunted her for eleven years. It was long past time for her to put those memories to rest where they belonged—in the graveyard of might-have-beens.

She wouldn't allow herself to care. Not anymore. *If you don't care, why did you bring that dress with you* to wear to the reception tonight? she asked herself derisively. *What are you trying to prove? And to whom?* It was a daring gown, designed to be worn with absolutely nothing beneath it. Designed to be worn by a woman who knew herself irresistible. *Well, that's true, isn't it?* she asked herself even more cynically. Millions of men lusted after her on the silver screen, the way women lusted after Dirk.

Millions of men…but not one in real life. Not one man who saw the plain girl she'd once been inside the beautiful woman she was now. Not one man who saw her need to be loved for who she was—her inner character—not the way she looked. Not one man who could ignite the fires of passion in a body that was ice-cold. Frigid. Doomed.

*That's another thing to blame Andre for,* she realized. *He killed that part of me. He ruined me for other men. How he would laugh to know that!*

The man presented his card of invitation to get into the reception—hiding behind a facile smile his resentment that he had to prove his right to be in attendance at this royal function. Then was forced to walk through the portable metal detector set up at the entrance to the Great Hall with all the other guests—again inducing resentment he refused to display to the king's men on duty there, even though their deferential attitude should have mollified him. No one would know from his expression that inside he was fuming. *My blood is as royal as the king's—I should be exempt, just as he is. I should not have to submit to this insult.*

The metal detector had been installed in the palace years ago by the current king's father. When the king

had ascended the throne three years earlier he'd wanted
it removed, but his objections had been overridden at
the insistence of the Privy Council and the king's own
bodyguards—the metal detector had stayed in place.
Not that a metal detector could detect any and all weapons, but it had definitely thinned the potential dangers
the king's bodyguards had to be on the lookout for during public occasions like this.

He glanced around the vast room, already filling up
even though it was early in the evening. He saw one of
the stars of the movie—Dirk DeWinter—standing head
and shoulders above the circle of adoring female fans
surrounding him. But Juliana Richardson—the other
star—was nowhere in sight. He didn't place much re-
liance on his being able to distract Juliana's attention
from Andre—she'd never had eyes for anyone except
Andre when he'd known her eleven years ago. But he
would try. If he wasn't successful…there was always
the alternative.

Knowing Juliana—and it was unlikely she'd changed
that much in the past eleven years despite her international fame—there would be opportunities to silence
her forever should it become necessary…and make it
appear an accident.

Juliana hadn't intended to make a dramatic entrance
at the reception. But she hadn't been able to resist the
oversize marble tub in the lavishly appointed bathroom
in her suite, and she'd indulged herself for almost an
hour. She'd washed her hair and let it air dry, thankful
she'd never had to do much with it—just brush it out
and let her natural wave do its thing.

Then she'd lain down on the large, incredibly comfortable bed, intending to just rest her eyes before the reception. But the lack of sleep on the plane had done her in. *Not just on the plane,* she'd sleepily acknowledged as she dozed off. She hadn't slept well ever since she'd known she would be returning to Zakhar.

She'd slept dreamlessly for the first time in weeks, her body too exhausted to do anything else. She never heard the rapping on her door, never roused until Maddie crept into the suite and then into her bedroom and shook her arm with a hushed, "Juliana! You're late! Everyone's asking about you!"

Juliana leaped into action and sent Maddie down to make her apologies. The household maid the palace had assigned to her had long since unpacked everything and put her things away. The dresses in the closet had already been steamed and pressed, ready for her to wear. Now she pulled out the full-length violet silk sheath that nearly matched the color of her eyes. Could she carry it off? Could she wear it the way it was intended to be worn, with no bra, no panties—not even a thong—and no pantyhose? Nothing except silk fabric clinging to her bare skin like a lover's caress, a daring side slit to midthigh. She'd bought the gown when she'd known she was coming back here. When she'd known she would see *him* again. It was a dress designed to make him remember…and regret.

*And he* will *regret,* she promised herself as cold anger shook her. Naked, she slithered into the tight sheath and zipped it up, then stepped into the matching violet-tinted pumps. With shaking hands she added the diamond-and-tanzanite choker and earrings her father had presented her with after she won her first Best

Actress award, because, he'd said with fond pride, they matched her eyes.

She quickly brushed her hair, swiped on a touch of lip gloss and added a dab of violet eye shadow to make her eyes even more mysterious. She didn't use eyeliner or mascara—her lashes were naturally long, dark and double-lashed. Then she spritzed herself with her favorite perfume, which she rarely wore. Not at $695 an ounce. But tonight she was pulling out all the stops. *If it's the last thing I do, I'll make him regret.*

# *Chapter 2*

Juliana made an entrance as she hesitated at the top of the Grand Staircase leading into the Great Hall. Conversation stopped for a full thirty seconds as heads turned toward her. There were a few sharply indrawn breaths and a few gasps—from women, of course—at the sight of a dress few women would have dared to wear.

Somewhere down there she knew Dirk and Sabrina were making the rounds, and sprinkled throughout were other people she knew—cast and crew. But Juliana had eyes for only one man in the glittering crowd, and she saw him instantly. Even without the royal uniform he wore she would have known him in a heartbeat, and at the sight of him a shaft of pain rippled through her, as unexpected as it was unwelcome.

He turned at the sudden hush and saw her. Then he was moving toward her with obvious intent through

the crowd that parted for him like the Red Sea before
Moses. Tall, regal and handsome—just as she remembered him all those years ago. Just as she remembered
him when she was a shy fourteen and he was the Crown
Prince—eighteen and already a man—welcoming her
to the palace. So handsome in full dress regalia then as
now, with his golden-brown hair and finely chiseled fea-
tures. So kind. So gentle with the shy, tongue-tied girl
she'd been, coaxing her into talking with those smiling
green eyes that invited confidences.

*Don't remember that now,* she warned herself. *Don't.*

He turned to the bodyguard following him like a
silent shadow and said something—she couldn't hear
what—but the man nodded acknowledgment of the
order he'd just received and faded back into the crowd,
although his eyes never left the man he was guarding.

When Andre reached her side at the top of the staircase, she said, "Your Majesty," and curtsied to him. But
she refused to bow her head, matching him in pride.
Playing a role, she held her hand out to him in the imperious manner of a woman who knows her own beauty
and expects homage—something she'd never done in
her life. But she'd planned just what she was going to
do when she met Andre again, how she would act, what
she would say. Every sleepless night she'd spent since
she'd known she was coming back here, she'd sworn
he would never know how he'd savaged her heart. He
would never know how much courage it took for her to
face him again after the humiliating end to their relationship. She wasn't about to betray herself now.

He took her hand in his, staring down into her eyes.
"Andre," he murmured in dissent, then went on to remind her, "You were never so formal before." He bent

over her suddenly trembling hand and pressed a formal kiss on the back of it. At least that's what it looked like to the other guests in the room below. Juliana knew differently. It wasn't a formal kiss. Andre was seducing her right there, in front of hundreds of people. His lips were warm, firm and masculine, yet so tender and seductive she shivered and her nipples tightened beneath the raw silk. The fabric rubbed against those hard little peaks, making them tighten even more, until they ached unbearably.

When he raised his head from her hand she saw from the knowing glint in his eyes that he knew the effect he was having on her. He *knew*. And he smiled, the satisfied smile of a man who knows he's a man, and that the woman with him knows it, too. It was *not* the expression Juliana had sworn to herself he would wear.

He drew her closer and tucked her hand under his arm. When she tried to draw it back he refused to let her go, and she reluctantly let him lead her down the stairway and into the Great Hall. The only way Juliana could have escaped would have been to make a scene, something she wasn't willing to do. Not here. Not yet. If she did that people might suspect she had something to hide, and her pride wouldn't let her give rise to gossip. Not only that, Andre might suspect…something. And she was fiercely determined he would know…nothing.

Laughter and chatter swirled around them, and sly, sidelong glances were cast their way. The massive chandelier overhead glittered with a thousand points of light, reflecting off the gilded ceiling and walls. Andre steered Juliana through the crowd, stopping courteously as people greeted her. But he never let go of her arm. And he never lost sight of his ultimate goal—a quiet alcove on the far side of the room, to which he eventually led her.

He briefly stopped a passing waiter and took a champagne flute, which he formally offered to her before taking one for himself. Then he saluted her with his glass and spoke for the first time since he'd met her at the top of the stairs, and his voice was just as she remembered. Deep, tender, with that barest hint of an accent to his English. "You are more beautiful in person than any woman has a right to be."

She stiffened. Was he mocking her? He'd known her when she hadn't been beautiful. When she'd been plain and awkward. He seemed to read her mind and shook his head slightly. "No, Juliana. Beauty of face and figure will fade. But your eyes, those windows into your soul, will always be beautiful to me. Forever and a day."

Those last four words stabbed at her heart. Once upon a time she'd prayed to hear those words from him. Once upon a time she'd thought he felt them, even if he didn't say them. But she'd been wrong. Horribly, heart-wrenchingly wrong. She'd paid the price of loving unwisely, while he...

Desperate to wound him as grievously as he had wounded her with his comment, Juliana drawled cynically, "Ah yes, those immortal words, *forever and a day*." She raised her champagne glass to him in a mocking toast. "To love. Im*mor*tal love. Isn't that why I'm here?"

Andre's eyes narrowed dangerously. "What do you mean by that?"

"*King's Ransom*. A love story for the ages," she said flippantly. "A fairy tale. As if any man, then or now, ever loved a woman that much." She tried for a carefree laugh, but couldn't prevent a tinge of bitterness from creeping in. Couldn't prevent her own life's experiences from coloring her perspective. "As if *any* man in that day and age would take a woman back who had shamed him in the eyes of the known world. Not to mention a king who could easily have the marriage annulled and have his pick of women. Chaste women."

She faltered at the icy expression in his eyes and the danger that radiated from him, so palpable she could feel it. She stared up at him, remembering Andre telling her the love story behind *King's Ransom*, the story of the founder of the House of Marianescu, the first king of Zakhar. Remembering how she'd hung on every word. Remembering how she'd believed in the immortal love the story represented—once upon a time.

Remembering, too, how she'd yearned to be a woman like Eleonora, who had inspired that kind of love in her husband, the first Andre Alexei. How she'd dreamed of someday making *her* Andre love her that way. *My Andre?* she told herself with redoubled cynicism. *He was never* my *Andre. What a fool I was. As if I ever meant anything to him other than another conquest.*

The frightening look in Andre's eyes faded. Then he smiled faintly as he slowly, deliberately looked her over from head to toe, and she knew he was aware she was naked beneath her dress. Something flickered in his eyes. Possessiveness. Desire. The sleeping wolf awakening at the sight of a helpless fawn. "Throughout history men have taken women for a variety of reasons." His gaze held hers prisoner. "Love is only one of them."

A frisson of fear ran down Juliana's spine, and in that instant she knew Andre wanted her. More than that, he was determined to have her. In a different century he would have just taken her—*droit de seigneur*—whether or not she wanted him, whether or not she already belonged to another man.

*But that can't happen today...can it?* she reasoned with herself, but the sudden pounding of her heart refused to be calmed. Zakhar was one of the last absolute monarchies left in the world, and the man standing in front of her was its king. If she just disappeared...who would know what had happened to her? Who would dare to question the king?

Her eyes widened and her breath quickened as her body automatically shifted into full panic mode—muscles tightening in a fight-or-flight reflex that told her to...*run, damn it! Run!* Her fear must have communicated itself to him, because his smile faded, and a tinge of some other emotion entered his gaze, something she couldn't decipher. It almost looked like... pain. But that didn't make sense...did it?

"Do not run, Juliana," he said softly, reassuringly. "You have nothing to fear from me. You never did." It wasn't that easy, of course. She couldn't just turn off the panic at a word from him. Especially since his words didn't stop there. "When I make love to you," he said, his eyes suddenly blazing, his deep voice curling inside her, making her knees weak, "you will come to me of your own free will. You will come to me because you want me the same way I want you." *Naked and trembling.* He didn't say the words, but his vivid green eyes told her he remembered.

A memory flashed into her mind, a memory she'd resolutely suppressed until now. And suddenly she was seeing Andre as she'd seen him all those years ago, his green eyes in a shaft of moonlight, glowing with what she'd fooled herself into believing was love. She was hearing his voice, that deep, throbbing voice she still heard in her dreams, whispering in Zakharan, *"Now it begins."*

"Never," she whispered from a throat gone suddenly dry, fighting the sensual web he was weaving. Fighting herself. "Never again."

His faint smile returned and his voice dropped a notch. "You *will* want me again, Juliana. That is a promise, not a threat. And when I take you, you will understand why." With that parting shot Andre turned on his heels and strode away.

*Arrogant.* Breath hissed out of Juliana as she watched him mingle with his other guests, so suave, so debonair, so much the gentleman king. But he hadn't been a gentleman with her. He'd been an arrogant savage, albeit with a kingly mask cloaking his wolfish intentions. She downed the glass of champagne in her hand, needing something to cool her parched throat. But that was a mistake. She'd had nothing to eat all day and the alcohol went right to her head, making her dizzy. *Maybe it's not the alcohol,* she thought wildly. *Maybe it's him.*

He turned just then, his eyes staring at her from across the vast room. Even though she couldn't see the color of his eyes at that distance, she felt those green orbs stripping her dress off until she shivered. And trembled. The power in him was incredible. It pulled at her, drawing her under his spell the way it had always done. He was a man, first and foremost. The king was secondary. But that was just as frightening as the idea that he might kidnap her and hold her captive until he was ready to let her go.

If he ever let her go.

Movement out of the corner of her eye made Juliana tear her gaze away from Andre, and she sighed gratefully as she saw Dirk and Sabrina nearing. Sabrina was wearing a sequined sky blue tunic belted over a long silver skirt, with the delicate filigree sapphire necklace and earrings that suited her. Juliana knew Dirk had given them to her as a pledge of his love years ago from the money he'd earned in his first starring role, and she wore them often. Like Juliana, she had "matched her eyes" with her dress, and from a distance she looked as lovely as she always did. But close up her smile looked forced, and there were two tiny lines of pain bracketing her mouth.

"Bree, are you okay? You look—"

Sabrina's smile widened, but it was an effort. "It's nothing, just a twinge, that's all." She turned in the direction where Juliana had been staring when she walked up. "That is a dangerous man," she said softly, and Juliana couldn't hide her sharp intake of breath. "He's why you didn't want to return to Zakhar." The eyes of the two women met, and Sabrina's were knowing, sympathetic.

Dirk spoke for the first time. "So that's the king of Zakhar. I've seen the portrait of the first king in the portrait gallery, and I must say there's an amazingly strong resemblance. You'd think after five centuries the genes would be diluted to the point where the resemblance would be nonexistent, but no." He reached over and rubbed the backs of his fingers comfortingly against Juliana's cheek. "He wants you, babe," he added casually. "And he looks like the kind of man who always gets what he wants."

"Dirk!" Sabrina's tone chided her husband, and he gently patted her arm.

"Don't worry, Bree. I'm not telling Juliana anything she doesn't already know." He glanced back at Juliana. "Am I." It wasn't a question.

"No." Her voice was husky. "But he's not going to have me." *Not ever again.*

"Want me to pound him into the ground for you?" he teased.

She laughed as he had intended her to do, although a little shakily. "I'll fight my own battles, thank you very much." She glanced from Dirk to Andre across the room, and back to Dirk again. Both men were close in age, of a similar height and weight, and in superb physical shape. But still… "If I were you," she drawled, teasing him back, "I wouldn't be too quick to take him on. He's a fighter. He trained with the Zakharian National Forces, and he doesn't look as if he's lost his edge."

Dirk spluttered with laughter and looked down at his wife. "Did you hear that, Bree? I think she just insulted my manhood."

Now it was Bree who patted *his* arm. "That's okay. You're man enough for me, honey, and that's all that counts." Husband and wife stared into each other's eyes, private smiles forming as they retreated to their own little world, and a pang of pain darted through Juliana when she saw the unshadowed love for each other in their faces.

Andre watched Juliana from afar, watched as she spoke with the man he recognized as Dirk DeWinter, the actor who would be portraying his legendary ancestor in *King's Ransom* opposite Juliana. His gaze sharpened into something cold and deadly when the man caressed Juliana's cheek in a comforting fashion. Juliana's name had never been linked romantically with DeWinter's. Nevertheless, Andre didn't want him touching Juliana, not for comfort or anything else. If anyone was going to comfort her, it would be him.

His bodyguard tonight, Captain Lukas Branko, stood two feet away, alert to any sudden betraying shift in the crowd, his eyes constantly on the move. Andre forcibly relaxed his tense muscles and tried to distract himself by thinking of something—anything—else, and his bodyguards' warnings came to mind.

This kind of duty in a large, diverse crowd of people was a nightmare for any bodyguard, Lukas and Damon had told him more than once, much less anyone as fanatically devoted to their assignment as they were. It wasn't just the devotion of subjects for their king, Andre knew. It wasn't just the devotion to duty of men for whom duty was honor. Lukas and Damon were not without ambition, but their ambitions for the past three years had all centered around one object— keeping King Andre Alexei IV alive. Alive and ruling over Zakhar for many years to come. No matter what they had to do. No matter if they died trying.

It was the "die trying" part neither Lukas nor Damon cared for, Andre also knew. Even more than his other bodyguards, die trying was an excuse to them, an excuse for which they had no patience and no forgiveness. They *would* keep their king safe, no matter who else had to die. Even if it meant taking the law into their own hands. Even if it meant disregarding a direct order from the very king whose word was law to them.

Their stance on the subject had amused Andre at

times, so much so he'd even discussed that contradiction in terms with his cousin Zax in one of their private meetings. But Zax hadn't been amused, Andre remembered now. And he wondered why that memory had suddenly occurred to him tonight of all nights.

He searched the throng of people for his cousin's face. *Maybe Zax can help me keep my mind off Juliana.* But he couldn't spot him in the overcrowded room. Then—despite ordering himself not to—Andre's gaze wandered inevitably back to Juliana, still standing with her friends where he'd left her.

He stared at her across the distance that separated them, wanting nothing more than to sweep her into his arms and carry her from the noisy, glittering crowd into the quiet sanctuary of his bedroom, the way he'd longed to do since the first moment she'd appeared at the top of the Grand Staircase tonight. Wanting nothing more than to make Juliana see what she was to him, what she had always been. Wanting to erase that hard, bitter edge he didn't understand but that he *knew* had to be an act, revealing the genuine, loving woman he remembered.

But she had to come to him. He could not force her. He could not make her. He had done everything humanly possible to get her this far, but that was as far as he could go. Now it was up to her. He could only do whatever lay in his power to convince her she belonged here in Zakhar. With him.

Her career was a stumbling block. She was at the height of her beauty, the height of her talent and power. It seemed as if there was nothing she couldn't accomplish in her career. No role she couldn't play.

On the other hand, there was no man in her life now, and had not been for several years. He was sure of it.

But he had not relied on the tabloids for that information. She'd been under the covert protection…and surveillance…of his agents ever since he'd ascended the throne. Ever since he'd acknowledged that the unbroken line of Marianescus ruling Zakhar for over five hundred years would be broken, unless…

The Privy Council was again pressuring him to marry and beget heirs. Delicately, to be sure, and some members more than others, but pressuring nevertheless. He'd managed to maintain his composure in the face of the subtle and not so subtle hints thrown out by the Privy Council regarding the topic of his marriage. He'd never succumbed to the intense pressure his father had placed on him—he wasn't succumbing to the Privy Council's pressure now.

Since women couldn't sit on the Zakharian throne, Andre's heir wasn't his sister, Mara. That was his cousin Zax, the oldest son of his deceased uncle Evander—and a year older than he was. Andre had never worried overmuch about the succession when he'd served in the Zakharian National Forces, not even when his unit was deployed to Afghanistan. He knew Zakhar would be in good hands with Zax at the helm, although it would have meant breaking the unbroken father-to-son direct line. But in the years since then, he'd recognized the supreme importance of that unbroken line—not to himself or his yet-to-be-born son, but to the people of Zakhar.

The Zakharians firmly believed the good fortune and prosperity their country had experienced throughout the centuries was somehow tied in with the House of Marianescu and the monarchy's father-to-son direct descent, from the first Andre Alexei to his oldest son, Raoul, right up to the present day. Superstition? No question.

But the average Zakharian citizen vehemently opposed tempting fate by breaking with the time-honored tradition. So Andre had every intention of acceding to the Privy Council's fervent wishes in the near future. Just not the way they expected.

Andre knew there were eyes all around them, watching, speculating, as if his life and Juliana's were just food for gossip, grist for the tabloid mill. He tore his gaze away from Juliana and smiled easily at the little group of men and women around him, joining in the inane conversation. No matter what, he had to shield Juliana from the tabloids if he could, the same way he'd shielded his sister, Mara, until her husband had come along to assume that responsibility. Perhaps that was an outdated attitude in this day and age, but he was Zakharian right down to his fingernails, and like his famous ancestor he would change for no man.

Just because he wasn't looking at Juliana didn't mean he couldn't see her, however. That heart-shaped face; those violet eyes fringed with long, natural, sooty lashes; those lips that looked so passionate yet somehow unkissable until a man saw the way the hesitant curve of her smile betrayed her vulnerability; the long, silky, ebony tresses that wreathed her face like a dark wavy halo and cascaded down her back.

She was perfection itself now, but that wasn't why he loved her. He remembered her as a coltish teenager, unsure of herself, unsure of the changes her body was going through as she metamorphosed from a girl into a woman. He had first loved her when she was sixteen and he was twenty, had loved her when only her violet eyes had conveyed a hint of the beautiful woman she would someday become.

But he had not touched her.

He had not touched her when she turned seventeen and began blossoming into a diminutive beauty standing just as high as his heart, not even when she practiced her newly discovered feminine wiles on him. He had teased her gently, turning aside her natural curiosity about men and women, deflecting her innocent desire for him, keeping her at a physical distance in a way that wouldn't seem like rejection to her sensitive soul.

Even the summer she turned eighteen he had not touched her, though by then her beauty made heads turn on the street, made men openly lust after her with their eyes. His body burned to possess hers that summer. He knew he could have her—Juliana's expressive eyes betrayed she ached for him the way he ached for her. Desire made him toss and turn in his bed so that he took to riding his stallion through the countryside late at night until they were both exhausted, then camping out in the rustic hillside cottage he'd made his own. Far away from the palace. Far away from the sleeping streets of Drago. Far away from temptation.

And he had not touched her.

She had tested his willpower to the breaking point, but it had held. Until the night before she left for college. Until the night she came to him like a silken dream…

As usual when Andre thought of Juliana, his body responded with a fierce surge of desire. He'd had a wealth of experience controlling that desire, and he tried to do so now. But it wasn't working. Not this time. Because Juliana was right there…just across the room. For the first time in eleven years he'd spoken with her, watched up close as those violet eyes changed hue with her emotions, saw the sudden fear ripple through her body, making her tremble and her nipples tighten under the violet silk sheath that caressed her body the way he longed to do. The gown she'd worn with nothing beneath it, *knowing* the effect it would have on him and every man who saw her. And then…knew she was remembering, as he did, one perfect night.

*Do not think of that,* he warned himself. *Not here. Not now. Not with the eyes of the world fastened upon you like vultures on a carcass.*

When he'd ascended the throne and had Zax assign men to protect Juliana, his cousin had asked in his blunt way if it wasn't possible Andre had built his love for Juliana into something more than it really was. That if he saw her again in person he might be able to get her out of his system.

Well, he'd seen Juliana in person. Finally. And Zax was wrong. He would never be free of the hold she had on him—heart, mind, body and soul. She was in his blood. In his DNA. Not that he'd spent the past eleven years doing nothing—he'd built a life of purpose without the woman he loved and had accomplished great things in the few short years of his reign. But as he'd told his sister, Mara, without Juliana he would be forever incomplete. *Come to me, Juliana,* he prayed silently. *Come to me.*

# Chapter 3

"Change of plans," the man said, sipping from a wineglass and gazing in Juliana's direction. "That may well be your first target instead. Before anything else."

"Juliana Richardson?" the Russian standing with him asked dubiously, instantly recognizing the famous face. "How does removing her achieve your goal?"

"Let me worry about that," the first man replied, his eyes hardening. "Trust me, I have a very good reason. You just prepare to do what you are told…should it become necessary."

The Russian laughed, a short bark of laughter that held no humor. "It is your money." His eyes were cold, with no redeeming touch of humanity in them, not even when he laughed. "A target is a target." He shrugged. "A pity she made an enemy of you." His gaze displayed a hint of curiosity, but no hesitation. "Security?"

"Assuredly. See the two men standing against the wall just behind her, with their eyes glued to her? They are not guests, although they pretend to be. Their sole purpose is to guard her—and there is not a thing I can do about it. You will just have to take that into account." He took another sip of wine—a bigger one this time—using the alcohol to give himself courage. *He is a tool to be used,* he reminded himself, needing the false courage engendered by the alcohol. *Not an equal.* "But do no more than prepare until I give the word. It may not be necessary."

"It will be arranged." A slight touch of contempt colored the Russian's tone. "At no risk to you, of course."

The first man's voice held nothing but ice. "There had better not be. Not with what is at stake—for everyone concerned."

Dirk excused himself for what he said would be a brief discussion with the film's producer, but Juliana and Sabrina made humorous faces at each other. They both knew once Dirk got started on a topic of conversation it would be difficult to drag him away. While they waited patiently for his return, the two women wandered toward one of the tall windows open to the night air along one endless wall. They didn't say much—theirs was an easy yet intimate friendship that didn't require constant chatter to fill any silence—and both women were guarding secrets.

Juliana knew why she wasn't ready to share anything about Andre with Sabrina. She'd never told *anyone* about that time in her life and didn't intend to start now. But she wondered what Sabrina was keeping from her. Her friend looked strange, unlike herself, and it wasn't merely the pain Sabrina was obviously suffering that she tried her best to hide. There was just something about her, something Juliana couldn't put her finger on. The faintest trace of trepidation combined with… suppressed excitement?

A hand touched her bare arm and a voice said, "Juliana."

She whirled around, her heart suddenly pounding again, but then she relaxed. The voice was similar to Andre's, deep and strong, but there was just a touch more of a Zakharian accent to this man's English. She smiled as she recognized him even though she hadn't seen him for eleven years.

"Hello, Zax. Good to see you again," she said honestly. Then another man came up behind Prince Xavier, and her smile faded. "Hello, Niko. Good to see you again, too," she lied with a straight face. She turned to introduce the two princes to Sabrina. "Your Highnesses, may I present my dearest friend, Sabrina DeWinter. Bree, this is…" She hesitated a second and looked up at Zax. "It's Crown Prince Xavier now, isn't it?"

Zax shrugged dismissively, then smiled down at Juliana. "Yes, until such time as Andre marries and has male heirs, which will no doubt be soon. I place little stock in the royal title, to be honest. I much prefer my military title." He turned to Sabrina, shook her hand and murmured formal words of welcome.

Juliana managed to hide the slicing pain Zax's words caused. For years she'd expected to read about Andre's engagement and subsequent marriage, and had steeled herself against it. But hearing Zax talk about it as if it were imminent… *Who?* she wondered feverishly. Of all the names that had been bandied about over the years as the next Queen of Zakhar, who was Andre's chosen one? And why wasn't she here tonight?

Niko cleared his throat and Juliana quickly brought her thoughts under control. "I'm sorry, Niko. Bree, this is Prince Nikolai, also of the House of Marianescu. Zax and Niko are the king's first cousins on his father's side."

Niko bent over Sabrina's hand and said suavely, "Ah yes, Mrs. DeWinter. I had the pleasure of meeting your husband—a marvelous actor, by the way—when I ran into him in the portrait gallery this afternoon."

Sabrina raised her eyebrows. "Really? Dirk didn't mention it." She withdrew her hand as soon as practicable, and Juliana shot her friend a sharp glance. Apparently Sabrina was equally unimpressed with the younger Zakharian prince.

"How is your father, Juliana?" Zax asked. "Is he enjoying his retirement?"

She smiled as she thought about her father. "My dad is still going strong at seventy-five—I hope I'm that active when I'm his age. He volunteers as a tutor at the local high school two days a week and distributes "Meals on Wheels" to seniors even older than he is on the weekdays he doesn't tutor."

They chatted desultorily for a few minutes after that, and Juliana assessed her old acquaintances. Zax looked older than she remembered, of course, but he'd already been a man when she'd left Zakhar, and the years had touched him nearly as lightly as they had Andre. His face was austere, and his bearing was as military as it had always been—she wasn't surprised to learn Zax was now a Lieutenant Colonel in the Zakharian Na-

tional Forces, on detached duty as head of security for
the king.

But it was his younger brother's appearance that truly
surprised her. Niko was only two years older than she
was, which meant he was two years younger than Andre
and three years younger than his older brother. But there
were already tiny lines of dissipation in his face. And
though he was still a handsome man—the Marianescu
good looks hadn't passed him by—the overall impres-
sion was of a man who'd indulged too often. Wine.
Food. Women. And drugs? Juliana never liked to think
of people she knew using drugs, even people she didn't
care for, but she wouldn't put it past him. The press had
dubbed him the playboy prince, and they weren't far
off. The moniker *wasn't* a compliment.

Juliana suddenly remembered how Niko had ignored
her in the early days, only displaying an interest in her
once she started showing signs of the beauty that had
eventually made her world famous. So very different
from Andre, who'd never treated her as an imposition
when she and Mara used to trail after him, who'd never
made her feel as if either of them were in the way. *And
this is important why?* she asked herself. Andre-then
and Andre-now weren't the same person. Maybe that
held true for Niko, too. Maybe he'd improved with age,
had become less self-centered, less self-important.

*But probably not,* she mused with a touch of cynicism, although she maintained an air of sweet interest
on the surface. She'd always seen right through Niko,
had seen his pursuit of her years ago for what it was.
From his appearance and the avid way he was acting
now, he hadn't changed one bit.

* * *

Zax showed up on the set nearly every day, but Juliana put that down to the meticulous way he did his job and not a particular interest in her. As head of security for the king, he was responsible for—among other things—making sure the cast and crew of *King's Ransom* weren't a threat to the king's safety in any way. They conversed sometimes when she had a few minutes between scenes—reminiscences for the most part—including memories of Juliana's father, who'd been the US Ambassador to Zakhar when she'd lived here. Although Zax reminded her poignantly of Andre in the way he looked, the way he spoke, even his mannerisms sometimes, and though she could tell he appreciated the beautiful woman she'd become, there was no spark and he never went beyond the line. He never said anything to which Juliana could take exception.

Niko also showed up on the set frequently over the next few weeks, and his presence watching the filming didn't bother Juliana one iota, any more than Zax's presence did. Nor did his attempts to get her alone cause her anything but amusement. Niko was just another in the long line of men who pursued her because of who and what she was—a status symbol. She'd dated men like Niko back in Hollywood, men who thought she was an easy mark. Not as many dates as the tabloids had trumpeted to the world, but a few. Like those Hollywood Lotharios, Niko would soon learn Juliana was no man's conquest, and eventually he'd lose interest.

The problem was, Andre occasionally visited the set, too, much to Juliana's dismay. Every scene was doubly hard to play with him there, and she never knew when he would show up. She had a well-deserved reputation with directors for being the consummate professional, able to do most scenes in one or two takes. That was something else she'd learned from Dirk.

But when Andre was there it was nearly impossible to act naturally. And more than once she was forced to apologize to the director and her fellow actors for some stupid screwup on her part, especially her scenes with Dirk. She told herself to ignore Andre. Told herself he was nothing to her now, no more than any casual acquaintance, so she shouldn't let him upset her. Told herself she didn't care what he thought of her, that the respect of her director, Dirk, the rest of the cast and the crew was all she cared about. But she was lying to herself, and she knew it.

She was dreading the two intimate love scenes scheduled for filming tomorrow: the wedding-night scene, where Eleonora and her husband consummated their wedding vows just hours before Andre Alexei was almost slain and Eleonora was kidnapped; and the reunion scene years later, after the king finally ransomed his queen and her young son at a cost that beggared his kingdom. A stupendous cost equivalent to a king's ransom, not just a queen's. And then had brought them home to Zakhar...to him.

The scene where Eleonora bravely confessed everything to her husband and offered to enter a convent to hide her shame and his—an offer Andre Alexei had adamantly refused. The scene where he made love to his wife so gently, so tenderly, she was finally able to respond to his lovemaking despite everything she'd endured in captivity.

That scene reminded her poignantly of a scene between Terry O'Dare and Tessa in *Jetsam*. Dirk had said the same thing to her when he'd first read the *King's Ransom* script, and they'd already discussed just how they were going to play it. But that made it incredibly intimate, more than just the words in the script. It was supposed to a closed set, with only the bare minimum cast and crew necessary to film both scenes. But who on the set would have the nerve to tell the king of Zakhar he couldn't be there?

Andre knew his presence on the set was having a negative effect on Juliana's abilities as an actress, and it bothered him not at all. He welcomed it as a sign she wasn't as indifferent to him as she pretended. But the night before the scheduled love scenes he knew he couldn't be there. He couldn't watch Dirk DeWinter and Juliana making love, take after take, angle after angle, fully and partially clothed. He knew the scenes would be tastefully done—Juliana was never fully naked in any of her films. And he knew it wasn't real, that they were merely actors playing the roles of the first king and queen of Zakhar. He still couldn't watch it.

*I should have ordered the screenwriter to remove those scenes from the script,* he told himself angrily. But in his heart he knew the scenes were necessary. The audiences *had* to see the love scenes, both before and after their long separation, in order to understand the eternal love that bound the two together even through years apart. They were actually beautifully written— the screenwriter had outdone herself.

But Andre couldn't watch those scenes being filmed. He also knew he would never be able to watch the completed movie—not with those scenes in it. It was too personal, would remind him too much of the one magical night he'd shared with Juliana. And if Juliana never came to him again, it would be like watching the nails being pounded into his own coffin, knowing that unlike his renowned predecessor, somehow he'd failed to win back the woman he loved.

He opened the French doors onto his private balcony, hesitated for only a second as he heard his bodyguards' warnings in his head, then walked out anyway. It wasn't that he thought himself invincible, but he couldn't live his life always afraid of assassination, even though in the three years of his rule he'd survived two attempts by traditionalists who resented the political and military changes Andre was trying to implement. One of those attempts he'd used as an excuse to send his sister, Mara, to Colorado, where she'd met and fallen in love with the man who was now her husband. So at least something good had come out of what could have been a national tragedy for most Zakharians.

He was a little more cautious these days—the attempts on his life had shaken him more than he cared to admit, and he no longer took unnecessary risks. But here in the palace—even exposed as he was on his private balcony—he was fairly safe.

Andre breathed deeply and looked down upon the twinkling lights of the sleeping city where he'd been born and raised, the city that was such a part of him he knew he could never live anywhere else even if he wasn't its ruler. There were precious memories here, too—memories of himself taking fourteen-year-old Juliana and his sister, Mara, thirteen, from one historical site to another, relating the history of Zakhar to them as they listened, spellbound. Juliana, even more than

Mara, had been captivated by the love story of the first Andre Alexei and his beloved Eleonora, and never tired of hearing him tell the tale.

Even that long ago he'd been drawn to Juliana. Her lovely violet eyes set in what was then a plain face had glowed with an inner light that told him she understood far beyond her tender age the anguish of lovers torn apart for years. The longing. The yearning. The hope and despair. And then, incredibly, the joyous reunion, never to be parted again in life. Not even in death.

They had stood together at the lovers' mausoleum in the royal cemetery as he translated the Latin script carved upon the walls for her:

*Two hearts as one,*
*Forever and a day.*

He'd watched the words seep into Juliana's soul, watched her eyes fill with tears of empathy for what the lovers had endured before being reunited. She had *felt* the story, the same way he always had.

He'd been immeasurably wounded when she'd mocked the love story the night of the reception. The Juliana he remembered could never have said those things, could never even have thought them. He'd struck back with a statement calculated to flick her on the raw. But then he'd seen the fear in her eyes, and that had wounded him far more. He'd never given Juliana reason to fear him. Even when he'd taken the gift she'd offered him so many years ago he'd shown her nothing but tenderness, had shown her how precious she was to him.

Once upon a time Juliana had believed in immortal love—he knew it. He didn't know what had happened to change that belief, but if he had anything to say about it she would believe again. Somehow he had to find a way to reach her. *Come to me, Juliana,* he urged, closing his eyes as if that would help deliver his silent plea. *Come to me.*

Juliana studied the next day's script lying in a bubble bath with a half dozen scented candles surrounding her, her favorite way to memorize lines. But somehow tonight it wasn't working. Instead of the intimate, romantic dialogue between the newly wedded king of Zakhar and his queen on their wedding night and the poignant reunion scene she was supposed to be committing to memory, she kept hearing Andre's voice in her head like a siren's song, calling her to him.

She could have sworn she'd heard him calling to her eleven years ago, the night before she was to leave Zakhar, the same way she was hearing him now. The same way she'd heard him calling to her over the years. She knew it was just her own yearning—her own desires—projected in her mind as Andre's voice calling to her. Usually she was able to block him out by focusing on a script, but not here in Zakhar. Not where everything reminded her of him. Not where everywhere she turned memories tugged her into wondering what had happened to the beau ideal prince she'd known.

She tried to drag her concentration back to the script, but it was impossible—the script itself reminded her of Andre. Too much. Finally she gave up. *I'll just have to get up extra early tomorrow morning and memorize,* she told herself.

She got out of the tub and dried herself off, then slipped on one of the oversize cotton T-shirts she preferred instead of the silky, slinky, diaphanous gowns the public imagined she wore to bed. This one had a picture of a sleeping pink-and-white kitten curled up on the front, and it came down to her knees. She crawled into the comfy bed, set her little traveling alarm clock and tried to force herself to sleep. Tried to block out the eerie sensation that Andre was calling to her.

*Come to me, Juliana. Come to me.*

She remembered how she'd woken from a restless sleep hearing him calling to her eleven years ago, and she'd gone to him in secret. They'd shared one luminous night, a night she would remember on her deathbed. But she would never go to him again. Would never sleep with him again. Would never let herself be vulnerable to him again.

Would never let him break her heart again.

Dirk came over to where Juliana was trying to get into character as she waited for the set to be ready. Both of them were already in costume, their colored contact lenses in place. The makeup artists had done their jobs well, making them look years younger. History had it that Andre Alexei had been twenty and Eleonora had been seventeen when they were wedded. Dirk had needed to erase a few years of living from his face in order to play the twenty-year-old king in this scene. Juliana had no wrinkles, not yet, but camera close-ups could be brutal. Her face still looked like her when the makeup artist was done, but her mirror had given her a pang. She had looked just that innocent, just that eager yet untouched when…

"Are you okay?" Dirk asked her quietly. "You look… haunted. Yeah, I know your character's about to be kidnapped, but you're not supposed to know that ahead of time. You're supposed to be deliriously happy on your wedding night."

Juliana shot him a quick glance, taking in the bleak expression on his face. "You don't look much better. What's wrong?"

He shook his head. "Nothing. Nothing's wrong." But his voice lacked conviction.

"Don't lie to me," Juliana insisted, placing a hand on his arm. "And don't pretend everything's okay. Something's wrong, I know it. It's Bree, isn't it? Please tell me."

Dirk hesitated, then took a deep breath. "You're the first to know—I'm quitting the business."

"What?" She was shocked.

"At least for the foreseeable future. I almost backed out of this picture, but Bree wouldn't let me." He laughed without humor. "She'd heard about the legendary love story, of course. Who hasn't? She wanted to come here to experience it firsthand, despite…"

"Despite what?" Her voice was small.

"Bree's sick, Juliana."

She looked at him sharply, remembering. "The night of the reception…she didn't look well."

"Yeah." His eyes squeezed shut in pain, and when he opened them again she saw her friend's naked torment. "The doctors won't say it, but I think she's dying."

"No." Juliana shook her head in denial. "How…? What…?"

"Don't let on you know. She doesn't want me to tell anyone yet, but I…I had to tell you. Third-stage ovarian cancer."

"Oh my God. Cancer? Third stage? Why didn't she tell me?"

"I don't think she'd even have told *me* if I hadn't forced it out of her."

"But…can't they do something? Anything? Surgery? Radiation? Chemotherapy? Cancer's not the death sentence it used to be. I know there's no guarantee, but Bree can't just do noth—"

His mouth was a hard line as he cut her off. "She won't even consider anything at this point." His voice was strained and ironic when he said, "She's pregnant. Just about ten weeks."

"Oh, Dirk…" Juliana looked at him helplessly, knowing the DeWinters had been trying for a baby almost as long as she'd known them. Very few people knew they'd pursued every avenue no matter how slim, even in vitro fertilization, with no success. Until now.

"When Bree heard the doctors say surgery can cause a miscarriage, she said surgery was out until the baby is born," Dirk said, reaching for stoicism. "When she heard chemotherapy isn't considered safe for the baby until the pregnancy is at least fifteen weeks along, she said chemo wasn't an option right now. And radiation treatment has to wait until the fetus is 'viable.' I asked Bree's doctors what the hell that meant, and they told me it means when the baby is far enough along to survive outside the womb—at least twenty-one or twenty-two weeks." His face twisted in agony. "I told her…" He took a deep, shuddering breath. "I told her I didn't care about the baby. All I care about is her. I want my wife, damn it! I would sacrifice our baby in a heartbeat if it meant saving Bree. But she won't even discuss it with me."

"She loves you," Juliana said softly, compassionately, understanding Sabrina's dilemma, and her choice, in a way that Dirk obviously didn't. Her own life? Or the life of the child she desperately wanted to give the man she loved? "So what are you going to do?"

"As soon as this picture wraps I'm taking Bree away. I don't know how much time I have left with her, but I want every minute, every second. She's mine until God takes her away from me, and I'm not going to waste a moment acting in some meaningless picture. We don't need the money. Even if we did, no amount of money could make it up to me for the time away from her." His face hardened. "And the minute she gives birth she's having surgery and going into chemo. I don't give a crap about bonding and breastfeeding, and all the other Holy Grail things of motherhood. I'm not giving her up without a fight no matter what. I can't force her to sacrifice her baby, but—"

Juliana's administrative assistant came over at that moment. "They're ready for you on the set, Juliana. And you, too, Mr. DeWinter."

Maddie cast a shy, adoring look at Dirk, one Juliana knew she had no idea was so obvious. *So young,* she thought sadly. *So vulnerable. Just like I was once upon a time, wearing her heart on her sleeve. At least with Dirk she'll never think he loves her. Not like I—*

She refused to let herself complete that thought. "Thanks, Maddie," Juliana said kindly. "Come on, Dirk." She took his hand in hers. "Let's go make love like there's no tomorrow." *I think we can both understand what that feels like.*

The man picked up the phone and dialed a number he'd been forced to memorize. *"Nothing in writing,"* the Russian had insisted. As he listened to the ringing on the other end, he told himself he had no choice. Juliana was no more immune to Andre now than she'd been eleven years ago—her reaction when Andre appeared on the set was a dead giveaway. To him, at least. As was Andre's reaction to her. So he would not let himself feel regret over what had to be done to safeguard his secrets. Juliana had brought this on herself. As had Andre.

Andre and his cousin Zax walked alone in the royal garden, watching silently for the most part as the sun set behind the mountains, casting long gray shadows over them both. Although they usually spoke their minds when they were together with a freedom they'd exercised since boyhood, now they guarded their innermost thoughts from each other. And Andre mourned what increasingly seemed to be the loss of the confidant he'd always relied on, especially since becoming king.

There was no man he trusted more than his cousin, but Zax was a traditionalist. The old ways were good enough for him, and he deplored many of the sweeping changes Andre was implementing. No matter what position Zax took in private, though, no matter how much he opposed what Andre proposed, in public he never said a word in criticism of the king. "The king has spoken" was Zax's usual reply to any reporter who dared to ask Zax's opinion on a new policy he disagreed with. *The equivalent of "No comment,"* Andre thought now will a rueful smile.

He cherished Zax's loyal support in public, just as he cherished his cousin's friendship. He just wished they didn't clash so often in private these days. And though at one time he'd confided his hopes and dreams about Juliana to Zax—something he'd recently confided to his sister, Mara, but to no other man—they hadn't spoken of Juliana since she'd returned to Zakhar to film *King's Ransom* other than to discuss the security surrounding her.

Not once had Zax asked Andre if there was any progress in the campaign to win Juliana's heart. Not once had he expressed empathy for the difficulties he knew Andre faced where she was concerned. And though Zax was not a man to display his emotions—he was too old-school Zakharian for that—not once had he shown by word or deed that he cared one way or the other if Andre was successful.

Not once. And Andre didn't know what to make of it.

# Chapter 4

Juliana woke early, knowing she had a free day from filming and wanting to make the most of it. None of the scenes scheduled that day involved her. She considered seeking out Sabrina and discussing with her friend what Dirk had revealed, but decided against it. Dirk had told her his wife didn't want anyone to know she was sick, possibly dying. Juliana couldn't betray Dirk's trust that way. *I'll have to think of a way to get Bree to confide in me.* In the meantime, she had something she needed to do on her own.

She dressed quickly in a long-sleeved silk blouse in a becoming shade of amethyst—a color she wore often because of her eyes—then neatly tucked it into her slacks and rolled up the sleeves for coolness, since the day promised to be warm. She considered doing something with her long hair, then shrugged and left it unbound but slid a clip into her purse—she could always twist her hair up later if it got too hot. She settled on comfortable walking shoes, then slipped away down the long hallway before most of the palace's residents were stirring.

Priceless objets d'art were on display everywhere—in glass cases as well as out in the open. And masterpieces by Rembrandt, Titian, Botticelli and a host of other famous painters hung in splendor from the walls she passed—paintings she remembered from the four years she'd been a constant visitor to the palace. She and Mara, Andre's sister, had been only a year apart in age. They'd attended the same private school and had been best friends for those four years—losing Mara's friendship had caused Juliana nearly as much heartache as losing Andre.

*You didn't lose Andre,* she reminded herself sternly. *He was never yours to lose.*

The guards were on duty, of course, but their job was to keep people out, not keep them in, so they didn't say anything to Juliana as she approached, just opened the massive doors for her so she could walk through. Then the guards on the gate did the same thing.

Once outside, Juliana took her time, wending her way through the narrow streets she remembered so well. Little had changed in Drago in eleven years. There was still that sense of walking in a sixteenth-century fairy-tale city, albeit one with strict sanitation rules that a real sixteenth-century city wouldn't have had. She chuckled to herself. Drago embodied the best of both worlds—she hadn't forgotten, not really—but she hadn't let herself remember because memories of Drago were all tied up with memories of Andre.

Juliana stopped for breakfast at a small café not too far from the royal cemetery—her eventual goal—and was glad to find the café she remembered was still there and hadn't made way for progress. She sat outside at one of the tiny tables and ordered coffee and a croissant. The square slowly came to life around her, and Juliana watched, enjoying the good memories it brought back.

When her breakfast arrived she thanked her smiling waitress in Zakharan and was rewarded with an even bigger smile. She knew the waitress recognized her as Juliana Richardson, but somehow it was different here in Drago, and her few words in the native language— rusty or not—carried more importance than her international fame. It would have been impossible for her to go most places by herself in the United States, but here in Drago she was relatively safe on her own. She'd known that even before she'd started out this morning. There were paparazzi here to be on guard against, just as anywhere in the world, but the average Zakharian citizen would respect her right to privacy.

Juliana continued to watch the activity in the square, remembering when Andre had brought Mara and her here on school holidays. Remembering feeling so honored to be with him. The citizens of Drago had loved their approachable, down-to-earth prince, and Andre had always lived up to their ideals.

He'd treated Juliana with the same gentle kindness he showed his own sister—teasing her gently, listening to her inchoate hopes and dreams, giving her advice on everything from her schoolwork, to horseback riding, to hiking the mountains around Drago, to the Zakharian boys who asked her out, including his own cousin Niko.

Until the summer before she left Zakhar to return

to the United States to start college. Until one unforgettable night…

Juliana's smile faded. That time in her life seemed so far away now, as distant from her as the emotions she refused to let herself feel…except when she was acting. That was different. When she was acting she could let her emotions run the gamut. Maybe that was why the critics loved her performances—all her pent-up emotions were allowed free rein. Joy and sorrow. Passion and pain. And agony. No one, the critics claimed, could portray agony the way Juliana could. Agony was easy. All she had to do was think of Andre.

She drank the last of her coffee and refused a refill, but she wasn't ready to leave, not quite yet. Tomorrow was the deathbed scene, and though she didn't really want to, she needed to visit the lovers' tomb in the royal cemetery. Needed to remember the story as Andre had related it to her when she was a young, impressionable teenager. Needed to remember how she'd understood Eleonora's actions that long-ago day, when the husband she loved more than life itself lay dying. She just wasn't quite ready for it, although she didn't want to acknowledge what that reluctance meant.

Juliana sighed eventually and rose, paid her bill and added a generous tip, then headed in the direction of the royal cemetery. She was just thinking to herself that Zakhar was blessed not having the kind of traffic that made driving in Hollywood and Los Angeles such a nightmare, when she stepped off the curb into the cobblestone cross street to the sound of a revving engine and squealing tires.

"Watch out!" A hard, male body tackled her, knocking the breath from her body and dragging her to safety

as a callous villain in her mind for years, and she didn't want to see him as vulnerable because then it would be difficult—if not impossible—to hate him.

*Hate?* The word bounced around in Juliana's mind and she caught her breath at the sudden realization. The opposite of love wasn't hate; it was *indifference*. Hate meant Andre still had control over her emotions. Hate meant those feelings of love weren't dead; they were merely suppressed. Pushed down to where they weren't a raw, open wound. But those wounds he'd inflicted weren't healed. Scar tissue had formed over them, but they were still tender, still aching to the touch. And she kept touching them. Couldn't help touching them. "No," she whispered, dismayed.

## Chapter 5

Soft footsteps sounded behind Juliana and she whirled. Andre stood there, his face wiped clean of emotion. "Why are you still here, Juliana?" he asked. "Waiting to twist the knife again?"

She gasped at his unexpected verbal assault and shook her head. "He…he wouldn't let me out." She raised a hand, indicating the elderly gatekeeper. "He said you told him to bar the gate."

"Ahhh. I see." He turned to the gatekeeper and spoke softly in colloquial Zakharan.

The old man nodded and quickly hobbled over to the gate, unlocked it and swung it wide. He bobbed his head at Juliana and muttered something she didn't understand, but his apologetic smile told her what he must have meant. "It is nothing," she assured the man in Zakharan with a smile, knowing it wasn't his fault. "A simple misunderstanding."

She passed through the gate and started to head back the way she came. Then she saw the magnificent black stallion tethered not far away, standing quietly. And just a few paces away was another man on horseback—Andre's bodyguard, the one she'd wondered about when Andre came to her alone in the cemetery. She knew the stallion had to be Andre's mount, but she was drawn admiringly to the horse's side. "Oh, you're a beauty, aren't you?" she whispered softly, careful not to startle the animal as she approached. The stallion let her caress his velvety nose, then run her hand along his withers under his ebony mane.

Forgetting for just a moment, she turned to Andre, not realizing this was the first real smile she'd given him since she returned to Zakhar. "What's his name?"

He stared silently down at her as if mesmerized for so long her smile faded into solemnity and she stared back at him. Finally he said, "His name is Charlemagne. He is half brother to Mara's horses, Alexander the Great and Suleiman the Magnificent."

Her brows drew together in a question. "Mara's horses? But didn't I read somewhere that Alexander the Great was *your* horse? Didn't he win the Grand National for you one year?"

His lips twitched into a faint smile and he made the fencing gesture indicating a hit…and a point. "You are well-informed," he said. "Yes, Alexander was mine, but no longer. I sold him for a fraction of his value to Mara when she married earlier this year—he was her wedding gift to her husband."

"Married?" She tilted her head up in a question. "I don't remember reading anything about that."

"New Year's Day. Very quiet. Very private. It was Mara's wish, and I—"

"And you could never deny her anything," she finished for him. "I remember that about you." She studied him for a moment. "Who did she marry?"

That faint smile came and went. "An American bastard who does not even know his father's name." Shock reverberated through her at his words, then her eyes narrowed in accusing fashion. He accurately read her accusation and explained ruefully, "That is his own definition of himself. I would rather have described him as a man who would give the blood from his veins to keep Mara safe, because she is his whole world."

"Oh, I'm so glad for Mara," Juliana said swiftly. "I always felt guilty that I—"

"That you never called her, never wrote to her after the first two months when you went away to college. She suffered under the loss of your friendship, little one. She never said anything—you know that was never her way—but I knew just the same. I had not thought you so cruel, so careless. Not to Mara."

She was stung by the accusation, knowing there was some truth to it, and at the same time startled and wounded by the use of his pet name for her so long ago—*little one*. She'd always been petite and seemingly fragile, but she had strength of will and a stamina that could put many men to shame. Next to Andre, however, who'd always towered over her since the first day she met him, *little one* had been an obvious endearment. And at the time she hadn't minded. On the contrary, she'd welcomed his having a pet name for her, the same way he'd had one for his sister. *Dernya*, which meant "little treasure" in Zakharan, was what he'd always called Mara. *Kolinya*, or the English translation, "little one," had been his choice for Juliana. It had made her feel precious. Cherished.

But Juliana hadn't expected to hear it on his lips ever again. Thrown off stride, she tried to defend herself. "I just *couldn't* remain friends with her. Not after…" She couldn't bring herself to say the words. Couldn't bring herself to talk about that terrible day she'd learned the truth about Andre…and about the fairy-tale world she'd been living in for two months.

His eyes darkened. "So I am to blame for that, as well?"

Pain welled up with such overwhelming force she couldn't hold it back. It slashed across her face, and the backs of her eyes prickled as a precursor to tears. She blinked rapidly, not wanting him to see her cry again. He closed his eyes, and if she hadn't known better she could almost have believed he couldn't bear to see her pain. But he'd authored her pain so many years ago maybe he'd forgotten. Was that possible? *Could* he have forgotten? Maybe he just *wanted* to forget, the way she wished she could. *I would give anything to forget,* her heart cried.

When Andre opened his eyes again Juliana saw that he had somehow retrieved that iron control over himself she remembered so well. "How did you come here, Juliana?"

If he could control himself and speak in a normal voice, so could she. "I walked."

"All the way from the palace?" He raised his head to look at the palace in the far distance, several miles away at least. "All by yourself?"

"I like walking."

He didn't smile, but his eyes softened. "I remember. But I cannot imagine you do much walking in Hollywood. Not alone."

"Not so much," she agreed, forcing herself to a semblance of a casual smile. "Fame carries a price." She indicated Andre's bodyguard. "I'm sure you know all about that."

Andre untied Charlemagne and quickly mounted with a creak of saddle leather. Then he held his hand out to her in imperious fashion. "Come. I will take you back."

She stared at his hand, suddenly afraid. It wouldn't be the first time they'd ridden double, with him mounted behind her. But she didn't think she could bear it. Didn't think she could bear the memories it would evoke of Andre and her in the soft light of early dawn, cradled lovingly, protectively in his arms. Or so she'd thought at the time.

She looked up at his face now and his eyes betrayed him. The memory she wanted so desperately to avoid was fresh in his mind, too. She stepped back, away from the memories, away from pain, and shook her head. "I'd rather walk."

Andre watched Juliana walking away from him, her head held high. He noted with passing approval that shortly after her departure a discreet shadow picked up her trail and followed her from a safe distance. In a corner of his mind he wondered why there weren't two shadows, but knew he'd get a report before too long that would explain the divergence from orders. But that wasn't really what he was focusing on.

He'd seen it in Juliana's eyes the way he knew she'd

seen it in his—she remembered as clearly he did the ride together down the mountain the day she left Zakhar so long ago. The first fingers of sunlight had not yet crept over the eastern sky, but dawn had already begun paling the dark blue of night. They'd ridden down together, even though Juliana had ridden her own horse up the mountain. He just couldn't bear to be parted from her one minute before he absolutely had to. And so he'd cradled her in his arms as they rode, the additional slight weight nothing to a fully rested Balthazar. Juliana's gelding had trailed along behind them on a leading rope.

*Do not go there,* his heart warned him. *Not now.*

By some miracle he managed to suppress that memory as he cantered back to the palace, his bodyguard a half length behind him, then took up the pressing duties that awaited him. The memory stayed successfully buried the rest of the day by sheer will. He met with the Privy Council as arranged for several hours that afternoon and managed to keep his mind on the serious business of running the country.

He met briefly with his cousin Zax to discuss the current threat assessment—and was perturbed by what had nearly happened to Juliana that morning. But he trusted Zax as he trusted no other man, and when he immediately ordered increased security he knew he didn't have to spell it out—Zax would know what needed to be done and wouldn't delay carrying out that command.

His appointments with the head of the Zakharian branch of the Red Cross and the delegation of international businessmen who were seeking investment opportunities in Zakhar went off without a hitch. A three-hour reception and state dinner with his cousins and the ambassadors of half a dozen countries, all vying for favored-nation status—Zakhar was small but strategically situated at a crossroads—was followed by a performance of the Zakharian Symphony Orchestra in the new Drago Performing Arts Hall in the ambassadors' honor.

Only Andre knew that all the while he was smiling politely and conversing with the ambassadors over dinner, he had no idea what he was eating. Only he knew that he heard nothing of the reportedly magnificent performance by the symphony orchestra beyond the opening bars of music. He'd stood to applaud when the ambassadors in the royal box stood, and had shouted "Bravo!" along with the rest of the audience. In between he fought a protracted battle with himself to hold back the memories that threatened to swamp him.

But when he finally slept he could no longer deny the one memory that had haunted him for years. The memory that had finally caused him to start setting things in motion three years ago to bring Juliana back to Zakhar. The memory Juliana so obviously wanted to forget.

Then the dream engulfed him.

Andre sighed and turned over, the simple cotton sheet rustling beneath him. It wasn't going to work tonight. He had ridden Balthazar until he'd finally taken pity on the horse and returned to this lonely, empty cottage, knowing it wasn't enough. That he wasn't exhausted enough to keep his desires at bay. Not tonight.

*One more night,* he'd told himself sternly as he groomed Balthazar, then led him into the stall, fed him and covered him with a blanket. *And then she will be thousands of miles away. Safe from herself...and me.*

But it had been a mistake to let himself think of Juliana, even in this way. Because thinking of her made him want her. Wanting her made him need her. And needing her was driving him insane. His body throbbed and ached for release. Not the release he could give himself, which he'd resorted to on far too many nights already, but the release he knew he could have with Juliana. Only with Juliana.

*She wants you,* an insidious little voice said inside his head as he turned over again. *You could have her. It would be so easy.*

Easy in one way, yes. Juliana loved him, and she would give him her body as willingly as she had given him her heart. He could make love to her as he'd yearned to do for the past two years. But he'd been having this same argument with himself—and winning—for those same two years. He wasn't falling into that trap now.

Because he knew himself, knew his constant nature. Knew he was like the first Andre Alexei, who had loved his Eleonora beyond all reason, even unto death. Making love to Juliana would seal his fate…and hers. He could never make love to her until it meant as much to her as it meant to him. Until she knew there could be no going back after that moment. Until she acknowledged she belonged to him the same way he belonged to her.

Forever and a day.

Eventually he dozed fretfully, only to dream of her. *Come to me, Juliana,* he dreamed. *Come to me.*

He woke to the sound of hoofbeats and a horse neighing softly. At first he thought he'd dreamed it, although that wasn't how his dreams usually ended. Then he heard a voice that was both dream and reality calling his name. He pulled on his riding breeches and was outside the cottage even before she'd dismounted.

"What are you doing here, Juliana?" he demanded harshly, his hand automatically grasping the reins below the bridle. She just gazed down at him in the moonlight, and she didn't have to say a word. He knew. "No," he told her, steeling himself against temptation.

She slid off her horse's back before he could stop her, and then she was standing so close to him he could feel her trembling. "Please," she said, her voice barely above a whisper. "I know you want me, too. I *know* it. I heard you calling to me. I can't go away without…"

"No," he said again, leading her horse to the tiny stable, putting distance between them as he cared for the horse. When he looked up from his task she was nowhere in sight.

"Juliana?" he called, but she didn't answer. He put the currycomb down and walked outside. Still no sign of her. But the door to the cottage was open the way he'd left it when he'd come outside. And he knew where she'd gone. "No," he whispered to himself. But the insidious little voice inside his head insisted, *Yes. Yes!*

The open doorway pulled him, lured him, and when he stood on the threshold he saw by moonlight what he'd known in his heart he would see. Juliana was sitting on the edge of the single bed, her clothes a pile on the floor where she'd dropped them in her haste to disrobe. If she'd been completely naked he might have been able to resist her. But she'd pulled the cotton top sheet so it was draped over the most vulnerable parts of her body, and that one insecure gesture pierced his defenses as nothing else could have.

"Juliana…" he said helplessly, his body reacting in

predictable fashion, blood pooling between his thighs, until he could count his heartbeats in the pulses.

"Please, Andre...I love you...and I have to know..."

From the safety of the doorway he said in a guttural voice, "You do not know what you are asking."

Her face resolved into a maturity that was unexpected, and the pleading look changed into determination. "Yes, I do know," she told him quietly in the voice of a woman, not a girl. "If you care for me at all, don't let me leave tomorrow without knowing what it means to be yours... just once. Please give me tonight. And let me give you tonight, too."

It swept over him like a tidal wave, the wanting and not having, the desire to hold her tight and never let her go, the need to show her how precious she was to him. And something more. The sure knowledge that he could no more walk away from the gift she was offering than he could walk out of his skin. He was shaking with the force of his desire, but one shred of sanity remained. One last chance for both of them. If he could make *her* run...

He quickly unzipped his riding breeches and stripped them off, letting her see him naked, letting her see the enormity of his need. Then he slowly walked toward her, until he stood only a step away. "*This* is what you are asking for, little one," he said softly, grasping himself crudely. "Is this really what you want? Me, inside you?"

He had hoped to shock her with his words, his size, with the realization of what was to come and the very real possibility of pain, but he was the one who was shocked. Without hesitation she reached out a hand and touched him, and a spark of electricity passed between them. Andre felt her touch everywhere, sizzling through him, leaving him gasping. His erection swelled even more, the skin feeling as if it would burst. And then it was too late. It had already been too late from the moment he'd seen her wearing nothing but moonlight and a cotton sheet.

Naked and trembling, he knelt before her, gazing deep into her eyes as he reached for the sheet…and tugged gently. Then she was naked and trembling, too, but not with fear. Desire. Desire that matched his. Her eyes told him she wasn't afraid, but they also told him what he already knew—this would be her first time with a man. Which meant he had to go slow. He had to build her desire to fever pitch before he did anything else.

If he could hold himself back. If it didn't kill him.

He reminded himself she had led a sheltered life. Her mother had died when she was a little girl, and though she was close to her ambassador father, it wasn't the kind of closeness a girl had with her mother. She might know the basics of what went where—impossible not to know that in this day and age—but he doubted she had any idea of everything he wanted to do to her. Would he shock her? Offend her? Or would she listen to her heart and know that every way he touched her was *right*… because he loved her?

She made room for him on the bed, her eyes on him betraying a nervousness she wouldn't acknowledge. She didn't know what to do with her arms, her legs, and they shifted restlessly. Then she lay back against the pillow and hesitantly parted her legs. He laughed softly, shaking his head. "No, little one. That is not the way. Not your first time. Not even your thousandth time." He brought his body gently over hers, feeling her tremors of uncertainty. And suddenly it wasn't so difficult to hold himself back. He smiled down at her and his voice was little more than a deep whisper when he said, "Let me show you, Juliana."

Juliana tossed and turned restlessly in her sleep, moaning to herself. The dream had come despite her stern warning to herself at bedtime. She wanted to stop the dream, but she couldn't, and now it was too late. The dream consumed her, controlled her. *Naked and trembling.*

Juliana knew the moment Andre surrendered to her… to the desire racking his beautiful body. His eyes, his face were transformed, and she thought, *He loves me. He couldn't look at me that way and not love me.* It gave her the courage she needed to be a woman for him, and not a girl shrinking away from her first sexual encounter. *But this isn't sex,* she reminded herself with joyous anticipation. *This is love—mine and his.*

She slid sideways on the bed, making room for him. Nervousness returned out of the blue, but she lay back against the pillow and hesitantly parted her legs. Then was startled by Andre's soft laughter as he rose over her. "No, little one," he told her. "That is not the way. Not your first time. Not even your thousandth time." His voice dropped. "Let me show you, Juliana."

With exquisite care and knowledge of women she didn't stop to question, he showed her. His big hands roamed her body, slowly, achingly, caressing every inch of her skin, building her desire step by incredible step. He was hot and hard against her, but he seemed to have an iron control over his body, because he refused to succumb to her frantic hands, her desperate pleas that he take her now...*now.* Instead he wove a magic spell as his hands lightly touched her here and there, until she was weeping from the beauty he created, until she was shaking and crying for him to release her.

She clung to him as tremors pulsed endlessly through her body, and he kissed away her tears. Then he moved, positioning himself at the damp portal of her womanhood, and thrust deeply. There was a brief, sharp pain, and Juliana couldn't hold back her sound of distress. But he was kissing her again, swallowing her pain and making it his own; his lips, his hands apologizing for having to hurt her this once.

"Never again," he promised her, remaining motionless.

Juliana sensed he was waiting for her body to accommodate his, waiting while her inner depths stretched and contracted, accepting his invasion, waiting while a fine sheen of sweat broke over his body from the strain she only vaguely understood. He was so deep, so tight; she couldn't believe they had ever been apart. Then he withdrew slowly, agonizingly, and the emptiness was unbearable. "No," she breathed, clutching at his hips until he filled her again with another sure thrust. And another.

"Now," he whispered to her in Zakharan, his eyes alight in the darkness. "Now it begins."

Juliana woke with tears on her cheeks. "Andre," she whispered, her throat aching. She didn't understand, would *never* understand how Andre could have made love to her with such exquisite tenderness, and then...

*Remember the rest,* she told herself savagely. She impatiently threw back the covers and rose, then moved to the open window and stared out at the sleeping streets of Drago at the bottom of the hill. She was angry with herself for crying for the moon, for crying for a fairy tale that had no basis in reality. Angry for shedding tears after all these years for a man so cruel, so uncaring he could humiliate her by sending agents to tell her he wanted nothing more to do with her.

She couldn't control her dreams, but she could control her waking thoughts. And while she acknowledged he had never seduced her—*he didn't have to; you threw yourself into his arms, into his bed,* she reminded herself, the memory a humiliating scourge in her mind—she could never forget he didn't even have the common decency to tell her himself that the one night she'd begged him for was all they would ever have.

Juliana wrapped her arms around herself as a cold hollow feeling settled in the pit of her stomach, remembering how she had wept through the night after his Zakharian agents had left—her heart breaking, her dreams shattered. Remembering how she'd asked herself again and again how the gentle prince she'd known for years, the tender lover who'd made her weep with ecstasy, could be the same man who had sent her *money* as a parting gift as if she had been a whore—used and discarded without a second thought.

No. Even if he could explain why he'd sent agents instead of telling her himself, she could never forgive him for the money and the degrading, soul-destroying words that had accompanied it. Never.

## Chapter 6

"Cut!" the director ordered.

"Save the lights," someone called out, and the hot lights were mercifully shut off. Juliana took a deep breath and expelled it slowly, evenly, letting the tension out at the same time. She wanted to wipe her forehead, but she knew better. The makeup team moved in quickly. One woman patted gently at Juliana's face, blotting the perspiration beading beneath her fluffy bangs. Somebody else handed Juliana a cold bottle of water, and she gave him a grateful smile before she drank thirstily. Work on her went on even as she drank— makeup touched up, hair brushed and the dresser assigned to her fussed over a streak of dust that had somehow mysteriously appeared on the back of her midnight blue velvet skirt. A few feet away Dirk was being given the same treatment.

The director came over to talk to Juliana and Dirk.

"That was good, really good, but not quite what I was hoping for. Let's try one more take, okay?"

"Sure," Dirk said.

"And this time, Dirk, see if you can add a little more…euphoria?…when you hear the news Eleonora gives you. I mean, this is the first child whose paternity won't be questioned. The first child after Eleonora was ransomed. Not to mention neither of you were sure Eleonora could even have more children after everything that happened to her."

Dirk was quiet for a moment, and Juliana gave him an anxious look. Then he smiled. "Sure thing."

After the director walked away, Juliana waited until everyone else had walked off the set, too, then said softly, "You okay?"

Dirk's smile faded, and the eyes he turned on Juliana were bleak. "It would be easier to express euphoria over Eleonora's pregnancy if I wasn't praying Bree would…"

"I know." She put her hand on Dirk's arm, wishing she knew what to say to him. "It would be easier for you to understand if you were a woman," she told him, her heart aching. "When a woman loves a man, really loves him, she wants to give him the immortality only his child can give him. No price is too high to pay, not even her own life." She breathed deeply, searching for something more she could share to make him see things from Sabrina's point of view.

"But that's not all," she said eventually. "To feel another life growing inside you, knowing it was created from the love the two of you share…this is what Bree is experiencing. I know it. Not that she doesn't want to live," she added, blinking hard against the emotions welling up in her, not wanting to ruin her makeup, "but we all die at some point. And giving you this gift means that no matter what, your love will live forever."

Dirk stared down at her, an arrested expression on his face. "I didn't think of it that way. I just… Thanks." He lifted her hand and kissed it. "Come on," he said. "Let's get this scene in the can so I can go find Bree and tell her I understand…finally."

Juliana and Dirk took their places on the set. When she turned her head she was startled to see Andre standing in the shadows, watching, his face hard and cold, one of the bodyguards who followed him everywhere right behind him. *How long has Andre been there?* she wondered. *And why is he upset?*

She thought about what she'd just told Dirk. The words had somehow poured out of her, and she realized she hadn't just been talking about Sabrina. She'd been talking about herself, too, about the way she'd felt toward Andre…once upon a time. At the time she'd prayed she was pregnant, wanting his child with an intensity she hadn't really understood until she found out it wasn't going to happen. But then she'd told herself it was probably for the best, that there would be other chances for them.

That was before she'd learned the truth. Before she'd learned that one chance was all she would ever have. And not just because Andre would never be hers. There would never be a child for her because there would never be another man whose child she would want to bear.

Andre watched Juliana touch DeWinter's arm and stare up at him, an expression of pleading on her face. He couldn't hear what she was saying, but whatever it was seemed to move DeWinter. When DeWinter raised Juliana's hand and kissed it something cold and terrifying sliced through him.

The fingers of Andre's right hand unconsciously curled into a fist. *DeWinter touched Juliana at the reception, too,* he remembered, *with his wife standing right there. Are they having an affair?* His cousin Niko's offhand comment yesterday about the apparent closeness and obvious affection between the two movie stars had flicked Andre on the raw, and he'd been hard-pressed to hide his reaction from his cousin's curiously intent stare. Somehow he'd managed it, had managed to present a front of casual indifference, but inside he'd been seething. He still was. Andre would never have believed the Juliana he knew could have an affair with a married man, but then…she had changed. She wasn't the woman he remembered. She was hard. Cold. Cynical.

Then he remembered her tears in front of the royal lovers' tomb and her well-known political stance as a children's rights activist, and he realized that despite recent evidence to the contrary she wasn't hard and cold. Cynical? Yes. But not hard and cold—she cared passionately. She'd been wounded, and the pain had turned her cynical. *Which of her lovers did it?* he wondered. *Which one broke her heart?* The tabloids, the celebrity magazines and the internet, his only sources of news of Juliana in the early years, had never even hinted her heart was broken. On the contrary, the stories had all indicated she was the original ice queen, moving from man to man but never giving her heart.

It was that last that had kept hope alive as year followed empty year. If Juliana had given her heart to no other man, then her heart could be won…by him. She had loved him once. She could love him again. He just had to find the key to unlock the mystery. If he knew *why* she had stopped loving him, he could change whatever it was in himself that needed changing. But if Juliana's heart had been broken it meant she had given her heart to another man. And if she had given her heart irretrievably—not just her body—then hope was dead.

He'd suffered the torments of the damned when Juliana dropped out of college after one year, went to Hollywood and took a lover instead of returning to Zakhar… and him. He could still remember the murderous rage that had possessed him when he returned from his tour of duty with the United Nations peacekeeping mission in Afghanistan and learned what Juliana had done. Could still remember finding himself standing in the midst of the wreckage he'd made of the cottage where they'd shared one luminous night—with absolutely no memory of taking it apart, piece by jagged piece. Only his hands, bruised and bleeding, bore mute testimony to what he'd done.

Then the madness that had gripped him evaporated, and sanity had returned. He'd fallen to his knees in the ruins and wept for the first and only time in his adult life. Not just for the loss of the woman he loved, but for the frightening glimpse of his true self, for the gentleman he *wasn't*. And he'd known even as he wept that somehow he'd brought this on himself, that if he hadn't surrendered to temptation as he'd sworn he wouldn't do, he wouldn't be paying for it now. That if he'd been a better man he wouldn't have lost Juliana.

That had been the turning point in his life. He'd vowed never again would he let himself lose control.

Never again would he succumb to temptation. Never again would that murderous rage be let loose. Somehow he would find the inner strength. And in doing so he would change himself into a man who deserved Juliana's love. Just as the first Andre Alexei had done, he would find a way to bring her back to him, no matter the cost. Somehow he would find a way to regain her love.

"Cut! And that's a wrap! Great job, Dirk. You, too, Juliana. Let's call it a day."

The director's words broke into Andre's consciousness, and he realized he'd been so caught up in his thoughts, his memories, that he hadn't even observed the scene that had just been filmed. Now he looked over to where DeWinter had stood with Juliana minutes before and was surprised to see the other man gone already. Juliana was still there, talking to the director about something, but as he watched she finished her discussion and started to leave. Grips were already tearing down the set, the lights, and moving the cameras preparatory to setting up the following day in another location within the palace. Juliana picked her way carefully through the disarray, holding her skirts up to avoid tripping over the wires everywhere.

Andre moved to intercept her, his bodyguard following him like a determined shadow. When Juliana saw who it was she stopped and looked up at him. He was so disconcerted by the pale blue color of her eyes, different from her normal violet hue, that at first he couldn't say anything. He slid his right hand into his pocket, feeling the small box there, and the reminder grounded him. Conscious that whatever he said would be overheard, he spoke a few carefully chosen words. "I need to talk to you."

Juliana blinked a couple of times. "Can it wait? I need to get out of costume, get this makeup off, and I really need to take my eyes out—they're starting to bother me." It was so unexpected he chuckled, and so did she. "I didn't word that quite right," she said, still laughing softly. "I need to remove my contact lenses. That's what I meant to say."

"How long will all that take?"

"A half hour? Maybe less. I need a shower, too, but if it's urgent I can wait for that."

"It is important, but not urgent. Have your shower. I will wait for you in the little library."

Even if the cast and crew of *King's Ransom* hadn't been shown over most of the palace in the early days, Juliana would have known where the little library was on the second floor, not far from Princess Mara's suite. She and Mara had often studied there when they were young. Mara had been a much better student than Juliana in just about every subject, but especially in math—Juliana had been hopeless and Mara had been gifted. Mara had tried to tutor her in math, but it was a lost cause.

The only area Juliana had excelled in was in recitation. She could speak blank verse as if it were simple English, and at one point had dreamed of being a Shakespearean actress like her famous mother—the mother who'd had a whirlwind romance with Juliana's ambassador father and died when her daughter was barely four. But the demand for Shakespearean actresses being what it was, when Juliana had decided to forget college and become an actress she'd headed for Hollywood.

Dressed in a floating sleeveless pale primrose summer dress belted around her tiny waist, sandals on her slender feet, her hair piled atop her head for coolness and held in place with a pair of cloisonné butterfly clips, Juliana hurried toward the little library forty minutes later. Andre's bodyguard was standing in front of the closed door, but he opened it and moved aside as she approached—he'd obviously received orders to let her pass without challenge. Then the door was quietly closed behind her.

"Little library" was a misnomer. It was little only in comparison to the Royal Library on the main floor. Andre was ensconced in one of the large, comfortable easy chairs scattered around the room, reading what looked to be official dispatches. Juliana remembered him doing something similar years ago while she and Mara studied, their books spread out on the antique table in the center of the room.

"I'm sorry I'm late," she said. "I couldn't resist taking a bath instead of a shower. The suite I'm in has the most amazing marble bathtub."

"The Queen's Suite," he said easily, closing the portfolio of dispatches with a snap. "Yes, the bathtub there is the biggest I've ever seen—it is bigger than mine."

Startled, she said, "The Queen's Suite? I didn't realize... Mara once said your father had that sealed off after your mother died and no one was allowed inside. We never even dared to sneak inside for a peek."

"Yes, it was closed for years, but it was reopened at the time of my coronation. I believe the Queen of England occupied it at that point, but no one since." His voice dropped a notch. "Eleonora's suite has been waiting for you, Juliana."

Something in his tone disturbed her, but she couldn't

put her finger on it. For something to say, she asked, "Was it really Eleonora's?"

"So legend has it, but all the queens of Zakhar in recent memory have occupied it. It has been extensively remodeled numerous times over the years, of course. Candle sconces replaced the torches. Then gaslight replaced the candle sconces. What was then modern plumbing was added, although a plumber today would laugh at it. Then electrical wiring replaced the gaslight. And truly modern plumbing was added in my grandmother's day. My mother loved it—I have vague childhood memories of her in that suite when I was very young—and she added her own touches." He smiled at her, a smile of singular sweetness. "You are comfortable there?"

"Incredibly. I've felt like a queen since the very first day."

His smile grew. "That was my intention."

Suddenly nervous for no reason she could think of, Juliana wandered over to the table in the center of the room. "How well I remember this table," she said, running her hand over its polished surface, loving the smooth feel of the wood beneath her fingertips.

"Yes, I imagine you would."

Her gaze fell on the portrait of Andre's father done at the time of his coronation, his wife at his side—both staring out at the world in haughty superiority. She'd met Andre's father, of course, but his mother had died when Mara was born. It was one of the things she and Andre had in common—he'd lost his mother at a young age, too. Now as she contemplated the picture she realized just how much Mara resembled her dead mother physically, if not in any other way. Regal beauty was reflected in the face of the woman in the portrait, but no sweetness, unlike her daughter. There had been a sweetness about Mara, Juliana remembered, an emotional vulnerability that had made Juliana want to shield her from hurt...just as Andre had always tried to do.

"So tell me about Mara," she said, succumbing to the sudden longing to know how her onetime friend was doing. "How is she? I remember reading that she received her PhD in math from Oxford University. That was her dream, I know. I was so happy for her I—" *Almost called her,* Juliana nearly said. But for some reason she didn't want Andre to know how tempted she'd been to reconnect with Mara despite everything.

"Mara is a professor at the University of Colorado. She and her husband live in Boulder."

Juliana laughed a little, shaking her head. "I still can't believe she's married and it never made the news. I didn't even know she was in the States."

Andre smiled as if at a private joke. "I sent her there."

"Why?"

"Because I hoped she would find there what she could never find here—and she did."

Juliana wanted to ask what that was, then realized she and Andre were conversing as if they were old friends. As if what had happened eleven years ago had never happened. She wandered toward the bookshelves, running her fingers over the leather bound tomes, then took a deep breath, and with her back to him asked as casually as she could, "So why did you want to talk to me?"

"I need to know. Are you and DeWinter lovers?"

Juliana whirled around, her face pale with shock. "You have no right to ask me that."

He considered her answer for a moment, then nodded thoughtfully. He stood and placed the portfolio on a side table. Then he walked toward her, stopping a few feet away, his hands in his pockets, his stance casual. "Then answer me this. Are you in love with him?"

"You have no right to ask me that, either." Her voice was tight with repressed anger. *"Your Majesty."* She threw those last two words at him as an insult.

"Perhaps not. But I am asking anyway. And you will not leave this room without giving me an answer." His seemingly indifferent tone was belied by his words… and his eyes. His eyes were bright green, blazing with some emotion she couldn't put a name to, and she knew he meant exactly what he said. Whether he had the right or not, Andre was just stubborn enough to keep her there until she responded, one way or the other.

She took two steps toward him. "No. I'm not in love with Dirk. And no, we're not lovers. We've *never* been lovers." Her eyes burned with tears of humiliation she refused to shed as her anger built. "He's my friend. His *wife* is my friend. How *dare* you ask me that!" Her chest was heaving with anger, hurt and a half dozen other emotions that swirled through her.

He didn't respond at first, just stood there watching her in that assessing way he had. Then he asked quietly, "If you are not in love with him, then why were you pleading with him between takes this afternoon?"

Her hand came up to her throat, where she could feel her pulse racing. "Because…" she began, but didn't go on because Dirk had told her about Sabrina in confidence and she wasn't about to betray it. Especially not to Andre.

"Because why?" His voice was quiet but implacable.

"That is absolutely none of your business."

He shook his head. "You are wrong, Juliana," he explained patiently. "*You* are my business. Anything to do with you is my business." Her mouth dropped open in amazement but she was too stunned to say anything. "If I must ask DeWinter, I will."

"Don't you dare ask Dirk anything!"

"Then you tell me."

"You have no right!" She was almost shouting now.

"I have the right you granted me eleven years ago," he said softly, evenly.

Every drop of blood drained from her face, and she felt light-headed, dizzy. And cold. The warm summer day vanished, and she shivered violently. "How dare you use that night to justify your actions now," she whispered, wrapping her arms around her waist to keep from shaking uncontrollably. "How dare you!"

"Juliana, I..." Suddenly she found herself in his embrace, his arms tight bands around her, her head pressed against his chest. And though everything in her rejected the idea of accepting *anything* from him, especially comfort, for a brief moment she stayed where she was. His heart was beating, beating, beating beneath her ear, and she remembered lying close beside him in that single bed in the cottage, her head pillowed on his shoulder, hearing his heartbeat exactly the same way.

"Tell me, Juliana," he whispered, his strong hand stroking the nape of her neck with exquisite, insidious tenderness. "If not DeWinter, then who? Someone hurt you. Someone broke your heart. Tell me, little one," he coaxed. "Tell me who it was."

She jerked herself out of his arms, appalled at both herself and him. Appalled at herself that she could let him hold her even for a minute. And appalled at him that he had the gall to ask her that question. How could he not know? After what he'd done, how could he possibly think anyone but he had broken her heart? "You," she said, wanting to hurt him as she was hurting. "It was you."

His brows drew together in a frown, and his face was stern. "Do not lie to me, Juliana. Your heart was not broken when you chose to go to Hollywood instead of returning to Zakhar that summer."

She gasped at how he was twisting the facts, and in defense she resorted to sarcasm. "And of course I would have known you wanted me to return to Zakhar because of your numerous phone calls, your impassioned pleas. Oh, that's right," she said, snapping her fingers. "You never asked me to return. Instead you—"

The flush on his cheekbones was the only sign her sarcasm had hit its target. "You should know why I never asked you to return. I expl—"

Juliana cut him off as he had done to her. "You're right. I do know." *You didn't love me. You didn't want me. You sent your men to tell me to stop bothering you with my love letters and emails. And you sent me money. You had to know that would be the most hurtful thing you could do to me, giving me money for—*

She couldn't even finish the thought—the wound was still too painful, even after all these years. "So don't pretend you don't understand why I didn't return to Zakhar," she threw at him.

Now his anger rose to match hers. "And taking a lover? What was that? Experimentation? Comparison? Wanting to see how I measured up?" Her hand came up of its own volition to slap him, but he was too quick for her, and he caught her hand before it could make contact. "No," he said implacably, forcing her arm down. "I may have deserved it at one time, but not for this." His whole body tensed. "I was not…sane…when I heard what you had done."

Denial rose to her lips, despite the fact that he had no right to know anything, no right to question her actions. No rights at all where she was concerned. "I didn't—"

*"Do not lie to me!"*

Immeasurably wounded by his accusation that she was lying despite telling herself not to be, she shot back, "Believe what you want. I don't have to justify myself to you. But believe this, too," she said fiercely. "You may have been the first, but that doesn't give you ownership of me. Whether I've had a hundred other lovers or none, it's not your concern. It never was. Not then, and certainly not now."

"That is where you are wrong, Juliana." He'd quickly regained his control, but his face was steely with resolve when he said, "It was always my concern. You belonged to me then. You belong to me now. The same way I belong to you—forever and a day. And from this moment on you will have no other lover but me. That is not a threat. Just a fact." He turned and strode toward the library door, scooping up the portfolio on his way out. He paused on the threshold and looked back, his eyes blazing. "Count on it."

## Chapter 7

Andre stormed into his secluded private office off his suite of rooms and slammed the portfolio of dispatches on his desk. "Out!" he ordered his bodyguard with unwonted harshness, unexpectedly irked by the lack of privacy he normally took for granted—at least until Juliana had reentered his life. As soon as he was alone he uttered an earthy, Zakharan curse, and it felt so good he repeated it, but the second time didn't give him the same satisfaction.

Too wound up to settle, he paced the large room, back and forth, back and forth. Angry with Juliana. Angry with himself. More angry with himself than with her because he hadn't meant to confront her, hadn't meant to accuse her. And he damned well hadn't meant to throw the threat at her that he had every intention of being her lover again...now and forever. Because it *had* been a threat, no matter what he'd told her. A threat. A promise. A plea.

He stopped pacing and sank into the leather-and-ebony chair behind his desk, disillusion battling with despair for dominance. *This is not working out the way I had hoped,* he thought sadly. *The way I had planned.* He drew the small box out of his pocket and flicked it open, then set it on the desk before him and stared at the ring it contained for several seconds, the central stone reminding him poignantly of Juliana's eyes. *Why did I think it would be easy after all these years?*

He couldn't get it out of his mind there was something he wasn't seeing with regard to Juliana. Something she wasn't telling him. Something important. He still thought it had something to do with DeWinter despite her denials. And if she wouldn't tell him, he would just have to get his answers out of the other man. No matter what he had to do to get them.

Andre left the ancient dining hall where the household staff was serving a buffet dinner to the cast and crew of *King's Ransom.* He'd already learned neither DeWinter nor his wife were in attendance. Nor Juliana for that matter, but for once his eyes weren't seeking her out. He was going to get answers. If not from Juliana, then from DeWinter. To that end he'd ordered his bodyguard to stay behind—over the man's vehement objections—because he needed privacy for what he was going to do, what he was going to ask.

But before he could head up the Grand Staircase, his cousin Zax caught up with him. "Andre! A moment, please!"

He paused with his foot on the first step and turned. "Can it wait, Zax?"

"No."

Andre sighed, but not so his cousin would notice. "What is so urgent?"

Zax's normally austere expression was even more forbidding than usual. "What is this rumor I hear that you are considering allowing women in combat?"

"It is no rumor. I intend to bring it to a vote before the Privy Council later this week."

"You are pushing too far too fast, Andre," Zax warned. "Was it not bad enough your first royal proclamation threw open the doors to allow women to serve in the military?"

"Are you still on that? It has been three years."

"Auxiliary service behind the line was bad enough. But now you want women in combat? Serving alongside men?"

"Combat service will not be mandatory," Andre explained in his reasonable way. "That was never my intent. Just as military service is completely optional for women, so, too, will combat service be optional. You have no sister, so perhaps you do not see this the same way I do. But Mara is right when she says women should make the decision for themselves—that career path should not be arbitrarily denied them merely because they are women."

Zax ground his teeth. "Mara is wrong. Combat is no place for women. You should know that—would you have wanted women serving beside you in Afghanistan? I certainly would not, not even as chopper pilots doing search and rescue as I did, or medevac. You are asking too much of the people this time. And the military—"

Andre cut his cousin off. "What of the military?"

"The men have remained loyal to you through all the other changes you have implemented, politically and militarily. But this may be the last straw."

Andre gave Zax a steady look. "It is the right thing to do. If I must compromise my conscience to retain my throne, I will surrender the throne and keep my self-respect."

Zax made a gesture of frustration. "It is not a matter of surrendering your throne—nothing so easy as that. You are playing with fire, Andre. Two assassination attempts in the past three years by traditionalists—"

"Like you."

His cousin's eyes hardened but he nodded. "Yes. Traditionalists, like me. Men who opposed the changes you implemented. Two attempts—foiled by the grace of God."

"The grace of God—and the devotion of the men guarding me," Andre corrected. "The would-be assassins are dead and I am still alive."

"And I am ultimately responsible for keeping you safe despite yourself. Despite your actions that make you even more of a target than you would otherwise be. Do you know how difficult that is? Hell, Andre, I can think of a half dozen ways to kill you myself, at no risk to me."

Andre smiled his faint smile. "Then it is a good thing you are on my side, is it not?" he said gently. He placed a conciliatory hand on his cousin's shoulder. "We can discuss this further, but not now, if you please. Come see me tomorrow morning—marshal your arguments and I will listen to what you have to say, I promise. Tell my appointments secretary I said to make room in the schedule for you."

He waited for Zax's reluctant assent and watched until his cousin was out of sight, a slight frown furrowing his brow. Things had grown so strained between them these past few weeks. And now he wondered how Zax had heard about his latest proposition. Someone on the Privy Council must have talked—there was no other explanation. Had whomever it was hoped Zax could dissuade him from pursuing this course?

He continued on to the DeWinters' suite and knocked on the door, mentally shelving one problem to confront another, but his sharp rap wasn't answered immediately. Impatient, he knocked again, harder this time.

"Just a minute!" The solid oak door was jerked open suddenly, and DeWinter stood there, a casually inquisitive expression on his face that turned into surprise when he saw the king framed in the doorway. The surprise quickly turned into something else. "I'll be damned," he said softly. "Bree was right."

"Accept my apologies for the intrusion on you and your wife." Good manners dictated the apology, but despite Zax's earlier interruption Andre was riding with his emotions on a curb bit, so his tone was perfunctory. "I must speak with you…about Juliana."

"Who is it, Dirk?" Sabrina came up behind her husband. "Oh." She glanced from Andre's hard, set expression to her husband's dawning smile, and she put a restraining hand on his arm. "Honey, I don't think—"

He cut her off. "I know you don't, but it's okay," he reassured her. He looked back at Andre and cocked a questioning eyebrow. There was also a bit of a challenge in his eyes, in his stance. "What did you want to know…about Juliana?"

Andre's gaze slid toward Sabrina. "Privately," he insisted after turning his attention back to DeWinter. The two men assessed each other like gamecocks, each noting the strengths in the other man…and seeking out the weaknesses, the chinks in the other's armor. Then came the realization in both sets of eyes that there *were* no weaknesses to exploit. Andre inclined his head slightly, acknowledging an equal. "Walk with me," he demanded softly.

"Dirk, I—"

"It's really okay," he told his wife. "I'll be back shortly. I promise."

The two men strode silently but purposefully back down the East Wing's lengthy hallway, then down the Grand Staircase, the king leading the way. The two guards at the front doors snapped to attention and saluted when Andre came into sight, but he turned away to a side corridor. "This way," he said, leading the other man into the music room.

Andre locked the door and stood with his back to it for a moment, watching silently as DeWinter wandered toward the grand piano on a dais in one corner of the room, sat down and began playing. Then, his voice hard and unrelenting, he stated, "Juliana tells me you and she are not lovers."

DeWinter's hands paused in midstroke, and he looked up at Andre. "You've got stones, I'll give you that."

"I would know if that is the truth."

One corner of DeWinter's mouth quirked up in a half smile. "Far be it from me to contradict a lady."

Andre took a step forward. "Are you saying you *are*

lovers?" he demanded coldly, clenching his right fist despite his promise to himself not to lose his temper. Had Juliana lied to him about this?

"No, I'm saying you've yet to prove to me it's any of your damn business." DeWinter obviously wasn't about to back down to anyone, king or commoner. There was a long tense pause, during which DeWinter seemed to reach a decision. "I've known Juliana for ten years," he said finally. "I've been married for twelve." His voice was as cold and hostile as Andre's had been. "That's all the answer you should need. And it's all the answer you're going to get."

Eventually Andre nodded. "Fair enough. But you are an intelligent, observant man, so answer me this. Is Juliana in love with you?"

DeWinter laughed suddenly, and Andre slowly let out the breath he was holding. No man could sound that unconcerned if there was any truth to the question. Not where someone as devastatingly beautiful as Juliana was concerned. "Juliana's a brilliant actress. On screen she's loved me since our first movie together—her Tessa to my Terry O'Dare was incandescent. Incomparable. And if she looked at me in real life the way she looks at me on the set of *this* movie, as if I'm her whole world and her only chance for salvation, I'd be hard-pressed to walk away from her. Although I'd like to think I'd remain faithful to Bree," he added drily. "But that's all there is between us. Make-believe. She's not, nor has she ever been, in love with me." The confident, forthright way he made that assertion convinced Andre his suspicions were wrong. Dead wrong.

Relief flooded him. *Not DeWinter. Never him. Someone. But not him.*

"Now I've got a couple of questions of my own," DeWinter said, closing the keyboard with a decided thud and rising to his full six foot two. "Juliana didn't want to return to Zakhar to film this movie. She wouldn't tell us why, but it's obvious to me...now. It's also obvious you maneuvered to get her here. Why? And who the hell do you think you are to break her heart?" Now his stance was a threat.

Andre considered both questions for several heartbeats and chose to answer the last one first. "I never broke her heart." He hesitated for another couple of heartbeats. "*She* left *me*."

"Well, that answers the first question, too," DeWinter replied. *"Why,"* he answered as Andre lifted a questioning eyebrow. "You want her back. That's why you went to all this trouble and expense to get her here." When Andre didn't answer, just folded his lips tighter together, DeWinter said, "The screenwriter you picked is a friend of mine. She let it slip who commissioned the screenplay. When I asked the studio about it they played dumb...but I'm not stupid. I offered to take a substantial cut in salary for a piece of the film, but I was smugly told they had all the financing they needed. And I wasn't even here a week before I started putting two and two together and coming up with some very interesting answers."

Andre didn't want to ask, but he had no choice. "Have you said anything to Juliana?"

DeWinter shook his head. "She's having a hard enough time with things as it is." He took a deep breath and exhaled slowly. "Juliana and I have been nothing but friends since the day we met. But I'll be honest. From the very beginning I told myself I could heal her...if I were free."

He let that sink in, watching Andre with sharp eyes before continuing. "But the flip side is that if I *had* been single and hunting her, we wouldn't be friends. Juliana doesn't let men get close to her—not in that way. Someone did that to her. Some man. I've always known it—I just never knew who it was...until now."

Andre shook his head decisively. "It was not me."

DeWinter grunted, but whether in denial or agreement, Andre couldn't be sure. And now that DeWinter had confirmed he and Juliana weren't lovers, now that he'd denied Juliana was in love with him, Andre needed time. Time to reassess, to consider what it all meant. Time to figure out why Juliana would accuse him of breaking her heart. And why DeWinter had been misled into thinking the same thing.

But there was still one question he wanted answered. "What was Juliana telling you this afternoon on the set?" It still ate at him, the pleading expression on her face as she looked at the man opposite him, the way she'd touched him with intimate purpose.

DeWinter cursed fluently, and suddenly the two men were standing toe to toe in confrontation, neither one backing down. "That is none of your damn business."

"That is what she said, too." Andre's eyes narrowed. "If you have lied to me—"

"What Juliana said is private, and has nothing whatever to do with you, or her, either, for that matter. It concerns my wife. And that's all I'm going to tell you." Eyes clashed; steely resolve met steely resolve. Then DeWinter shouldered Andre aside and stalked out.

At first Juliana had been so angry at Andre she'd gone for a long walk in the gardens surrounding the palace, needing to expend all the excess energy that had built up during their confrontation. But then she realized she should warn Dirk. She wouldn't put it past Andre to ask Dirk the same questions he'd asked her earlier… *To see if our answers match,* she thought derisively. *Damn him!*

She hurried inside, smiling at the guards at the door as they let her in. In her haste she didn't see the shadowy figure that had followed her into the garden now follow her up the stairs and down the corridor to the DeWinters' suite, pretending to continue on without hesitation when she stopped and tapped on the DeWinters' door.

Sabrina opened the door. "Oh, it's you," she said, a worried frown on her face. "I thought it might be Dirk."

Surprised, Juliana asked, "He's not here?"

Sabrina shook her head. "He went off with the king twenty minutes ago."

"Damn! I didn't warn him soon enough."

Sabrina cocked her head to one side. "You know why the king wanted to see Dirk?" Hot color seeped into Juliana's cheeks, and Sabrina pushed the door wide. "You'd better come in and tell me about it." She led Juliana into the sitting room and curled up gingerly in a corner of one of the sofas, waving a hand to tell Juliana to sit wherever she wanted.

But she couldn't sit. And at first she thought she couldn't tell her friend what Andre had accused her of. *What if deep down Bree suspects that, too?* Juliana felt like crying. She didn't want her friend to think she would betray her trust. *I don't have that many friends in Hollywood that I can afford to lose Bree…and Dirk,* she thought with dismay.

Sabrina made it easy on her. "So the king thinks you and Dirk are lovers?"

Juliana gasped. "How did you know?" Then she stumbled over herself to deny there was any truth to Andre's accusation. "Not that we are… We aren't… I would never… Dirk wouldn't…"

Sabrina laughed, and it was such a carefree sound it put to rest Juliana's sudden suspicion that her friend might have thought… "You're right. You wouldn't. And Dirk wouldn't, either. But I don't think the king knows that." Her smile turned empathetic, but it wasn't just for Juliana. "I think he looks at you…and he doesn't think at all, he feels. And he transposes his own feelings for you onto every man around you." She patted the sofa beside her, coaxing Juliana to sit next to her. When Juliana perched on the edge, she said kindly, "Don't you think it's time you told me what this is all about?"

Warmth surged up into Juliana's cheeks again, and she couldn't meet her friend's eyes. "I don't know what you mean."

"Dirk and I have eyes, you know," Sabrina said softly. "He told me you freeze on the set whenever the king shows up. He affects your performance, which isn't like you—no man *ever* makes you flub your lines like that. And we saw the two of you together at the reception, don't forget that. Add up everything we've seen, throw in the fact that you never wanted to come back here, and it's obvious there's history between the two of you. I hope you know I would never betray a confidence you gave me. Not even to Dirk."

Juliana linked her fingers together and twisted them subconsciously, then glanced over at Sabrina. "You're right," she admitted in a tight little voice. "Andre and I knew each other a long time ago."

"He's part of your mysterious past?"

Juliana's tone was harsh. "He's all of it." Sabrina made an encouraging sound, and she continued. "I was eighteen. He was twenty-two. I thought he loved me. He didn't. End of story."

"Nice try," Sabrina said drily. "Try again."

Juliana took a deep, shuddering breath. "We had one night together. One. Then I went back to the States to attend college in Virginia. I wrote to him…more than once. Love letters. Emails. Pouring my heart out to him. It makes me sick now to remember just how pathetic I must have seemed to him." She stopped, unable to continue for a minute. "He never wrote back," she said finally. "No letters. No emails. I waited for him to call me. He never did." Her eyes filled with tears. "So I called him. Several times. But he never answered. I thought he loved me, even though he never said the words. I was so *sure*. But—"

"He *does* love you."

Juliana rubbed the heels of her hands against her eyes like a little girl, wiping away the tears. "He wants me. Just like nearly every other man in the world except Dirk. He thinks I've slept around and figures why shouldn't I sleep with him, too? After all, I did once before."

Sabrina's smile was gentle. "What makes you think Dirk doesn't want you?"

## Chapter 8

"*What?*" Shocked, Juliana stared at Sabrina.

"Don't get me wrong. I trust Dirk completely. I know he would never cheat on me, would never have an affair with you or any other woman." Sabrina's eyes shone with her complete confidence in her husband's loyalty. "But he's a man—very much so. And you're an incredibly beautiful and sexy woman. He's held you in his arms. He's kissed you. He's made love to you on-screen, sometimes with very little in the way of clothes between you. He wouldn't be human if he hadn't thought about it at times."

She waited for Juliana to digest that. "But that's as far as it goes. Even if he wasn't married to me, you've got Touch Me Not signs everywhere. And Dirk is too much of a gentleman to ever risk hurting you. He knows there was a man in your murky past who shattered your trust in men. And since we've been here in Zakhar, I'm sure he's figured out who, the same way I have. Just not why."

At the tail end of that last sentence Sabrina suddenly caught her breath and pressed her fingers to her side. Juliana reached over and placed a comforting hand over her friend's hand. "Bree, what is it?"

Sabrina made a sound of pain and her eyes squeezed shut. "It's nothing…just a twinge," she said at last.

Juliana knew it wasn't *just* a twinge. It was the cancer. But she was torn. If she told Sabrina she knew the truth, knew about the cancer and the pregnancy, Sabrina would know Dirk had told her. And she didn't want to betray Dirk's trust. "Do you have something you can take for it? Aspirin? Ibuprofen?"

"Aspir— Oh!" She whimpered in a little voice, "It hurts."

"Aspirin? Is it in the bathroom? Tell me where it is, Bree, and I'll get it for you."

"Bathroom."

Juliana flew into the adjoining bathroom and scrabbled through toiletry and makeup bags until she found a bottle of aspirin. She ran water into a glass, rinsing it out before filling it halfway, and flew back into the sitting room. She put the glass in Sabrina's hand, then fumbled with the bottle until she got the childproof cap off, and shook several tablets into her hand.

"How many? Two? Three?"

"Two."

"Stick out your tongue." Bree did so, and Juliana deposited two tablets there. "Sip the water," she ordered, "and chew the tablets but don't swallow. Put them under your tongue for as long as you can—they'll be absorbed faster that way." When Sabrina was done, Juliana took the glass from her hand and set it on the side table. Then she knelt in front of her friend, clasping her hands. "Can I do anything else?"

"Dirk," Sabrina whispered. "I just want Dirk."

Juliana sprang to her feet and whirled toward the door, but just before she reached it the door burst inward and suddenly Dirk was there. His face was white with repressed anger, but before Juliana could say anything he took everything in with one comprehensive glance, and his anger was replaced with concern.

"Bree..." He was at his wife's side in an instant.

"Dirk..." She reached up to him, her lips pressed tightly together to hold in the pain. He swept her into his arms and swiftly carried her to their bedroom.

Juliana stood rooted where she was, not sure if she should wait or leave the two of them alone. Wishing there was something she could do. Soft, deep murmurs from the bedroom told her Dirk was comforting his wife, and she turned to go. But then Dirk came back into the sitting room, softly shutting the door to the bedroom.

"Don't go yet," he told her. "Bree's resting now. What happened?"

She shook her head. "I really don't know. We were talking, and then...all of a sudden, she got this sharp pain."

"Did you tell her you know?"

Juliana shook her head. "I just got her some aspirin. I felt so helpless. God, it's just not fair. Bree doesn't deserve this."

Dirk's mouth twitched into a travesty of a smile that

didn't reach his eyes. "No. She doesn't. At least I had the chance to tell her I finally understand what she's going through right now, before we were interrupted."

"I'm so sorry about that," Juliana said. "I didn't think Andre would really..." She trailed off. She glanced at Dirk uncertainly. "What did he ask—"

"What did he ask me? Don't you mean what did he accuse me of?"

She cast him a wounded look before turning away. "I'm sorry," she said again. "I told him it wasn't true. I guess he didn't believe me."

"He's very possessive of you," Dirk agreed. "So... are you going to tell me why?"

"He has no right to be possessive," she said, still with her back turned. "Maybe eleven years ago, but not now."

Dirk considered her statement, then shook his head as if something didn't make sense. "According to him, you left him."

"That's a lie!" Juliana whirled around, anger rising to the top. "He—" She cut off the rest of her sentence, unwilling to admit—even to Dirk—the scars Andre had left on her heart. It had been hard enough confessing to Sabrina the few things she'd shared with her. She couldn't tell Dirk what she couldn't bring herself to tell Sabrina, what she'd never told *anyone*.

Dirk looked as if he were going to say something, but then thought better of it. He reached out one hand, tucking behind her ear a strand of hair that had fallen down. "He believes it, babe. I don't know what your history is with him, but I can tell you this. He believes you deserted him. Despite that, he's determined to win you back."

* * *

"It's a lie," Juliana told herself as she stormed back to her own suite and locked the door behind her with a savage twist of the bolt, something she didn't usually do. "A damned lie." A lie she was shocked to discover Andre had told Dirk. *Why are you shocked?* she asked herself. *A man who will do what he did to me has no honor. None. So lying about it shouldn't be a shock.* But it was. Andre had never lied to her—not in so many words. And he'd never lied to Mara as far as she could recall. In fact, she couldn't think of a single instance when he'd lied. "Except by his actions," she reminded herself with a cynical twist of her lips. "Except when he let you think he loved you the night he made love to you."

*No, he didn't make love to you,* she corrected herself. *He had sex with you. That's all. Lovemaking on your part, yes. But just sex for him. Fantastic sex, maybe, but sex all the same.*

Still, she couldn't deny Andre's growing tension and possessiveness. The edge of command, of a hint of savagery, was clear beneath his royal restraint. And she was responding to it. To him. Since the moment she'd seen Andre at the reception, she'd wanted him—a visceral response she'd fought that night…and every moment since. Her body had recognized what it wanted, what it needed, even though her brain said no. What she feared most wasn't that Andre wouldn't take no for an answer—he would never force her—but that her traitorous body wouldn't take no for an answer. And that he knew it.

Still thinking about ways and means to protect herself from herself, Juliana wandered into the bedroom, where the bed had already been turned down by the maid assigned to her from the palace staff. She made her way to the dresser and pulled out a nightshirt to get ready for bed. It was early, but it wouldn't hurt her to have a quiet night. She shut the drawer, laid the night-shirt on top of the dresser and unbuckled her belt. She'd just unbuttoned the line of tiny buttons running from neck to waist when out of the corner of her eye she caught a movement in the old-fashioned cheval mirror standing in one corner. She turned toward the mirror, then swung sharply around. Andre stood there in the middle of her bedroom. Watching her. Just watching her as she undressed.

She was so startled to see him there that at first she couldn't speak. Anger, outrage and fear—of her own weakness where he was concerned—surged through her in a riptide. Then she found her voice. "Get out!"

He didn't say anything, but he didn't move, either. Just stood there, his gaze sliding from her face downward, lingering on her bared skin, and then back again. Juliana clutched at the bodice of her dress, holding the two edges together in sudden desperation. Only then did he move, walking toward her with an unhurried gait. She backed away, unable to tear her eyes away from the determination in his face, but she didn't have far to go before she backed up against the wall.

She wanted to say, "Don't touch me," but she couldn't get the words out because he was already touching her, caressing her cheek with fingertips like the brush of a butterfly's wings. Not an overtly sexual move, but unbearably arousing all the same.

"Do not be afraid of me, Juliana," he said. "You know I would never hurt you."

"You are," she whispered. "You did."

"When?" he asked softly, his hand sliding down to cup her breast through her dress, and the nipple tightened of its own accord beneath that sure but gentle touch. His breath rasped in his throat. "When did I hurt you? When I took you that first time? But I made it beautiful for you first, yes?" He kissed her just behind her ear, then her neck. Then his lips moved tantalizing to the open bodice of her dress, kissing her between her breasts but making no attempt to go further. "You knew there would be pain the first time. But did I not promise never again? And did I not prove it to you that night, twice over?"

"Don't." It was just a thread of a sound, and it was directed more to her treacherous body than it was to him. *Don't respond to him,* she was saying. *Don't let him make you want him. Don't let him do this to you again.* But his words, his touch were bringing all those memories vividly to life, and she shuddered as a wave of heat began in the core of her being and swept outward, bringing her body to life along with the memories.

His warm, caressing hand left her body, but he didn't move away. "'Don't?'" he asked softly. "'Don't?' That is not what you told me then," he said, his deep, seductive voice telling her he knew what he was doing to her. His head moved until his lips were a tantalizing inch away from hers when he whispered, "'Please.' That is what you said to me that night. 'Please.' Do you remember, Juliana? I do. 'Please, Andre.'"

"Please, Andre." Was that her voice saying those words? That breathless, desperate, *needy* sound? Her brain wanted to retract her plea but her lips refused to obey, and then it was too late.

His lips took hers. Warm. Firm. Sensual. Seducing her with no more than a kiss. "I did please you, little one," he breathed when he raised his mouth from hers. His tongue touched her lower lip. "Each time." His teeth caught her lip and tugged delicately. "Every time."

She shook her head. She wasn't denying his statement; she was trying to tell herself no, not to let him seduce her this way.

"Yes, Juliana. Do you think I could not tell?"

His hands slid beneath her skirt, pulling it up until it bunched at her waist. Then he lifted her effortlessly, sliding her body against his until she could feel him at the crux of her thighs—throbbing through the scant protection of her panties the way she remembered. Only then there had been nothing between them. Nothing but hard male flesh against tender female flesh. More than anything she'd ever wanted, she wanted him in that instant. Wanted him to rip away the barriers between them, to thrust himself into her the way her body ached for him to do. Wanted him to take her with that controlled male power she remembered so vividly, and in taking give and give and give.

"No!" She wrenched against him and he let her go immediately, let her slide down his body, then stepped back. She put distance between them, and her trembling fingers buttoned as many buttons as she could as quickly as she could. "You have no right," she told him, panting a little, trying to catch her breath. "No right."

"You gave yourself to me once," he told her, an unreadable expression in his eyes. "I would have let you go untouched. But you came to me." His jaw tightened. "Do you think it was easy for me? Two years. *Two years* I fought against taking you, knowing I had no right. I was one day away from letting you leave Zakhar a virgin. But then you came to me and you gave me that right. You cannot take it back. Not now. Not ever."

He turned on his heels and strode toward one of the wall hangings, not toward her sitting room, where the door to the outside corridor was. Juliana's gaze flew to the outside door just visible through the sitting room doorway, and she realized it was still firmly bolted. *How did he get in?* "Andre!" she called. He paused and turned back to her. "How…how did you get into my bedroom?"

The corner of his mouth curved upward in a faint smile. "Are you just now asking yourself that question?" he said, unexpected amusement in his face.

"I want to know," she insisted.

"You are occupying the Queen's Suite," he told her, as if that should be answer enough. When she shook her head, puzzled, he lifted a hand and raised the heavy tapestry on the wall, revealing a doorway cunningly concealed in the masonry behind it, with an ancient wooden door that opened inward into a passageway. "The King's Suite is at the other end," he said, letting the wall hanging fall back into place.

When she gasped in comprehension, he said, "The passageway lends credence to the legend that this suite of rooms began as Eleonora's. I discovered it when reading some old manuscripts from that era. After I ascended the throne and occupied the King's Suite that had been my father's, I located the passageway and had it cleaned out. At the same time I had the iron hinges on both doors oiled, and the rust removed from the locks and keys."

"You mean you can just walk into my bedroom whenever you want?"

That faint smile came and went again. "Whenever I want," he agreed.

"You can't," she protested angrily. "I won't stay here. I won't! Even if I have to move out of the palace, I won't stay where I have no privacy."

At first he didn't say anything, as if assessing the sincerity of her threat. "No need," he told her finally. "I only came to apologize for not believing you about DeWinter. But then…" He shrugged his shoulders. "You are a temptation that is hard to resist, little one."

"Don't call me that!" she said sharply. "Don't call me 'little one,'" she insisted, hurt by the memories it evoked of happier days with Andre.

"I cannot promise that," he told her in his deepest voice. "It is what you are to me—small and precious. But I *can* promise I will never again use the passageway to come to you." He indicated the key in the ancient lock. "Lock this door, and your privacy will be inviolate, Juliana. I will not use my key." His words, his tone, the expression on his face told her he meant it. "But know this—I will not lock my door against you. You are welcome to use the passageway to come to me, if you choose. Anytime. Day or night."

"Never." She shook her head, remembering telling him the same thing at the reception. "Never again."

Again there was that faint, tantalizing smile that reminded her of how she'd responded to him only a few minutes ago. Of how her body had fought her mind and had almost won. Of how much her body still wanted him, even now, even when he wasn't touching her. But he didn't say anything—he didn't have to. He merely turned, moved the tapestry to one side and disappeared into the darkness.

## Chapter 9

Back in his bedroom Andre paced until his body calmed down, until his heartbeat slowed and the blood no longer raced in his veins. But a flicker of hope had been ignited. He'd been so close. So close to having Juliana again he hadn't wanted to let her go when she'd struggled against him—but he had. Instantly. He'd sworn to himself he would wait until she came to him.

He hadn't intended to seduce her. Hadn't intended to touch her at all. He honestly had gone to her room merely to apologize. He'd considered going to her suite via the main corridor, but he hadn't wanted to compromise her. In addition to his own bodyguard and the ones assigned to her—the ones she still didn't know anything about—anyone could have seen him in the hallway, knocking at her door, and at that time of night it would seem…curious. Possibly suspicious. Certainly worthy of comment. While his bodyguards were discretion personified and the household staff knew better than to gossip outside the walls about anything going on in the palace, he didn't want backstairs gossip making the rounds about Juliana.

He hadn't seen her in the corner of her bedroom when he'd first entered it through the passageway, and he'd thought she wasn't there. He'd planned to enter the sitting room to wait for her return, apologize for not believing her about DeWinter and leave. Simple. Straightforward. But when he turned and saw her reflection in the mirror, saw her undressing, he'd been frozen. Unable to move. Unable to speak. Then she'd seen him. Ordered him to leave. And when she'd clutched the bodice of her dress like an outraged virgin, he'd moved. Not to leave, as his brain told him to do. But toward her. Needing to touch her the way he needed to breathe.

To hear her accuse him of hurting her had been more than he could bear. He had to remind her of what it had really been like all those years ago. Had to remind her that *she* had come to *him*. But when he touched her, when he smelled the delicate scent that rose from her heated skin, he couldn't stop. His brain kept telling him to stop, but his body refused to obey. Because every word he whispered to her reminded him of what it had been like to make love to her. What it had been like to know she loved him enough to come to him.

And her body had responded to his. Finally. She didn't want it to—oh yes, he could tell she was fighting her body's response—but he knew she wanted him, too. At last. Not enough. Not yet. But it would happen. He knew it in his heart. He could wait until then. He'd waited all these years, hadn't he?

With that realization he finally let himself grow calm enough to focus on something else. Something that had been weighing on his mind for several days. Juliana was in danger. She didn't know it, seemed totally oblivious to the fact that someone had deliberately tried to run her down the day she'd visited the royal cemetery. But he was as sure as a man could be. The Mercedes had turned out to be stolen. That meant someone had planned the attack on her.

Should he tell Juliana? Warn her? If he did, would she believe him? *Not unless you tell her how you know,* he admitted to himself, and he wasn't ready to do that. Not yet. Because he didn't know how she'd react when he told her his men had been guarding her for the past three years. That his men had surrounded her in the first-class cabin on the plane bringing her here. That she hadn't taken a single step since she'd been in Zakhar without men following her, keeping her safe.

Not stalking her. That wasn't it at all, but she might feel that way. Might feel it was an unwarranted intrusion into her life, and he couldn't take that risk—he *had* to keep her safe no matter what.

He'd already doubled the surveillance and protection on Juliana, which meant he ran the risk she would notice she was being guarded. But that was better than the alternative.

Juliana tossed and turned, unable to sleep. Unable to erase the evening from her mind. Not just Andre appearing in her bedroom, but earlier, in the little library. All the different ways he'd looked at her. The way he'd held her in her strong embrace, his voice tenderly coaxing her to confide in him while his heart beat so reassuringly beneath her ear. The emotions in his voice, his face, his eyes. Sweet, then autocratic. Demanding, then tender. Gentle, then implacable. All the facets of his personality she remembered from her growing-up years. Her beau ideal prince.

Then she remembered him saying, *"Do you think it was easy for me? Two years. Two years I fought against taking you, knowing I had no right. I was one day away from letting you leave Zakhar a virgin. But then you came to me and you gave me that right. You cannot take it back. Not now. Not ever."*

That made absolutely no sense. The way he talked now sounded like the Andre of old, the one from eleven years ago. The man she'd fallen in love with. The man she'd been so sure loved her. The man whose children she'd wanted to bear. If she didn't know better, she'd think he loved her now. If she didn't know better, she'd think he'd loved her then, too, had always loved her.

But she did know better. She knew he hadn't loved her then. She knew because of the money he'd sent her as a parting gift. The money and the words of rejection. Not just a rejection of her, but of everything she'd ever wanted to give him. He could never have done that if he loved her. Never.

Andre looked around the conference table at the Privy Council. "We are agreed, then, gentlemen?" he asked politely. Not by a flicker of his eyelids did he betray they had spent far more time than he'd allotted for discussion of this issue, and that the conclusion the council had nearly reached after much dithering was the one he'd already reached the week before, despite Zax's powerful arguments against it.

Bringing Zakhar into the twenty-first century had entailed far more than bringing in new industry and technology. Far more than instituting sweeping policy changes. Andre had long since determined Zakhar also needed to modify its political structure. Absolute monarchs were passé in this day and age, but the Zakharians had stubbornly clung to their traditional way of life, and that had included a fierce, unshakable devotion to the much-loved monarchy. Zakharians were proud that the House of Marianescu had reigned over Zakhar in an unbroken line for centuries, from father to son, and were resistant to change.

Zakhar had been extremely fortunate the House of Marianescu had been just as devoted to Zakhar as the Zakharians had been to it, and that the kings of Zakhar had—to a man—been worthy to rule. Some more than others, it was true, but Zakhar had never had a truly bad king. Andre's own father had ruled with a fair and just hand, despite his own personal shortcomings as a father and a husband. It wasn't common knowledge, but Andre's father had been instrumental in his wife's death by insisting on another son to ensure the Marianescu legacy, despite the queen's doctor warning against a second pregnancy. But as a king Andre's father had been above reproach.

The Privy Council advised, but the king had final authority. And the Privy Council had always been appointed by the king, so it was unlikely the council would provide any advice that ran contrary to the king's wishes. That was the way it had been right up through his father's day. But in the three years since Andre had ascended the throne he had slowly but surely started placing more power—and responsibility—in the hands of the now-elected Privy Council, another change he'd instituted over the objections of nearly everyone, including his cousin Zax. That meant having the patience of a saint at times, something Andre struggled to attain. But he knew it was the right thing to do...for the long term. In the short term, however, he often had to grit his teeth and smile.

He glanced in the direction of his cousin Niko lounging indolently on the other side of the large conference table. Niko had been a mistake, a big one. Andre hadn't intervened when Niko had stood for election to the council. He'd figured the electors would see Niko's obvious moral weaknesses and unsuitability for the job the same way he did, and would reject his candidacy without Andre expressing an opinion one way or the other, something he was loath to do in the new political process. *I just didn't count on the Zakharians' devotion to the royal family,* he acknowledged privately. He wouldn't make that same mistake the second time around.

Niko had easily won his election despite the stellar qualifications of his opponent—a man Andre had really wanted on the council—and had been a royal pain ever since. Andre had hoped Niko's new responsibilities on the council would steady his erratic younger cousin the way military discipline had shaped his cousin Zax, but that had been a fleeting hope at best. Niko still skated through life like the petulant boy he'd once been. And he delighted in obstructing change, even when it was change for the better.

Not that Niko would ever openly take a stand against Andre any more than his brother would...but for entirely different reasons. Nothing would have been more fatal to Niko's nascent political career—in a showdown between the king and his younger cousin there was no contest in the eyes of the Zakharians. But Niko agitated the Privy Council in private, raising specious objections to Andre's best ideas, and encouraging the council to drag its feet on one issue after the other, especially when it came to changes potentially limiting the monarch's absolute authority.

Andre wondered—not for the first time—if Niko's opposition to any lessening of royal power and privilege had its roots in his assumption he might one day inherit the throne. But every time the thought occurred to Andre he dismissed its relevance. If anything happened to him, Zax was first in line. The brothers were only three years apart in age, and Zax was in far better physical shape than the self-indulgent Niko. It was highly unlikely Niko would outlive Zax, even assuming Andre had no heirs of his own body to supplant both Zax and Niko in the line of succession.

That train of thought led directly to Juliana, and Andre sighed inwardly without letting it show on his face. He'd planned to drop in on the filming this afternoon, but it was highly unlikely that would happen now. Not unless the Privy Council could get off the stick and reach a resolution.

Dirk caught Juliana and lifted her effortlessly into his strong arms, cradled her, then carried her the few steps to the massive bed. He laid her gently down, kissed her tenderly, then lifted his head to bellow for the servants and the midwife.

"And cut!" the director said. He glanced at his watch.

"And I guess that's a wrap for today," he said with reluctance.

Dirk grinned down at Juliana as a flurry of work went on around them. "Oh, my aching back," he told her, pretending her featherweight had given him a backache.

"Ha ha ha," she responded, struggling to sit up, the bulky padding she was wearing to simulate a late-term pregnancy giving her trouble. "It's not my fault we had to do that scene six times."

The first take, Juliana's special padding had shifted noticeably and alarmingly just as Dirk placed her on the bed, and he'd dissolved into laughter. An extra strap had been added to Juliana's gear to prevent that from happening again. One of the arc lights had gone out during the second take before he'd taken two steps, and they'd had to wait while that was replaced. The third take, Dirk had stumbled and almost dropped her, making her yelp, then giggle. One of the overhead microphones had unexpectedly shown up in the main camera shot just as the camera was panning out during the fourth take, and that had involved much cursing and pointing the finger of blame.

The fifth take had been a near disaster when one of the overhead lights had inexplicably come crashing down in the middle of the bed, right before Dirk was to place Juliana in it. If they'd been two feet closer, Juliana, and most likely Dirk, too, would have been seriously injured or killed by the impact. That had taken almost an hour to repair—especially picking the glass out of the bedding and off the floor where it had scattered in all directions—and both the director and the producer had been furious. The director because of the delay; the producer because of how this might affect the insurance on the film. The producer was still fuming, vowing to fire whomever had been so criminally negligent, but everyone in earshot was disavowing responsibility.

Juliana had shrugged it off; Dirk not so much. Accidents happened no matter how careful people were, but as a man who'd gotten his start in movies as a stuntman, Dirk had never been one to leave things to chance. Juliana had caught him eyeing the lighting setup a few times while the cleanup went on around them, as if trying to figure out exactly how it had happened.

By the sixth take everyone in camera range except Dirk and Juliana was holding his or her breath, wondering what would go wrong this time. But the sixth take had worked like a charm, from Juliana's initial gasp of pain as labor started, to Dirk's final bellow. The scene that would end up as roughly thirty seconds in the final cut had taken the remainder of the afternoon to film.

Dirk put his arm around Juliana's shoulders, helping her to straighten up. "Is it really that awkward?" he asked. "Pregnancy, I mean."

Juliana laughed. "I can't speak from experience, but that's what I've heard. I've had friends tell me it's like carrying around a bowling ball. But you'll know soon enough when Bree—" She stopped abruptly, realizing she had no idea if Sabrina would be able to go full term.

Juliana and Dirk had been shooting on location for almost ten weeks, which meant her friend was nearly five months pregnant and definitely showing. Sabrina had finally confided in Juliana about her pregnancy, but she hadn't mentioned one word about the cancer, and Juliana—true to her word to Dirk—hadn't said anything, either. But things had been going well for Sabrina so far, and Juliana was praying they'd stay that way, that her friend would safely deliver her baby four months from now.

Dirk's expression turned troubled. "I hope you're right," he said roughly. "Because it's not one baby she's carrying. We just found out it's twins. And because there's a tendency toward premature delivery with chemo, she's resisting that idea, even though she's now safely in her second trimester and doesn't have to worry about the chemo causing birth defects."

"Oh God," Juliana said helplessly before she pulled herself together. Twins, she knew, usually had lower birth weights, which would explain why Sabrina didn't want to risk premature delivery at this stage. "Think positive," she told Dirk stoutly. Her assistant, Maddie, came up to them just then, with bottles of water for both of them.

"I'm trying," Dirk said. "I've got plans for tonight. There's a full moon and I've arranged to take Bree sightseeing…in a horse-drawn carriage."

Juliana's face softened. "That's so romantic, Dirk." She raised her hand to cup his cheek. "Bree is lucky to have you," she said, blinking back unexpected tears. "I wish…" She never got the chance to say what she wished, because all at once she saw Andre standing off to one side watching her. Watching Dirk. A brooding expression on his face. She drew her hand away from Dirk's cheek sharply, as if she'd been caught doing something she shouldn't. It had been an innocent gesture, but Andre wouldn't know that.

"Come on," Dirk said, helping her off the bed. "Let's get these duds back to Wardrobe before we hold them up."

*I haven't done anything wrong,* she told herself as

she walked past Andre toward Wardrobe with her head
held high, refusing to look in his direction. *No matter
what he thinks, I haven't done anything wrong.*

"How the *hell* did it happen?" Andre demanded of
his cousin Zax in the privacy of his office, cold anger
making him pace and ramping up his blood pressure.
"Do you have any idea? Who was guarding Juliana? I
thought you doubled the security around her. How did
security break down?"

"Be reasonable," Zax said, answering the last of the
machine-gunned questions first. "Who could have pre-
dicted this? You cannot blame the men guarding her any
more than you can enclose Juliana in a bubble to keep
her safe from *every* possible threat."

"If she were yours, Zax," Andre said fiercely, "you
would not say that."

Zax waited until Andre calmed down enough to listen to reason, then offered up what evidence had been
collected so far. "It was no accident. That much we
know. The anchor points were nearly filed through on
two sides, leaving enough to bear the light's weight for
a time, but eventually gravity would cause a stress failure. Other than that…"

Andre stopped pacing to nail his cousin with an
angry flash of his eyes. "Who is responsible?"

Zax shook his head. "It could be anyone. One of the
crew…or not. According to the producer, those lights
were set up yesterday in preparation for today's filming. Again, according to the producer, it was not necessarily aimed at harming anyone. Filming of that scene
was expected to be completed long before the light ac-

tually fell, so it might have been merely someone with a grudge against the film. According to the producer."

"No, Zax. Juliana was targeted, the same way she was targeted when she was nearly run down weeks ago. Follow the money trail. Someone was paid to do this." Andre clenched his fist as tight as his jaw. "Somewhere there is a record. Find it for me, Zax. Find whoever is trying to kill Juliana."

## Chapter 10

"Another failure." The man tried to hold on to his temper because the Russian's cold stare unnerved him, but it wasn't easy. "That makes twice you have failed to eliminate the threat Juliana Richardson entails."

"The first failure—yes," the Russian nodded, "I will take responsibility for that. My man failed to run her down. He should have been successful despite the interference—we will not be surprised like that again. But *you* were the one who wanted to try the 'accident' on the set," the Russian reminded him. "Not us. We arranged it…at your insistence." His expression clearly conveyed what he thought of that amateurish attempt.

"Juliana's death has to appear accidental," he justified. "With the tight security around her, what else could we have done? I cannot afford to—"

"Yes, yes," the Russian said, cutting him off. "You

cannot afford to show your hand in this, not if you are to achieve your goal. I am aware. But the head of my organization is displeased with the lack of progress in the overall plan. Not the woman—he cares nothing for her—it is the king who stands in his way. And when Aleksandrov Vishenko is unhappy, unpleasant things happen…to everyone."

The deadly tone in the Russian's voice sent a chill down his spine, and his bowels cramped. *I should never have gotten involved with the Russian Mafia,* he realized now. Now…when it was too late. But he could not draw back at this stage. He could not become *uninvolved* with the Brotherhood. And the reason he'd cut a deal with Vishenko in the first place—that reason still existed.

*No,* he acknowledged with a grimace, attempting to calm his fears, *I have no choice. Not anymore.* Because his ultimate goal—to take his destined place as king of Zakhar—that goal was still attainable…but only with the *Bratva's* help. "So what are you going to do?"

"The *Pakhan* says," the Russian stated flatly, referring to Vishenko, "that the woman has distracted you— us—from our real goal long enough. It is time to forget the woman, and return to the original plan."

Alone and restless, Juliana stood on the balcony outside her bedroom, looking up at the full moon. Somewhere out there, she knew, Dirk and Sabrina were riding in a horse-drawn carriage beneath that full moon, and once again she felt an ache of envy. Even knowing the precariousness of Sabrina's situation, she would have traded places with her friend in a heartbeat. Not to be with Dirk, but to be with Andre. To know herself loved the way Dirk loved Sabrina. To be carrying Andre's children, even at the risk to herself.

"No!" she whispered in a desperate undertone, appalled at where her thoughts had strayed. *How can you even think that? Haven't you learned the hard way that Andre doesn't love you?*

But she wanted him to. It wasn't just that her body craved his touch. Her heart yearned for him, too, despite everything. And her desire for Andre's children was a part of that yearning. The scene they'd filmed this afternoon had brought that desire achingly to life.

She wondered if Eleonora had ever faced a situation like this. It seemed unlikely, but you could never know for sure. The chroniclers of the time had painted the first Andre Alexei with a heroic brush, granting him all the virtues and none of the vices. Had he really been faithful to Eleonora for nearly five empty years?

There was nothing in the history of the day to suggest otherwise. *In other words, no bastards attributed to him,* she thought with a wry tilt to her lips. And that was at a time when royal bastards were an everyday occurrence and rarely hidden. It wasn't as if he didn't have what it took sexually—Eleonora had conceived their first night together, and then had borne him six more children in the sixteen years after she'd been ransomed. So it seemed likely Andre Alexei had remained faithful.

But had he really paid a king's ransom to redeem her and her son, the son whose paternity had yet to be proved? Again, relying on the historians at the time, it seemed probable. Andre Alexei had beggared his kingdom—that was a known fact.

And Raoul *had* been his son, she remembered from the story Andre had told her and Mara so long ago, although it had taken a genetic defect to prove it—a crook in the pinkies of both hands, in father and son. A dominant gene—one that had come down through the centuries, but that hadn't impaired their fighting abilities. Both Andre Alexei and Raoul had been fearsome warriors. Mara hadn't inherited that defect; her fingers had all been perfectly straight. But Andre had.

Juliana remembered examining his hands minutely the night they'd become lovers, fascinated by the little thing that had made such a vast difference in whether or not Zakhar accepted Raoul as Andre Alexei's legitimate heir. Wondering if the children she would someday give him would have the same odd but endearing genetic defect.

*The children I will never have,* she reminded herself. The thought was nearly unbearable.

Alone and restless, Andre stood on the balcony outside his bedroom in defiance of his bodyguards' wishes, looking up at the full moon. Wondering if bringing Juliana here had been a terrible mistake. Danger for himself he could accept. Danger for Juliana he could not.

He'd lost his temper with his cousin—fear did that to a man. Not fear for himself. Never that. But fear for Juliana, which was becoming his constant companion. Just as he'd wanted Mara safely out of the country after the second assassination attempt and had accomplished two goals by sending her to the United States, now he wondered how he was going to keep Juliana safe here in Zakhar. Not just during the filming of the movie, but forever and a day.

Seeing her on the set this afternoon, her body rounded with the pregnancy she was faking for the movie, he'd suddenly realized just how much was at stake. Not just Juliana, but any child they might have. If she stayed in Zakhar, if she married him, if they created a child from their love…the risk of assassination would be there.

Whoever was behind these attempts on Juliana's life had to be caught. He could not be allowed to remain a threat to Juliana or their child…assuming they had a child. Assuming Juliana ever grew to love him again enough to make that a possibility.

He breathed sharply. Even if the man behind the threat to Juliana was caught, he still wasn't sure if she *would* ever love him again. Yes, her physical attraction to him was undeniable. But would he ever know the joy of hearing those simple words from her that had thrilled him when she'd first said them? Thrilled him at the time and then haunted him over the years. *"Please, Andre…I love you…and I have to know…"*

He closed his eyes as a wave of desire shuddered through him and his body came roaring to life. He wanted her in every way a man could want a woman. Not just as his lover. Not just as his wife. But also as the mother of his children. He craved that closeness, that bond of the flesh, that pledge for all eternity. Would he ever have a son to inherit the throne? Or would the monarchy's direct descent from father to son end with him? "God only knows," he whispered to himself, fighting the despair that crept in unawares, "because I surely do not."

Time was running out. The producer of *King's Ransom* briefed him daily on the film's progress, and they were on schedule. Another few weeks and the cast and crew would withdraw, returning to Hollywood to finish up whatever odds and ends remained that didn't require filming on location. And Juliana would leave with them.

*No,* he told himself, steely determination sweeping through him. *She will not leave. Not now. Not ever. She belongs here in Zakhar. With me. Whatever I must do to keep her, and keep her safe, I will do.*

He would never *know* she was safe...always...unless he was at her side. Unless he could listen to her quiet breathing as she lay next to him in the deepness of the night. If he hadn't promised Juliana her privacy would be inviolate, he could slip into her room this very minute to assure himself she was safe. Then do the same each night that followed. Every night of her life. An assurance even more critical now, after the recent attempts to kill her. But he *had* promised, so that avenue was closed to him...for now.

*Which leaves what?* he asked himself.

He could seduce Juliana into staying, into sharing his bed. He knew that much. She'd been fighting herself as much as she'd been fighting him the other night. He could make her want him. He could drug her with sensual pleasure so she would willingly give him her body—a body he yearned to have now even as he'd yearned when she was sixteen...seventeen...eighteen.

But it wouldn't be enough. He would always live in fear that someday it wouldn't be enough for her, either, and she would leave again. He couldn't do that to his people, to his kingdom. No matter the cost to him personally, he couldn't do that to Zakhar. She *had* to come to him of her own free will.

*If she came to me I would know she loves me again, that she has come full circle. I would know that all the other men in her life were meaningless. If she came to me...*

He couldn't let her go, but keeping her by seduction or any other form of coercion would destroy the dream. And the dream was all he had left. "Come to me, Juliana," he whispered to the night, to the moon. "Come to me."

*Come to me, Juliana.* Andre's voice in her head made Juliana shudder with treacherous longing. *Come to me.*

"Stop it!" she told herself desperately, covering her ears with her hands as if that could prevent her from imagining she was hearing Andre calling to her. She'd imagined it like this eleven years ago and through all the intervening years, but never so strongly. Never as if his hands were caressing her body as he said the words. Never as if his lips were pressed to her ear, whispering in Zakharan, melting her insides as he'd done that first night…and then into the wee hours of the morning. Each time. Every time.

Desperate to escape the memories of Andre and the sound of his voice in her ears, Juliana threw off the covers and stomped out of bed, tearing off her nightshirt as she went. She grabbed a pair of jeans from the dresser and angrily tugged them on, followed by a bra, then rummaged in the drawer for her cotton knit short-sleeved shirts. The first one she pulled out was in a shade of emerald green that matched Andre's eyes. *Don't think about that now,* she warned herself, thrusting the green shirt back and pulling out a white one with tiny blue forget-me-nots embroidered all over it. It wasn't much better as far as reminders of Andre went, but at least it wasn't the color of his eyes.

She stepped into a pair of espadrilles, bundled her hair up quickly and slipped quietly from her room.

The palace at night looked very different than it did in the daytime. Sconce lighting spaced periodically through the halls allowed Juliana to see her way clearly, although there were shadows enough to spook anyone who wasn't familiar with the palace at nighttime.

Juliana was. She'd spent enough nights here with Mara—giggling together as teenage girls did during sleepovers—to become familiar with certain sections of the palace on the second floor. And Mara had occasionally spent the night with her in the ambassador's residence not that far from the palace. *Andre's doing,* she remembered suddenly. Andre had wanted his sister to have all the normal experiences young girls had growing up, and had actively encouraged Juliana's friendship with Mara. He'd stood up to his father, too, especially on Mara's behalf. Fighting Mara's battles with their father because Mara had been too insecure.

*Don't think about that now,* her heart warned her. *Don't think about Andre.*

She passed the little library, her feet making no sound on the thick carpet runners that lined the hallways, resolutely thrusting away the memory of her encounter with Andre there the day before. *Don't think about that now.*

She laughed under her breath, a ghost of a sound. Those words were becoming her mantra—*don't think about that now.* As if she could ever *not* think about Andre, especially here in the palace.

A slight sound behind Juliana had her whirling around in sudden panic, her heart jumping.

Her eyes frantically searched the shadows as well

as the patches of light all the way down the corridor, but she saw nothing. No movement. Nothing to be afraid of. "Old buildings creak," she muttered. "That's all it is."

She turned back and continued making her way toward the suite that had once been Mara's. She knew it was unoccupied. She'd run into the master of the household the week before—she'd remembered him as well as he'd remembered her—and they'd chatted about those long-ago days and about Princess Mara. The old man had always had a soft spot for Mara and Juliana, indulgently overlooking their teenage girlish pranks—more Juliana's doing than Mara's, who'd always tried to be so perfect to please her father, although that had been impossible. After several minutes the master of the household had told Juliana he'd intended to house her in Princess Mara's old suite for sentimental reasons.

"But the king overruled me," the master of the household had said in his formal way. "I trust you are comfortable where you are?" At the time Juliana hadn't known why the king had overruled him, but it made sense now she knew of the connecting passageway between her bedroom and Andre's.

Just before Juliana reached the door to Mara's suite she mentally kicked herself as she realized her quest was most likely for naught—the door would probably be locked, especially with all the strangers—movie people—being housed in the palace for the duration of the filming. And she didn't have the key. Sure enough, when Juliana tried the old-fashioned latch it refused to budge.

"Damn!" It wasn't so much that she was desperate to revisit the scene of some of her happiest teenage memories with Mara—although she would have liked to see the suite again—but she'd wanted something to distract her from thoughts of Andre that stubbornly kept popping into her head. Something to block out his voice calling to her.

She jiggled the latch, but it held firm. "Damn," she said again, but without heat this time. When she reluctantly turned around to head back to her own suite, she froze when she saw four men surrounding her. Guns drawn and pointing at her.

The phone call hadn't wakened Andre. He hadn't been to bed yet—hadn't even undressed. "Miss Richardson is on the move, Sire," the voice on the other end of the phone had said. "It is after midnight, and I thought you would want to know."

"Destination?"

"Unknown. But she does not appear to be leaving the palace. She is still on the second floor."

"Good man. Stay with her. I will be with you shortly."

Four men in camouflage clothing and desert-style boots confronted Juliana outside the door to Mara's suite. She had no idea how they'd managed to creep up on her with such stealth, and sudden terror brought the metallic taste of fear in her mouth. When the man closest to her—obviously the leader of the team—recognized her he lowered his weapon, but the other three still kept their guns pointing in her direction. "What are you doing here at this time of night, Miss Richardson?" the leader asked.

Juliana opened her mouth to answer, but no words came out because her heart was pounding too hard and she could scarcely catch her breath. Then she saw the badges they wore on the arms of their camouflage uniforms—Zakharian National Forces—and was able to breathe again. Only then did she remember the security briefing she'd received along with everyone else staying in the palace. *Motion detectors in the common areas are operational from midnight to 5:00 a.m.,* they'd all been warned. *Please do not leave your suite during this time.*

The motion detectors weren't the only security in the royal palace to protect the priceless antiques, paintings and other objets d'art owned by the king, Juliana remembered now from the security briefing. All the paintings on the walls were wired for touch, as were the numerous display cases. And the crown jewels were housed in a separate area of the palace—strictly off-limits to visitors except by appointment—guarded by electronic eyes as well as human guards. By leaving her suite after midnight in violation of the warning, she'd set off the silent alarm.

"An innocent mistake, I am sure, Sergeant," said a deep voice from the shadows. All four men immediately recognized the king's voice—as did Juliana—and at a sign from their sergeant the other men holstered their weapons, turned toward the king and saluted.

Andre moved out of the shadows and into the light, flanked by two men, neither of whom Juliana recognized. "At ease," Andre told the security guards. "Thank you for your diligence, gentlemen, and your quick response, but I think Miss Richardson is no threat. You may return to your posts."

"Yes, Sire," the sergeant said quickly, snapping another salute before he and his men departed with military precision.

Andre's eyes never left Juliana as he waited for the security guards to leave. Then he said, "I am sorry they frightened you, but were you not warned about the silent alarms?"

Juliana nodded, then found her voice. "I was. But I wasn't thinking. I just wanted…" She wasn't about to tell Andre she'd been trying to distract herself from thinking about him by revisiting old haunts, and had completely forgotten the warning until it was too late. Especially not with two strangers listening to every word she said.

A faint smile touched Andre's lips, and he lifted his chin in the direction of the doorway behind her. "You were trying to enter Mara's suite. A trip down memory lane?"

She swallowed hard. "Something like that."

Without turning his head, he said, "Privacy, please, Dmitri. Yakov."

"Yes, Sire," both men responded before moving several paces away, out of earshot.

Andre took a step toward her. "You could not sleep, either, little one?"

His tender voice was as tangible a caress as if he'd touched her, and Juliana shivered and backed away. "Please don't," she begged. "Please."

She wasn't sure what she was asking, except that she couldn't bear knowing she was as vulnerable to Andre as she'd been eleven years ago. And that he knew it. That he would take advantage of her when she had no defenses against him.

His smile faded, and his eyes darkened. "No, Juliana.

Since you ask it, I will not. Nor will I impose myself on you any further tonight." He turned and strode away with his determined tread, saying as he went, "Dmitri, please escort Miss Richardson back to her suite."

# Chapter 11

Once back in the Queen's Suite Juliana paced. No more able to sleep now than she had been before. But it was worse now, because seeing Andre tonight had brought home an undeniable truth she could no longer escape—whether he loved her or not, whether he deserved it or not, her heart irretrievably belonged to him. *Forever and a day.* She had to accept that...and move on.

*So what do I do now?* she wondered. She looked down the years of her life and realized she had come to an end of sorts. *King's Ransom* could be her swan song, just as it would be Dirk's. She wasn't under contract for anything yet, even though she'd received half a dozen scripts to read and offers were on the table. She didn't need the money any more than Dirk did. She'd never lived lavishly, so she'd saved enough money to retire comfortably even though she was only twenty-nine.

Even if she hadn't saved her money, she'd inherited a trust fund from her mother—a highly successful stage actress before she'd married Juliana's father—that would support her if she needed it. She'd never been a starving artist, not even when she first started out in Hollywood. And eventually her father's money would come to her, too. *But not for a long time,* she prayed. She couldn't really remember her mother, so her father was the only parent she'd ever known. Money could never fill the void in her life the loss of her father would bring.

But the bottom line was that she didn't need to support herself with her current career, had never needed to work at all. Not for money anyway. She *had* needed to work to escape.

She still had her charity work. She was on the governing boards of two organizations related to children's rights—one advocating strict child labor laws in developing countries similar to laws in the United States, and one fighting the sexual exploitation of children. They'd invited her for marquee name value to raise awareness of the issues, not realizing just how actively involved she'd become—because anything related to safeguarding children pushed all her buttons and always would. So she still had that to focus on.

Maybe she'd give stage acting a shot, too, although that was very different from acting in the movies. Once upon a time she'd daydreamed of following in her mother's footsteps and becoming a Shakespearean actress—maybe now she'd give herself the chance to find out if she could do it or not.

Daydreams. Once upon a time she'd daydreamed of Andre, too. But not anymore.

\* \* \*

The helicopter hovered over the site of the landslide for a moment as Andre stared at the shocking devastation below. "Take her down," he called to the pilot through the headsets they both wore, the noise of the rotors making headsets a necessity. The pilot nodded acknowledgment, his eyes searching for a good spot for the helicopter to land. Andre spotted it first. He touched the pilot's arm to draw his attention, then pointed silently, and the pilot nodded again.

Once down, Andre wasted no time. He jumped out, followed by his bodyguard, but Andre didn't wait for him. Both men bent over until they were out of range of the still-whirling rotors, then picked their way over the rough ground from the landing site to the houses that had been hardest hit. A fire-and-rescue crew was already there, frantically digging through the rubble, searching for survivors. Other crews, including teams from the Zakharian National Forces, were working on other houses. Andre saw them helping the surviving victims, sorting through those who were injured and those who were merely badly shaken when half the mountainside had unexpectedly come down upon this tiny village, nearly wiping it out.

There were other victims, too, he saw, his brows twitching together. Bodies laid out side by side in the sunlight, blankets drawn over them to give them a measure of dignity in death. Six of the blanket-covered mounds were much smaller than the rest, and Andre felt a pang in the region of his heart. Children. Six of the known dead were children. *How many more?*

A bell tolled frantically from the church tower of Taryna. The church itself had suffered extensive damage, but the bell tower was miraculously still standing with no apparent structural damage amid the rest of the devastation, and Andre hoped that sound would carry through the mountain passes and call the men back from the mountain meadows. Most of the villagers were sheepherders, making their livelihood from the mountain the way their ancestors had for centuries. But even in this day and age of cell phones, coverage in these mountains was spotty at best, and the bells were still the best way to send an urgent message.

Water mains and sewer systems hadn't been affected—anything below ground was apparently still intact—but electricity was out because the power lines had come down. And natural gas had been shut off at the pumping station to prevent fires from breaking out through the ruptured gas lines in the destroyed buildings.

A sudden wailing drew Andre's attention to a dust-covered woman picking up a small body that had just been pulled from under a beam that had once held up a roof. A body that didn't move, even though she clutched at it and begged it to answer her. Before he knew it he was there beside her. "Let me take him," he told the woman kindly, lifting the slight weight into his own arms, quickly feeling for the pulse he knew wasn't there.

Pity swept through him. Pity for the child, whose eyes were half open but would never see again. And pity for the mother, whose child was forever lost to her. With one hand he closed the eyelids so the child appeared merely to be sleeping. Then he stroked the tousled hair into a semblance of order and brushed the dirt away. "Come," he said, walking toward the tent the Zakharian Red Cross was already setting up over the bodies laid out in what had once been the town square.

He surrendered his precious burden to a Red Cross aide, then turned to the silently weeping woman behind him. In that moment they weren't king and subject. They were just two people in the midst of tragedy, and Andre held her for long moments as she wept her heart out in his arms. Finally, when the first torrent of tears abated, he asked her, "What was his name, madam?"

The woman raised her head. "Stepan," she said brokenly, then dissolved into tears again. "Stepan."

"A good name for a son," he told her, wishing there was something more he could do other than hold her. Wishing he had the words to comfort her.

A group of men rushed down the road just then, returning from where they'd been tending their flocks of sheep in the high mountain meadows, obviously starting their return when they'd heard the mountain rumble ominously, followed by the frantic tolling of the bells. A man with a dazed look about him broke away from the others and rushed to where Andre stood with the grieving mother. "Katia?" he asked anxiously. "Katia? Where is Stepan? Where is our son?"

The woman turned from Andre and threw herself into her husband's arms, weeping anew. Muffled words answered him, and the man's face contracted over his wife's head on his shoulder as he grasped the truth he didn't want to hear. His eyes met Andre's.

"I am sorry for your loss," Andre said gently, laying his hand on the man's other shoulder and squeezing firmly.

The man shuddered once, but kept his emotions in check. "Thank you, Sire," he said gruffly. He glanced down at his wife. "And thank you for…"

Andre shook his head. "It was nothing. Do not think

of that. Just comfort your wife. Stay with her. Be strong for her." He squeezed the shoulder one more time then removed his hand. "I will pray for your son," he said sincerely. "And for your wife. And for you."

The other man blinked back sudden tears. "Thank you, Sire."

Andre turned away to give the man some privacy in his grief and almost ran into his bodyguard. "Get their names, Damon," he stated quietly for his bodyguard's ears alone. There was little enough he could do for the couple. Money to rebuild their house, yes. Money to replace the possessions they'd lost. *But that will not bring back their son,* he thought sadly. He breathed deeply several times, preparing himself mentally for more bad news. Then he headed back to the ongoing rescue effort.

The fresh-faced palace maid assigned to look after Juliana and who went by the name of Daphne had been and gone, tidying the room, drawing Juliana's bath over her protests, asking her what clothes she wanted to wear for the evening and then laying them out, again just ignoring Juliana's protests with a patient smile. Juliana wasn't used to being waited on this way.

Yes, she had her personal assistant, Maddie. Maddie was a necessity to deal with fan mail, to run interference, to perform little errands such as taking clothes to and from the dry cleaner's and to do the hundred and one other things Juliana didn't have time to do for herself as a general rule. But not to wait on her hand and foot. Not to do things Juliana was perfectly capable of doing for herself, like laying out her own clothes and drawing her own bath.

But all Juliana's protests were ignored, and Daphne

continued doing whatever she felt it necessary to do on Juliana's behalf, and eventually Juliana had given in with as good grace as she could muster. She had just finished luxuriating in the perfumed bath Daphne had drawn for her after a long day of filming when there was a sudden loud rapping on her door. Juliana pulled on clean underwear and quickly wrapped her robe securely about her, knotting the belt firmly. The rapping continued, more forcefully than before.

"Okay, okay," she called, but she wasn't sure if the person on the other side of the door could hear her or not, so she hurried to answer it. Dirk stood there, his face a study in worry.

"Got a minute, babe?" he asked Juliana, not waiting for her assent, just moving into her sitting room.

"Sure. What's up?" She turned around to face him as he paced.

"I talked to the director and the producer about changing the filming schedule, and they're willing as long as you agree contractually. In other words, as long as it doesn't cost the film more money. But it means extending your stay in Zakhar."

She started to shake her head. No way did she want to stay a minute longer in Zakhar than she absolutely had to. But then she realized Dirk, the ultimate professional, wouldn't ask her to do this unless he had a really good reason. And the only reason that came to mind was Sabrina. "It's about Bree, isn't it?"

He nodded. "I want to take her back to the States for treatment. I've been talking to her doctors back there, and we've just about convinced Bree chemo will be safe for her *and* the babies now that she's closer to six months along. She's wavering on the surgery, but I'm working on that. I've got scenes to film that don't in-volve you—you know I was supposed to stay on after you leave. But if I can accelerate all my scenes into the next two weeks, my part on the movie will be wrapped up and I'll be free to take Bree back earlier rather than later. But that means the rest of your scenes without me will have to be postponed. Will you do it?"

"You know I will," Juliana responded without hesi-tation. "I don't have another picture lined up—I was going to take a vacation after *King's Ransom*, go visit my father. But he'll understand if I can't make it when I said I would."

"Thanks, babe," he told her, giving her a quick hug and kiss. "I'll tell the producer. He'll probably want you to sign something—you know how that goes. I'll call Marty and give him a heads-up," he added, referring to their lawyer agent. "I owe you big-time."

"Don't be stupid," she chided him. "I love Bree like a sister. I'd do this in a heartbeat for her, you know that. But even if that wasn't the case, I owe you far more than a little thing like this." She put her arms around him and held him tightly. "Think positive, okay? Bree's going to be fine." They walked arm in arm toward the door.

Just as Juliana reached for the old-fashioned door latch, a knock sounded on the door. Her heart skipped a beat and all she could think of was Andre. Andre knocking at her door because he'd promised her he'd never use the secret passageway between their bed-rooms. Andre… And she was alone in her suite with Dirk, wearing a bathrobe with nothing beneath it but skimpy underwear. Until this moment she hadn't real-ized how it might look. *I haven't done anything wrong,* she told herself stoutly. But would Andre believe it? Believe her?

Then she shook that thought off. *Why do I care? Andre doesn't believe me anyway.* Still, before she opened the door she called out, "Who is it?"

"It's Maddie," came the muffled response through the solid oak door.

Juliana let her breath out on a whoosh, and Dirk gave her a knowing look. "Thought it was him, didn't you?" he asked, not needing to specify who *him* was.

With heightened color, she said, "Don't be ridiculous," and opened the door. "What is it, Maddie?"

"Oh," the young woman said as Dirk exited Juliana's room without saying a word, just a smile and a wave. She watched him walk away, then turned her gaze back to Juliana, taking in the robe and Juliana's obvious lack of other clothing beneath it. "Oh, I…I didn't mean to interrupt." Her eyes betrayed what she was imagining.

"Come on in," Juliana told Maddie, leading her into the sitting room and past the open door to the bedroom, wanting her to see the bed completely made up, nothing in the room out of place as it would be if she and Dirk had just spent the preceding hour in a passionate frenzy. And the clothes laid out on the bed ready for her to don them. She smiled to herself when Maddie finally relaxed her tense scrutiny of both rooms.

"Dirk wanted to know if I'd agree to change the filming schedule, and I said I would. That means we'll be staying here longer than originally planned. Will that be a problem for you?" Maddie started to answer, but Juliana added, "If it is, don't be afraid to tell me. You can always go back ahead of me—I'm fine with that."

"Oh no!" Maddie shook her head emphatically. "I love it here. I don't mind staying. Honest."

Juliana smiled. "Okay, then. I'll need you to change our flight reservations, but I'm not sure exactly when we'll be leaving. I have to talk to the producer and the director first, get the revised filming schedule. I'll let you know when I know." She changed the subject. "So what did you come here for? What's up?"

Maddie looked confused for a few seconds, then her confusion cleared. "Oh, I was going to ask if you heard about the landslide."

"What landslide?"

"There was a terrible landslide in the mountains west of here. I saw it on the news. I mean, I saw the pictures, but I had to ask someone what it all meant because I couldn't understand the announcer. They told me a whole village was pretty much wiped out. I don't know how many are dead, but…it's pretty bad."

"Oh my God!" Juliana's hand covered her mouth, and the only thing she could think of was Andre, how devastated he would be by this. These were his *people*. He would take the loss personally—she knew him well enough to know that. Her first instinct was to seek him out, comfort him however she could, but almost immediately she realized that was ridiculous. Andre didn't need her. Not for comfort, or for anything else. "Oh my God," she said again. "Do you know anything more?"

Maddie shook her head. "All I know is what I just told you."

Juliana hugged Maddie quickly. "Thanks," she said. "Thanks for letting me know. I probably wouldn't have found out until tomorrow if you hadn't come to tell me right away."

After Maddie left, Juliana stood in the middle of the room for a moment. Her first instinct—to go to Andre—had been suppressed, but her second instinct was to pray. Pray for the villagers who were suffering tonight. And pray for those whose suffering was over, but who left behind grieving family members. *The chapel,* she thought suddenly. *There's a chapel just downstairs.*

She moved swiftly, ignoring the casual outfit she'd planned to wear that was laid out on her bed, searching instead for a dress in the closet. *Sleeves,* she reminded herself as she rejected first one dress and then another. *Nothing sleeveless for church.* Maybe that was old-fashioned nowadays—she knew most Americans were a lot more casual in their church attire now—but that's the way her father had raised her. And besides, Zakhar hadn't moved with the times the way the United States had. Women still covered their heads in church here, and both men and women still dressed with care for church.

Satisfied with her choice at last, Juliana donned the dress, searched in the dresser for a scarf she could use, then hurried out. Her feet skimmed down the steps of the Grand Staircase, her hand just lightly touching the gilded handrail. She knew where the chapel was on the main floor, in the older part of the palace. She'd been there before when she was younger, but never like this. Never with a desire to alleviate suffering with prayer.

The chapel door was open, and Juliana checked on the threshold, startled. Someone else was already inside. Two someones, actually—both visible in the glow cast by the lit banks of votive candles. One man was kneeling on a prie-dieu in front of the altar railing, his head bowed; the other man was standing a little to one side watching the first man, but not so intently he didn't see Juliana in the doorway when she paused there.

She slipped the scarf over her head, then slid into the last pew, not wanting to intrude. In the few seconds before she bowed her head in prayer she realized who it was who was here before her. *I should have known,* she told herself. *Where else would he be?* Then she resolutely emptied her mind of everything except those she was praying for and began the comforting litany of formal prayers from her childhood.

She didn't know how long she prayed, just that—at the very end—Andre intruded on her thoughts again. Andre, who would be suffering tonight along with his subjects. So she added him to her prayer list. "Help him in his hour of need, Lord," she whispered. "Help him find the words to comfort his people. And help him be strong enough to bear this alone. Amen."

*Alone,* she thought. *So alone in his role as Zakhar's king.* He would comfort others, but who would comfort him? She'd wanted to be that woman all those years ago. Had believed she could be. And if only he'd loved her, she would have been. He wouldn't be alone now.

For the first time she saw not only what she'd lost eleven years ago, but what he'd lost, too. And in that instant a tiny thaw began. She didn't recognize it at first. Didn't realize that her thoughts of Andre at this moment…her prayers for him…and her presence here in the chapel were all reminding her that forgiveness was the path to true healing. She would never heal as long as she refused to forgive Andre. She would always be locked in the bitter past until she let go of her anger and pain, and to do that she needed to forgive him. Her heart would never be free until she did.

Juliana looked up just then and saw Andre rising from his kneeling position in front of the altar. Saw him turn tiredly toward his bodyguard and say something. Saw his bodyguard point in her direction, Andre's gaze following where he pointed. Their eyes met across the distance. Locked. Held. And in her head she heard the words that had haunted her for eleven years. *Come to me, Juliana. Come to me.*

But this time they weren't soft, seductive words. This time they weren't a sensual lure. This time they were the cry of a man in pain, a man who needed someone to take the crushing weight of kingship from his shoulders for a moment. Just for a moment. A man who could be strong in all the ways he needed to be…if only he could let go and be weak for just a moment. If only he had a woman who believed in him. A woman to lend him her strength for that one moment when he couldn't be strong on his own. *Come to me, Juliana. Come to me.*

Loving words. But not lying words. Not anymore.

## Chapter 12

Suddenly Juliana realized Andre and his bodyguard were walking briskly toward her up the chapel's main aisle, and she panicked. She slid from the pew and hurried out the door, her only idea to escape. Because she didn't know what she would say to him. Didn't know how she would react if he searched her eyes, not sure she could hide her feelings. She just knew she wasn't ready to face him, not with everything she'd just come to understand so fresh in her mind.

She raced down the corridor, not caring that her scarf flew off and fluttered to the marble-tiled floor, not caring if anyone saw her running. Not caring if Andre saw her running, either. Then she heard footsteps behind her, not soft like hers; the determined tread of a man who wasn't about to let her escape.

"Juliana!" he called. "Wait!" He caught her at the

foot of the Grand Staircase, snagging her wrist and swinging her around effortlessly to face him. His other hand held the scarf she'd dropped, which he must have stopped to pick up. He didn't say anything, just dropped her wrist so he could loop the scarf around her neck and tie it loosely. Then he stepped back, away from her, and she realized there were eyes everywhere. Not only Andre's bodyguard, who'd followed his king as he raced to catch her, but the guards on duty at the front door, household employees crossing the vast expanse and who knew all else.

She looked up at him, her heart beating wildly. Not just from running, but from the emotions chasing through her at the sight of him in a way she'd never seen him before. He was dusty, dirty, disheveled. His clothes were a mess and almost certainly ruined, rips and tears that could never be invisibly mended. There was a bad scratch across one cheek that looked as if it needed attention—it had drawn blood. And his hands with their long, straight fingers—all except the pinkies and their odd yet endearing defect—his hands were bruised and grimy, some of the nails broken off at the quick. He'd obviously come directly to the chapel from the site of the landslide, directly from the rescue effort without bothering to stop and clean up.

He whispered her name, and she asked the question foremost in her mind. "How many?"

He closed his eyes briefly, and when they opened again she saw the undisguised grief in their depths. "Ninety-seven." He breathed raggedly. "Ninety-seven dead, thirty-two of them children."

"Oh God," she whispered, appalled.

"The dead are mostly women and little children. The

older children were all in school—the village does not have its own school, thank God, so the schoolchildren are bused into Drago. Most of the men were at work and away from the village when the landslide occurred, but many of them heard the rumble as the mountain let go and hurried back. It was a good thing they did—we needed those extra hands in the rescue effort."

"How many wounded?" she asked softly.

"Nearly twice as many, some of them seriously. The seriously wounded ones are in hospital. The ones who had only minor injuries, or who were miraculously unharmed, are being housed in the surrounding villages and in Red Cross shelters, as are all the ones who were not there when it happened. The village of Taryna itself was destroyed. Not a single structure is safe to occupy." His face hardened. "And even if the buildings were safe I would not let anyone stay there. We do not know if the mountain is done."

"Do they know…? Have they found everyone?"

A muscle twitched in his cheek as he said in an undertone, "Do you think I would have left there tonight otherwise?"

And as he said it Juliana knew it was the simple truth. Andre wouldn't have left the site until everyone—every man, woman and child—was accounted for. How she knew this she wasn't sure. Eleven years had wrought changes in him she was just beginning to comprehend. He'd always had a compassionate nature—she couldn't have loved him otherwise. But the selflessness involved in a search like this—ignoring the risk to himself—the empathy he obviously felt for the suffering of his subjects, were new to her. Sterling aspects of his character she'd never really encountered before.

She ached for him, knowing his pain as if it were her own. She wanted to raise her hand and brush away the dust from his golden-brown hair. Wanted to take a warm, damp cloth and soak the blood from his cheek. And she wanted—desperately wanted—to hold his head against her breast and let him ease his suffering in the shelter of her arms. But all she could do was gaze at him, her heart in her eyes. Telling him without words everything she yearned to do for him.

Andre caught his breath and mouthed her name. And the little thaw that had begun in the chapel turned into a strong Chinook blowing warmly across the frozen wasteland that was Juliana's heart.

She would never forget this moment, she knew. Would never forget the need in his eyes. Not a physical need. This wasn't *wanting*. This wasn't desire. He felt those things for her, too, of course. He was a man, after all. She'd known he wanted her, desired her the night of the reception. But this wasn't anything like that. This was raw, emotional need. Need, like the way a man admitted he needed a woman to complete him. Need, like the way a strong man needed a woman he could be vulnerable with. The kind of need that went hand in hand with love. The way Andre had looked at her eleven years ago, his brilliant green eyes alight as he whispered, *"Now it begins."*

He would never forget this moment, he knew. Would never forget the soft compassion in Juliana's eyes, would never forget the yearning he saw there. Not a physical yearning, but rather a desire to hold, to comfort, to heal. The way a woman looked at the man who held her heart when she knew he was suffering, the desire to take away his pain. The way Juliana had looked at him eleven years ago, when she came to him in the night, saying, *"I heard you calling to me... Please, Andre... I love you... Let me give you tonight..."* Her beautiful violet eyes telling him she loved him even without the words.

If he were just a man she would be in his arms now. If he were just a man he would carry her up the stairs to his bedroom, and then she would tell him the words he longed to hear again, the words he'd craved for eleven years. He would lose himself in her arms, then awake refreshed, strong, able to take on the weight of the whole world. If he were just a man he would have gone to her years ago, taking whatever she offered...however little or much that was. If he were just a man...

But he wasn't just a man. He was a king. A king in chains—chained to his duty, his responsibility, his subjects. He couldn't ask his people to accept a queen who might leave him someday. Divorce was out of the question. Juliana *had* to come to him. Did she understand? *Could* she understand? For himself it would not have mattered. But for Zakhar he could not take that risk.

So instead of blurting out the words in his heart, he merely said, "Thank you."

A puzzled look crept into her eyes. "For what?"

Unsmiling and with deep sincerity, he said, "For your prayers."

She let out her breath in a soft little rush. "It's little enough. I couldn't think of anything else I could do when I heard the news."

He shook his head. "Not a little thing, Juliana. You care. You care about the people around you. You hurt for them. Feel their pain. Your prayers are heartfelt. No, it is not a little thing, your prayers."

"Is there anything else I can do?"

He hesitated. "The Red Cross will be making an appeal for donations. Your face, your name is well-known. If you would…?"

"I'd be happy to. That, and anything else you can think of."

"Thank you." He stared at Juliana for endless seconds, wanting to say more, but knowing now wasn't the time and place. Knowing they needed privacy for what was in their hearts. But he was comforted by the knowledge that the time was coming. He could sleep tonight for once, knowing the time was surely coming. Juliana would come to him, and then they would say everything they needed to say.

When Juliana woke the next morning, her first thought was of the tragedy that had occurred the day before. Her second thought was of Andre. His face last night. Vulnerable. Defenseless. Needing her the way she'd once believed he needed her. Loved her. Could she have been wrong about him all these years?

*Forgive me,* he'd begged her that day at the cemetery. Did he regret what he'd done years ago? Had he subconsciously been asking forgiveness for that as well as his rough treatment of her in front of the lovers' tomb? But she had still been too wounded to forgive. She'd still been clinging to her own anger and pain. She'd lashed out at him and told him she would never forgive him.

But it wasn't true. In her heart of hearts hadn't she already forgiven him for almost everything? Could she remember their one night of love so poignantly if she hadn't?

Everything he did, everything he said, the way he'd

looked at her last night—needing her in such an elemental way her heart had responded instinctively—
everything told her that even if he'd never loved her
all those years ago, he loved her now. And love was
too precious to waste.

*Too precious to waste.*

Juliana walked out of her meeting with the producer
and director of *King's Ransom* with a new shooting
schedule in her hand and a copy of a legal document
that had already been scanned and emailed to her lawyer agent, Marty Devens. The time difference between
Zakhar and California meant that Marty was still sleeping. He wouldn't have had a chance to review the contract modification and give it his blessing. But she
already knew even if he didn't she would sign it. For
the first time in their ten-year friendship Dirk needed
her help. Dirk and Sabrina had given her so much—
now when they needed something from her in return
she wasn't about to refuse.

She glanced down at the schedule. She'd already reviewed it with the producer, but she just wanted to con-
firm what he'd said, that she had no scenes to shoot for
the next three days. All the scenes involving Dirk alone
had been escalated. For the next three days Dirk would
be playing Andre Alexei during the time Eleonora was a
captive far away. Including his lightning raids on neigh-
boring kingdoms for the treasure he needed to ransom
his queen. They would also be shooting the daring final
raid, the one where Andre Alexei was fatally injured.

She was free until Friday, when she and Dirk would
film the scene that took place between the first king
and queen of Zakhar right before that final raid, among

others. The scene where Eleonora begged her husband not to go after the ransom he'd paid for her sixteen years earlier. Not to try to exact vengeance for something so far distant.

But Andre Alexei couldn't let it go. Recovering the ransom was secondary, he'd told his wife. Someone was going to pay in blood for everything she'd gone through. Someone was going to pay in blood for every scar she bore, every nightmare that still haunted her. Someone was going to pay in blood for the humiliation and helplessness he'd suffered knowing his wife—the woman he loved—had been raped and tortured, and there hadn't been a thing he could do to prevent it. And now that the opportunity had finally presented itself, he was damned if he'd turn the other cheek.

*His fatal flaw,* she realized. The first king of Zakhar had carried that anger inside him for years. Not white-hot, but simmering below the surface. A powerful anger born of a powerful love. And because he couldn't forgive, because his thirst for vengeance had finally overpowered him, he'd died, and Eleonora had died, too. *Would he have done it if he'd known?* she wondered. If he'd known Eleonora would choose him, would choose death with him over life without him, would he have risked his own life merely for vengeance?

There was no way to know for sure, but she wanted to believe he wouldn't have done it. Wanted to believe his love was strong enough to put Eleonora's life above his own needs, the way he'd done years before when he ransomed her.

Her thoughts moved to Andre. *Her* Andre. And he *was* her Andre, she recognized with a shock. Maybe he hadn't been hers eleven years ago, but he was now.

For the time being anyway. Maybe he didn't love her the way she loved him. Maybe he didn't love her the way Andre Alexei had loved Eleonora. But he loved her *now.* Needed her *now. Maybe not forever and a day. But enough. Enough for now.* And on that thought she went in search of him.

Juliana finally ran Andre to ground, after much searching, in the official royal office suite that had once been his father's. She remembered his father as a stern, unsmiling man, who tolerated her friendship with Princess Mara merely because he barely tolerated Mara herself, and cared little for anything to do with Mara's life. It was different with Andre. All the then-king's hopes and dreams were tied up in his heir, and he begrudged anything that took Andre's attention away from learning the business of running the country. Zakhar first and foremost had been his credo, and Andre's father had demanded his son's attendance at nearly every official function.

The old king had bitterly resented any attention Andre had paid to Mara, too, not just to Juliana. Mara had never said anything, and neither had Andre. But Juliana had known. She'd contrasted her own father's loving treatment of her with the way Mara's father had brushed his daughter aside, time and again. She'd compared her own father's interest in the minutiae of her admittedly less than stellar school accomplishments with the complete indifference Mara's father had shown toward Mara's outstanding academic achievements and her brilliance in mathematics, and had pitied her friend.

She remembered now that Andre had never knuckled under to his father, not regarding Mara or anything else. Mara had told her once that Andre was stronger than anyone who went against him, and not just physically. The old king had ranted and raved against it, but Andre had insisted on serving the requisite four years with the Zakharian National Forces demanded of every other Zakharian male—and had done so.

He'd even voluntarily served an additional year when his unit had been called upon to go to Afghanistan on behalf of the United Nations, she remembered. She hadn't known it at the time, but she'd read about it when he ascended the throne—the tabloids had been full of stories about him and his exploits, and she hadn't been able to resist reading everything written about him.

The old king had also ruthlessly tried to separate Andre from Mara—and failed. Juliana had watched as Andre had quietly, but insistently, done his best to fill the void in Mara's life, and if she hadn't already loved him she would have loved him for that alone—for his tender, loving attitude toward his younger sister, for the protective shield he threw around her. The same way he'd treated Juliana, until…

And Mara had adored Andre. Wasn't that why Juliana had broken off her friendship with Mara, rather than disillusion her friend about her beloved brother? Because she couldn't bear the hero worship in Mara's voice when she talked about Andre? Because she'd wanted to scream the truth about him the last time they'd spoken on the phone…but couldn't hurt Mara that way? Couldn't destroy the only loving influence in Mara's life? Better to let her friend think Juliana no longer cared. Better to let Mara think Juliana didn't need her friendship anymore. Anything except tell Mara what Andre had done when he'd repudiated any relationship with Juliana.

Her thoughts in turmoil, Juliana entered the outer office, where three male secretaries guarded entrance to the inner sanctum with smiling but unshakable resolution. "I am sorry, Miss Richardson," the appointments secretary told her. "His Royal Majesty is extremely busy this morning. I could make an appointment for you at…" He looked at the computer screen, checking the calendar there. "Three o'clock tomorrow afternoon." He smiled, anticipating her acquiescence, his next question merely a formality. "Would that do?"

Juliana stood her ground. "His Majesty asked me last night if I would film an appeal for the Red Cross relating to the landslide. The sooner, the better, I thought. Could you ask him about it? He didn't give me any details when we spoke."

"Of course, Miss Richardson. Excuse me a moment." The secretary slid from his chair, knocked on the door to the inner office and waited for a response before opening the door, entering and closing it behind him. He was back in less than a minute. "Please come this way, Miss Richardson," the appointments secretary said. And while he'd always been respectful, there was a different intonation now, a deference that hadn't been there before.

Andre was on the phone when she entered, but he smiled his faint smile as soon as he saw her and indicated a chair in front of his desk. Juliana seated herself and looked around the room as she waited. She couldn't remember ever having been in the inner office before, but she imagined it had been completely redone when Andre ascended the throne, because it didn't look like the kind of office the old king would have had.

The furniture here now suited Andre somehow.

Not modern, not casual, but not stiffly formal, either. Comfortable. She imagined he spent a lot of time here. Zakhar wasn't a large country—*probably equivalent in size to the state of Vermont,* she thought abstractedly, although even more mountainous. But running a country wouldn't be a sinecure, not if you threw yourself into the job heart and soul, the way Andre did.

When she turned her head all the way to the right she saw Andre's bodyguard—not the one who'd accompanied the king in the chapel last night, a different one—sitting motionless in a chair in the corner. After she thought about it for a moment, she realized he looked like the same bodyguard who'd been on duty the night of the reception. She remembered him because after Andre had spoken to him he'd faded back into the crowd, but his eyes had never left the man he was guarding. And now that she thought of it, he was also the one who'd been on duty outside the little library the evening she and Andre had confronted one another.

She gave the bodyguard a friendly smile of recognition, but he didn't smile back. He merely acknowledged her smile with an inclination of his head and a slight softening of his expression, and with Andre still on the phone her thoughts went on a tangent.

Bodyguards. She'd gotten used to the necessity in the United States. There were crazies out there, and no one recognizably famous was safe. It had been refreshing not to need a bodyguard here in Zakhar, but then again, she was just an actress. She wasn't in Andre's shoes. Even though Zakhar was fiercely loyal to the monarchy, there was always a chance someone might try to assassinate him. There had been two attempts on his life since he ascended the throne—that had been front-page news; it had been impossible to avoid…even if she hadn't read everything she could about Andre over the years. But judging from the careful way this man watched over his king, Andre was in good hands.

*Only one bodyguard, though?* she thought, suddenly worried for Andre's safety, remembering the team of Secret Service agents who surrounded the US president whenever he went anywhere. *Shouldn't Andre have at least two people guarding him? Or more?* Maybe he did…when he was outside the palace. *No, that can't be right,* she reminded herself. There had been only one bodyguard in evidence at the cemetery.

Andre made one last forceful statement into the phone, and Juliana understood enough Zakharan to know he didn't agree with whoever was on the other end before he hung up the phone with a decided bang. She raised her eyebrows in a question, and Andre made a derisive sound. "That was my chief councillor. The Privy Council is dragging its feet…again." She saw the struggle for patience on his face. "As usual, Niko is… But that is not why you are here, Juliana," he said with another faint smile. "Thank you for coming so quickly to help with the disaster relief. But are you not needed on the set today?"

She shook her head. "I'm free until Friday. They've rearranged the schedule so Dirk can leave earlier."

He frowned. "Why is that? The producer never mentioned it to me."

"It just came up yesterday evening," she explained. "And you were otherwise occupied."

"But why?" Juliana's gaze slid in the direction of Andre's bodyguard, though she didn't say anything. But Andre got the message. "Lukas," he told his bodyguard, "would you leave us, please? I will let you know when we are done."

"Yes, Sire."

The man got up, casting a searching look over Juliana, as if he thought she might be concealing a weapon somewhere. *Although where he thinks it's hidden is a mystery to me,* she thought, suddenly amused despite the seriousness of the situation. She was wearing a lightweight summer dress similar to the one she'd worn the other night in the little library, but this one was in a deep shade of rose, a vibrant color that set off her ebony hair and made her skin look translucent. It had a fitted bodice and swirling skirt, but a skirt that clung to her figure, leaving no room for anything bulky hidden beneath it. Add to that bare legs and sandals, and she didn't think she looked like a threat. On the other hand, she didn't fault Lukas for his devotion to duty. Terrorists didn't always *look* like terrorists, and women could be assassins, too.

When they were alone finally, Andre steepled his fingers and touched them to his lips before asking, "Why?" And Juliana knew the time had come to tell him the truth.

## Chapter 13

"Dirk's wife, Sabrina, has cancer," Juliana said on a rush. "But there's a complication. She's also pregnant." She gave Andre an appealing look. "You can't tell anyone, not even Dirk, that you know. Bree has told people about the pregnancy, but she doesn't know Dirk told me about the cancer. He told me in confidence. I'm trusting you because—"

"So that is it," he said softly, interrupting her, and Juliana knew he'd made the connection between this information and all the seemingly intimate exchanges he'd witnessed between Dirk and her. "Why could you not tell me this before?" There was a strained note in his voice—not harsh, not accusing, more like…hurt. Hurt she hadn't trusted him enough to confide in him. And surprising to her, hurt and regretful he hadn't trusted her, either.

He got up and walked over to one of the bookcases

that lined the room, running his fingers blindly over the bindings. "I owe you an apology, little one," he said with his back still turned to her, his voice very deep. "And DeWinter, too."

"Yes, but you can't apologize to him. Not now. You can't tell him you know." She took a deep breath. "Anyway, that's why they're changing the schedule all around. Dirk wants to take Bree back to the States for treatment. Bree wants him to finish filming *King's Ransom* first. Dirk thinks he can be done in less than two weeks, and it's possible. But that means putting all my scenes without him off into the future."

"So you will be staying in Zakhar longer than originally planned?" Andre still hadn't turned around, but now he did. And there was an expression on his face that told Juliana this was good news to him.

"Yes," she confirmed. "And because the shooting schedule's been rearranged on *King's Ransom*, that means I'm free the next few days to film that appeal for the Red Cross you mentioned. And free to help in any other way I can." She looked him full in the face. "What can I do? How can I help?"

Juliana stood in the midst of the devastation, hearing Andre's voice from the night before, *"Ninety-seven dead, thirty-two of them children."* Looking at the houses knocked off their footings, some buildings seemingly exploded from the inside out and some just literally wiped off the face of the earth, it was hard to believe *anyone* had survived when the mountain had rumbled down on Taryna.

Electricity was still out, and the natural gas was still turned off, Andre had told her just before their helicopter had taken off. But large portable generators had been brought in to provide power for the cleanup crews, along with tents, cots and portable restrooms for their use. And there were a couple of Red Cross food trucks dispensing hot coffee and meals for the workers around the clock. Andre had mobilized a small army on short notice.

Juliana glanced down at the script she'd been given, in both English and Zakharan, but she'd already memorized her few lines that would be spoken on camera. The rest would be a voice-over, while the disaster footage the camera crew was shooting now was shown. For that she didn't need to memorize; she just needed to rehearse so it wouldn't sound as if she was reading from a script when she spoke her appeal for donations.

She looked over to where Andre was standing with a team of structural engineers, hydrologists and geochemists he'd carefully assembled to assess the damage and ongoing situation. They were all dressed in sturdy clothing and hiking boots, including Andre. Every resident of the small village had been accounted for, but there were still questions. When—if ever—would the survivors be able to return to retrieve their personal possessions? Which houses were safe to enter, if not to occupy? Would the records in the town hall be recoverable, the official lists of births, marriages and deaths that went back hundreds of years? And could Taryna be rebuilt where it was? Or was it just too dangerous? What had caused the landslide in the first place? And was there any way to tell if the mountain was done, as Andre had so succinctly worded it?

Two more victims had died that morning—an elderly woman and her infant granddaughter, who'd both been barely clinging to life when they'd been found in the wreckage of their home—raising the death toll to ninety-nine, fully a third of them small children. Juliana had been standing next to Andre, preparing to board the helicopter, when he'd received that unwelcome news. He'd folded his lips even more sternly, but that was the only reaction he'd allowed himself. And yet…she knew it was another blow to him, the same way it was to her. It *mattered*.

Now as she watched him walking about the ruins of Taryna with the assessment team she realized he wouldn't spare himself in this. He wouldn't ask anyone to take a risk he wasn't willing to take, wouldn't stand back while others did the work. He was a "Come on, men!" leader, not a "Go on, men!" king. She remembered the way he'd looked last night, remembered his hands particularly. Bruised. Filthy. Nails broken off. As if she'd been there beside him yesterday in the wreckage, she knew he'd been in the thick of the search for survivors, using his hands to dig out those who were trapped when using machinery would have been just too dangerous.

And then, when everyone who could be rescued had been rescued, he'd gone directly to the chapel in the palace. Bone weary, but not ready to give up until everything that could be done had been done. He would push himself until he collapsed, because that was the kind of man he was. The man she'd fallen in love with years ago…and still loved. Not cold. Not callous. Not uncaring. She'd been wrong about that. What else had she been wrong about?

Juliana and the film crew were long finished taping. The crew had packed up their equipment in the helicopter they'd arrived in and had headed back more than an hour ago. They'd willingly offered her a ride—she recognized the frank, male appreciation in their eyes, but she knew it wouldn't go beyond that, and that wasn't why she'd turned the offer down. She just wanted to wait for Andre, no matter how long it took. She'd come here with him and wanted to return with him. *Dance with the man who brought you,* she heard her father say in her head. And despite the tragedy that had occurred here yesterday—or maybe because of it—she couldn't help but smile a little at the quaint normalcy of her father's advice.

It wasn't a modern concept. But then, her father was nearly old enough to be her grandfather, so his mores were those of two generations earlier. He'd married late—he'd been almost forty-six when she was born, and since her mother had died when Juliana was four, she was his only child and the darling of his heart. He'd retired when she was twenty, barely a year after she went to Hollywood—Zakhar had been his last ambassadorial posting.

He'd been a good father, though. A good role model. Not perfect, but he'd done his best, and she loved him dearly. *I should call him,* she reminded herself, making a mental note. They were in constant contact via email, but that wasn't really the same he'd told her more than once. And no texting for him—he preferred hearing her voice—he was old-fashioned that way, too.

Some of the things he'd taught her growing up were definitely outdated, like the fact that the first and last dance of the evening belonged by right to the man whose date you were—hence the advice, *dance with the man who brought you.* Like the fact that good girls don't.

Her smile faded. *Good girls don't.* But she hadn't been a girl when she'd sought Andre out. She'd been a woman. A woman in love. She hadn't thought she was doing anything wrong by showing Andre how much she loved him. And he hadn't seemed to think anything bad of her because of it…not that night, and not the next morning. It was only later—when he'd sent her the money—that she'd writhed in humiliation at how easy she'd been. How cheaply he seemed to hold the gift she'd given him. How cheaply he seemed to value her.

And yet…that didn't seem to be the way he thought of her now. *"You gave yourself to me once,"* he'd told her the other night. As if she'd been a precious gift, one he treasured in his memory and wanted to keep forever.

Once again she realized that too many things didn't make sense. Too many contradictions between what she knew had happened then and what she was hearing now. Dirk telling her Andre believed she'd deserted him, but he was determined to win her back anyway. She'd been adamant Andre had lied to Dirk, but…what if he hadn't been lying? *"Tell me, Juliana,"* Andre had said that night in the little library even before he'd talked with Dirk. *"If not DeWinter, then who? Someone hurt you. Someone broke your heart… Tell me who it was."*

And when she'd accused *him* of being the one who broke her heart, he'd said, *"Do not lie to me, Juliana. Your heart was not broken when you chose to go to Hollywood instead of returning to Zakhar that summer."* She'd been shocked at how he was twisting things around. But…what if he wasn't? What if he truly believed it? Was it possible?

Nothing made sense anymore. Least of all the money he'd sent her. The money…and the motive behind it.

She could forgive him almost anything else now that he seemed to love her again. But the money was the one thing she was finding nearly impossible to forgive because it was the one thing she couldn't explain away.

It was nearly dark by the time Andre returned to the village with the assessment team, and the temperature had dropped with the setting sun. Even though it was summer, the average temperature in the mountains here near Taryna was twenty to twenty-five degrees cooler than it was in Drago, and Andre and the rest of the team had dressed accordingly.

His brain was fully occupied with the answers the engineers, hydrologists and geochemists had come up with for all the questions he'd originally posed to them, as well as the additional questions that had been raised as a result of what they'd uncovered. Exhaustion tugged at him, but he refused to give in to it. The rest of the team was dragging after the miles they'd hiked today, miles in the thinner mountain air that made it more difficult to replenish the oxygen their muscles burned.

But Andre knew no one would complain as long as he never showed even a hint of weakness, so he was careful not to show it. Still, he was glad to see the church tower of Taryna in the distance. He'd pushed himself to the limit yesterday, and today had been the same. He'd be glad to get back to the palace, glad for the simple luxury of being alone so he wouldn't have to hide his weakness from the world.

They passed through the village, and Andre stopped to talk with the man spearheading the cleanup operation— a colonel in the Zakharian National Forces and a whiz at organization. "Go on ahead," he told the other members of the team. "Do not wait for me. We will meet tomorrow at the palace at—" he looked at his wristwatch and amended his initial time "—9:00 a.m. I would like a written report from each of you detailing your observations and recommendations." He smiled at them. "Thank you. You are all invaluable to this team. I will see you tomorrow."

Dismissed, the rest of the assessment team headed to where the helicopters had been waiting since their arrival this morning. Andre's personal bodyguard stayed behind with the king, of course, and Andre mentally counted up the number of team members and the number of available seats in each helicopter, satisfying himself that everyone would have a seat in the three helicopters that had brought the team here, even though a couple of the structural engineers had arrived earlier this morning with the cleanup crew. He wouldn't hold anyone up by staying to get a progress report on the cleanup.

He spent twenty minutes with the colonel, committing relevant information to memory, and agreeing with the colonel's request for more manpower. "You will have it," he told the colonel in no uncertain terms. *Even if I have to disregard the Privy Council's wishes,* he thought with a sudden spurt of internal anger. *Again.*

When he was done Andre and his bodyguard headed to the royal helicopter. He suddenly thought of Juliana as they passed the spot where she'd stood in front of the cameras, a children's playground, where the playground equipment—swings, jungle gym and seesaws—were all half buried in dirt and rocks. He smiled to himself, remembering how she'd unerringly picked that spot as the most poignant, and the most likely to ap-

peal to parents the world over even without her saying
a single word. He'd watched the filming for a few moments before the assessment team had headed up the
mountain. Somewhere in the piles of wreckage that had
once been houses, Juliana had uncovered a battered and
filthy baby doll, and she'd cradled it in her arms as the
cameras rolled.

He'd already put in motion the soon-to-be-broadcasted
Red Cross appeal, both on television within Zakhar and
via the internet worldwide. Juliana's face, her emotive
voice, her appeal in both English and Zakharan, would
soften the heart of anyone, and donations would pour
in as soon as the edited film was available. He made a
mental note to check on that first thing in the morning,
before his meeting with the assessment team. The sooner
the Red Cross appeals began, the better for the Taryna
villagers, no matter how the Privy Council dragged its
feet on the relief effort.

His smile faded when they reached the royal helicopter and he saw Juliana huddled inside, curled up in
one of the seats, fast asleep. The military pilot, who'd
waited with the chopper the entire day, and one of Juliana's bodyguards—a man she wasn't aware was her
bodyguard—had both placed their jackets over her,
Andre noted. But even though she was a little bit of a
thing the jackets wouldn't stretch to cover her entire
body. She was wearing slacks and a long-sleeved shirt,
but she wasn't dressed for the mountains, not after the
sun went down and the temperature plummeted. He
cursed under his breath. *Why didn't Juliana return to
Drago with the film crew earlier?* he asked himself.
*Why did she stay here?*

He climbed in, hearing the men's apologies in a distant recess of his brain, and responding to them automatically. "Not your fault," he reassured them. "It was mine for not making sure she was dressed for the mountains before we left Drago. You did the right thing. Thank you for looking after her as you did."

He told himself he should wake her. Told himself anything else would be a mistake. But he couldn't do it. He picked her up effortlessly and sat down in her seat, cradling her in his arms for a moment, and that's when he realized she was still clutching the baby doll she'd used as a prop that morning. She'd brushed the dirt away but the damage wrought by the landslide was still evident.

She made an incoherent murmur and snuggled closer to him, closer to his warmth, but she didn't waken. If he'd been alone with her he would have kissed her awake. But he wasn't alone. And kissing her in front of the chopper pilot and the bodyguards—no matter how discreet they were—was out of the question. Even holding her like this was an indiscretion.

With a tiny sigh he lifted her over and deposited her in the seat next to him, then buckled her seat belt. She woke when he did that. Slowly. Her eyes fluttering open and staring up at him as if she couldn't figure out where she was or why she was there.

"Hi," she said, finally focusing, unable to suppress a sudden yawn. A yawn followed by an unguarded smile that took his breath away. "Everything done?"

"For today. Tomorrow is another day, but that will not affect you." He turned away from her and reached over abruptly to accept the wireless headset the pilot handed him over his shoulder, then fitted the headset in place and buckled his seat belt. He nodded at the pilot's questioning look, and the engines roared to life.

They were less than halfway back to Drago when one of the helicopter's engines began stuttering, like a car that wasn't firing on all cylinders. Juliana wasn't worried at first. But when the helicopter began bucking and swaying, when they began losing altitude and the pilot and André exchanged a quick flurry of words through their wireless headsets, she grew concerned. She wanted to ask what was going on, but knew now wasn't the time. Whatever the problem was, it wouldn't help for her to ask frantic questions. She just had to trust in André's military pilot...and André.

*Prayer won't hurt,* Juliana decided. She'd always been uncomfortable praying for herself, but she wasn't the only one in the helicopter. She closed her eyes and clasped her hands tightly together as she prayed, refusing to watch while the helicopter spun out of control and the earth came up shudderingly fast to meet them.

Juliana was grateful for the seat belt holding her in place, because otherwise she would have been thrown from side to side in even more sickening fashion with the buffeting the helicopter took. Then a strong arm slid around her shoulders and a large hand closed around both of hers, squeezing gently.

When she opened her eyes she saw André watching her with an expression she was hard-pressed to describe. Love was there, but so was reassurance. Reassurance they weren't going to crash. And even if they did, his eyes seemed to be saying, she would walk away from it. She knew it wasn't true. She knew if they crashed no one would walk away. But it helped. Not that she wanted to die, but it helped to know that Andre was with her, that she wouldn't die alone.

Then she gasped as something suddenly became clear to her. *That's why Eleonora did what she did,* she realized. *Not just because she couldn't bear life without her husband, but so he wouldn't die alone.*

She turned her hand and linked her fingers with Andre's, then she tightened her grip. This time when she prayed, she prayed for the courage to face whatever was to come—for both of them.

The pilot did something—Juliana was never sure exactly what—and the crippled helicopter stopped stuttering and shaking. Then slowly, agonizingly, as seconds ticked into minutes, they regained altitude, though their speed had noticeably slackened. She breathed suddenly, only then realizing she'd been holding her breath in anticipation of crashing.

Andre spoke through his wireless headset to the pilot in Zakharan, too quickly for Juliana to catch the words and translate them. And she couldn't hear the pilot's response. But she knew from Andre's tone that he was angry about something. Not angry with the pilot—that wasn't it at all. But he was holding on to his temper with fierce restraint.

They managed to make it back to Drago and land safely without further incident, but Juliana hadn't spoken the rest of the flight. Even when the crisis seemed to have passed, it would have been difficult to converse with Andre over the sound of the one remaining engine without raising her voice. She wanted to ask him what had just happened—what had failed and what the pilot had done to save them. But Andre's face was set in stern

lines, and she didn't want to bring up a topic that was
already a sore point with him.

There were other questions she wanted to ask—
unrelated questions. But they were complex questions,
needing more than just a yes or no answer. She wanted
to know what would happen to the village of Taryna.
Wanted to know the ultimate fate planned for the survivors of the landslide. The pilot had been in radio contact with his military superiors in Drago all day, so she
knew no one else had died, and she'd sent up a little
prayer of thankfulness every time he'd given her a status
report in answer to her questions. But he couldn't tell
her what the assessment team had found—only Andre
could do that, and she wanted to know. Not because she
was curious, but because she wanted him to share that
difficult part of his life with her, wanted to know what
he was thinking, feeling. Just as she had last night, she
wanted to be the one he confided in.

*Trouble shared is trouble halved,* her father used
to say when she was a little girl. It was a simple statement, but profoundly true. Nothing ever seemed quite
so bad if you could talk about it with someone else. It
had been true when she was a little girl, and it was still
true now. Hadn't it helped Dirk for him to confide in
her about Sabrina's illness? Hadn't it helped him when
she'd been able to give him insight into what Sabrina
was going through from a woman's perspective? The
dilemma she was facing and the decisions she'd made?

*And what about you?* she asked herself. *Didn't you
feel a tremendous sense of relief when you finally confided in Bree about what happened with Andre years
ago?* Not that she'd told her friend everything. But that
discussion had opened the door to a place in Juliana's

## Chapter 14

But Andre wasn't available to ask…anything. Once they arrived back at the palace's heliport in Drago, Andre spoke with the pilot in Zakharan too quick for her to catch. The man nodded—in understanding? In acquiescence? Juliana couldn't be sure.

Two additional bodyguards were waiting at the heliport for their arrival, probably in response to the incident with the helicopter engine that the pilot must have reported. Before he left in their company, Andre addressed the man who'd looked after her all day, making sure she had everything she needed. This time she understood what Andre was saying in Zakharan when he told the man, "See her safely into the palace. Let nothing happen to her." She was unexpectedly touched by his concern for her, although she knew it was misplaced.

Andre turned to her. "I must leave you here. I have

heart that had been locked for eleven years, had allowed her to look at things from another perspective. Andre's perspective.

So the questions about Taryna weren't the only ones she had. She also wanted to ask Andre about the money. The money he'd sent her eleven years ago, and the motive behind it. If she could bring herself to do that—and it wouldn't be easy, she didn't fool herself it would be easy even to ask the question, much less listen to his answer—that discussion would have a pivotal effect on her life. Because if she could forgive him for the money, she would stay in Zakhar. She would stay because she loved him and always would.

But if she couldn't forgive him…she would leave when *King's Ransom* was done, and she would never see him again. Her self-respect wouldn't allow her any other option. As much as she loved him, there were some boundaries she couldn't cross, and keeping her self-respect was one of them. Just as she couldn't stay with a man who physically or verbally abused her no matter how much she loved him, she couldn't stay with Andre without an explanation she could accept and forgive.

a meeting with the Privy Council already scheduled—they are waiting for my return."

"I understand," she replied quickly.

He looked as if he wanted to kiss her, but he didn't. He left with a hasty "Thank you again, little one" instead, words uttered in a caressing undertone that told Juliana he didn't want to leave her just then...but had to.

Juliana's escort took her into the palace, then left as soon as she entered the door to the Queen's Suite and closed it firmly behind her. Once there she realized she desperately needed to talk with someone about the chaos in her mind. Someone she'd taken her troubles to when she was a little girl, and who'd never failed to give her wise counsel. She wasn't a little girl any longer, but still...

She pulled her cell phone out of her purse and checked the time, thankful Maddie had obtained a sim card for her so she could use her phone in Zakhar. She mentally tried to calculate the time difference between Zakhar and Virginia but couldn't remember how many time zones she'd crossed on her flight here and whether you subtracted time or added it. Then she crossed her fingers in hopes it wasn't too early, and hit speed dial for her father.

When he answered, she said, "I hope I didn't wake you, Dad."

He laughed softly. "What time is it there, Juliana?"

She glanced at the ormolu clock on the mantelpiece. "Almost seven. In the evening."

"We're six hours behind you. Which means it's early afternoon here. So unless you were talking about disturbing my afternoon nap..."

Juliana winced. "Sorry, Dad. Math never was my strong point."

Her father chuckled in her ear. "That's okay, honey. I wouldn't have minded if you *had* woken me. It's good to hear your voice no matter what." He cleared his throat. "So what's wrong?"

"I don't just call you when something's wrong," she protested.

"No, but I've known you all your life," he reminded her. "And a father can tell when something's troubling his baby girl."

"Oh, Dad..." She laughed, more rueful than anything else. "That's just it. I'm not your baby girl anymore. And I..." *Good girls don't,* she suddenly remembered him saying, and realized this might not be such a good idea, after all.

"It's about Andre, isn't it?" he asked her gently.

She gasped. "How did you know?"

"You think I didn't know how you felt about him all those years ago? That I didn't know you loved him with all your heart when you left Zakhar to attend college? You think because I'm an old man I don't remember what it's like to be in love?"

"You're not old."

"I'm seventy-five, honey. That's old in anyone's book, especially mine. But I remember the moment I met your mother as if it were yesterday. I loved her then and I love her still. I always will. Her death didn't change that."

Her breath caught in her throat. "You...you've never really talked about Mom with me that way. You told me what she was like, but...not about how you felt. About..." She didn't know how to finish that sentence.

He was silent for a moment. "I waited a long time to

fall in love, Juliana. You know that much. And I only had your mother for five years before she was taken from me. But I wouldn't trade one moment of the time I *did* have with her for anything you could offer me. I wouldn't be surprised if you finally realize that's how you feel about Andre now that you've seen him again, and that's why you're calling me."

When Juliana didn't answer, he said, "I never brought it up at the time because I figured if you wanted my advice you'd ask for it. You always had before. But even though you didn't ask, I couldn't help but wonder what happened between the two of you. Wonder why you stopped loving him. *If* you stopped loving him."

The slight upward inflection on the last sentence turned it into a half question.

"I...didn't," she managed. "But he..."

"Don't tell me he stopped loving you," her father stated unequivocally. "Because I refuse to believe it."

"I... It's complicated," Juliana stammered out. "You don't know... I never told you, Dad, but..."

"But you slept with him the night before you left Zakhar." Stunned speechless, Juliana could only gasp again. "Oh, baby," her father said with tenderness, "did you think I wouldn't know?"

"But...you never said anything."

"What should I have said? It was your decision. I figured you knew what you were doing—or thought you did. I figured you'd gone to him—which was no more than your mother did when she sought me out."

"Mom did that?" Juliana couldn't believe what she was hearing. "But you said... You told me good girls don't."

"Girls, yes. But you weren't a girl by then, any more than your mother was when we fell in love." He hesitated. "Is that why you never asked me for advice on this? Because you thought I'd judge you harshly?" His voice softened with regret. "Oh, baby, I'm sorry. If I'd known…I would have said something."

His sigh sounded in her ear. "I never thought badly of you for what you did. I never thought badly of Andre, either, or that he took advantage of you—well, no more than I thought badly of myself for not being able to resist your mother when she came to me."

"Why didn't you ever tell me? About Mom…and you?"

"How do you think we ended up together? There were almost twenty years between us, and I tried so hard to be noble. Tried so hard to resist loving her. But your mother was having none of that." He chuckled softly to himself, and Juliana knew he was remembering her mother in a way she'd never envisioned her parents. "She came to me, told me she loved me, and the hell with my efforts to be noble and deny what was between us. Then she—" He halted abruptly, coughed and added drily, "You were born almost nine months to the day afterward."

Juliana's throat tightened with emotion. "Oh, Dad, I wish I'd known. All I could think of was you telling me good girls don't, and I didn't want you to know what I'd done."

"I didn't want you to take sex lightly, that's all. I wanted it to mean as much to you as it meant to your mother—a precious intimacy to be shared with the man you loved. I wanted you to grow up to be like her—strong, courageous and true. Fearless when it came to love. You weren't my little girl anymore that summer—I knew that. You were a woman, making choices you had every right to make for yourself."

He let that sink in. "And don't forget, I knew Andre. I knew the kind of man he was. Most important to me as your father, I knew he loved you more than anything, loved you enough to sacrifice his own desires for your benefit…to let you go…to give you time to grow up completely. You couldn't have picked a better man to love."

Thirty minutes later Juliana was still in a state of shock. Not just that her father knew about the night she'd spent with Andre, but that he adamantly refused to believe what she'd told him about Andre's actions afterward.

"There's an explanation, baby," her father insisted. "Give him a chance to explain. I can't and I won't believe it unless I hear it from Andre himself—and even then I'd have a hard time believing. He's too good a man." The conviction in her father's voice shook her to the core, and she couldn't have spoken even if her father hadn't continued.

"I never liked Andre's father, but you know that. I didn't like the way he treated his daughter, for one thing, as if she were worthless, when most fathers would have been immensely proud of Mara. And I didn't like the way he treated his son, either, as if Andre was just a *possession* to him, someone he could dictate to. But Andre never let what his father thought he should do control his actions—if he believed something was the right thing to do, he did it, and damn the consequences. That kind of moral courage is rare."

After she hung up the phone Juliana stood undecided for a moment, then abruptly headed for the DeWinters' suite. Needing to know she wasn't crazy to be thinking of staying in Zakhar. Hoping maybe Sabrina could help her make sense of the confusion of thoughts and emotions swirling through her. Especially since her conversation with her father had only raised more questions than provided answers.

Dirk opened the door to Juliana's knock. "Hey, babe. What's up?"

"Oh. Hi," she answered, her disappointment showing on her face.

Dirk laughed under his breath. "Well, that's a blow to my ego," he teased. "I take it you weren't looking for me."

She smiled appealingly and shook her head. "I was hoping I could talk with Bree."

"She's sleeping. The pregnancy's taking a lot out of her. I barely got back from the set when she pretty much passed out on my shoulder as I was telling her how today's filming went, so I put her to bed."

Suddenly concerned, Juliana asked anxiously, "Is that normal, Bree being so tired at this stage?" She tried to think about her other friends who'd gone through pregnancies. "I thought by the second trimester women weren't that tired. Is it related to the cancer?"

He shook his head slightly. "Not as far as I can tell. And Bree's taking all her prenatal vitamins, eating right, doing everything she should be doing at this stage of her pregnancy." Two of the palace's household staff turned a corner and began walking down the corridor toward them, and Dirk pushed the door open. "Come on in—this isn't a conversation I want to have in the hallway."

Once Juliana was ensconced on the sofa in the sitting room, he stood leaning against the fireplace mantel and continued. "Morning sickness is long past, thank goodness. But she *is* carrying twins, and that takes an extra toll on her body. Bree's been seeing an ob-gyn here in Zakhar—we found a woman Bree felt comfortable with—and she tells us things are progressing normally where the babies are concerned."

His face softened into incredible vulnerability. "I don't know if Bree mentioned it to you, but she's feeling the babies move already. Little flutters. And at her last checkup we heard the heartbeats."

He didn't have to say another word. The babies were real to him now in a way they hadn't been before. There was such an expression of paternal love and wonder on his face that Juliana knew he wasn't even thinking about what he'd told her the first time he'd talked to her about Sabrina's pregnancy, before they knew she was carrying twins—that he didn't care about the baby, that he would sacrifice their child without a second thought if it would save his wife. There was no way Juliana was going to remind him, either. He loved their babies now, maybe not exactly the same way Sabrina did, but he wanted them just as much. He wanted his wife, but he wanted their children, too, and he would no longer sacrifice one for the other.

Juliana closed her eyes and breathed deeply, realizing she had her answer even without talking to Sabrina. Her eyes flew open. "Thank you," she told Dirk. "You have no idea, but...thank you." She jumped up and crossed the room to hug him tightly, then headed for the door.

"Wait a second," Dirk called after her. "What did I say?"

She turned with her hand on the doorknob, her eyes shining. *Men can change,* she thought, free of the shackles of the past at last. *They can grow into love.* But she couldn't say that to Dirk, not without reminding him of how he'd first felt about Sabrina's pregnancy. She couldn't tell him that eleven years ago Andre had sent her money along with a cold, nearly unforgivable message—that the money was for an abortion if she was pregnant. And if not, the money would serve as his parting gift to her. She hadn't been pregnant, but those words had destroyed her make-believe world, the world where Andre loved her and would love any child they created.

But the money and the message he'd sent her eleven years ago didn't necessarily mean that was the way he felt now. Dirk hadn't wanted his own baby at first, even though he loved Sabrina with all his heart, but now he did. The same could hold true for Andre. "I can't tell you," Juliana told Dirk, her face radiant. "But I owe you anything you want to name. Just ask. Anytime, anywhere. And when Bree wakes up, give her a kiss for me and tell her I said she's so lucky to have you. I mean that."

Back in her own suite Juliana paced her bedroom restlessly. Glancing constantly at the tapestry on the wall, the tapestry that hid the door to the passageway leading to Andre's bedroom. He would never use it again. He'd promised her he wouldn't, and she knew he'd keep his word. But he'd also told her, *"You are welcome to use the passageway to come to me, if you choose. Anytime. Day or night."*

If she went to him, she would be admitting she forgave him for everything that had happened eleven years ago, for his rejection of her and the child they might have created that night. She would be admitting she loved him—had always loved him—and she would accept whatever he had to offer her, whatever role he would allow her to have in his life. Even if it wasn't the marriage she'd dreamed about at eighteen.

But she would also be admitting...accepting...they would never have a child together. Not ever. She loved Andre with everything in her, but she wouldn't deliberately bring an illegitimate child into the world. Maybe the world didn't care anymore, but she did, and she couldn't do that to her child. Their child.

And that meant she couldn't go to Andre without some kind of birth control, because she could never have an abortion. It didn't have anything to do with her personal beliefs about a woman's choice, and she would never judge another woman who made different choices for her life. It was just that for her it wasn't an option— if she conceived, she would bear the child. She knew that about herself, had known it since she was eighteen when she'd faced that possibility. She and Andre hadn't used anything their first night together—birth control had been the last thing on their minds back then.

But she wasn't an innocent eighteen anymore. She was twenty-nine, and she knew better than to take that kind of risk again. Then she thought, *I don't even know what kinds of birth control are available here in Zakhar, if any. Zakhar is fifty years behind the times in so many ways, maybe they don't even sell condoms over the counter. Maybe the patches, pills and shots available to women in the United States aren't offered here, either, not to mention all the other options.*

She wasn't on any kind of birth control now. She wasn't sexually active, and until Andre had reentered her life she'd had no intention of being sexually active, so she wasn't prepared to prevent an unwanted pregnancy. *Unwanted pregnancy. That's a laugh. If I were pregnant with Andre's child it wouldn't be unwanted. But it would break my heart under the circumstances.*

No, she couldn't go to Andre through the secret passageway until she was protected. And that meant either finding a doctor here in Drago, or waiting until she could see her own gynecologist in Los Angeles. And no way did she want to wait weeks before—

Then it occurred to her. Sabrina had an ob-gyn here in Drago. Juliana couldn't be certain, but Sabrina's ob-gyn was probably one of the few female doctors available, not only in Drago, but in all of Zakhar. *I need to get that name from Bree tomorrow, and see if I can make an appointment.*

Andre couldn't sleep waiting for Juliana to come to him that night. He lay on his back in his lonely bed, watching the shadows cross the room as the moon moved across the night sky, watching the tapestry against the far wall. But it never moved, never so much as twitched.

He'd been so sure she would come to him. *Why? Why were you so sure?* Because of the way she'd looked at him last night at the foot of the staircase, compassion mixed with yearning in her lovely violet eyes. As he'd stared at her he'd envisioned what it would be like to lay his burdens down temporarily and lie in Juliana's arms, finding the peace and comfort only she could give him. To absorb the emotional sustenance she would bring, and rise strong, reenergized, ready to take up his burdens again. And even more, knowing she would be there always. That when he needed her, she would be there, just as he would be there for her when she needed him. Forever and a day.

He lay in his bed waiting for her—hot, hard and aching—until the moonbeams told him it was long past midnight. Until he realized she wasn't coming to him that night. Maybe she never would. *No,* he told himself, pressing his lips sternly together against that defeatist attitude, turning over to find a cool spot on his pillow. *She loves me. I know she loves me. And she will come to me...someday. Someday soon. She will come to me because she wants me the same way I want her. She* will *come to me.*

But he was leaving Zakhar early tomorrow. A longstanding commitment to address the United Nations in New York, followed by a state visit with the President of the United States—neither of which could be rescheduled—meant his plane would depart long before Juliana awakened, and he'd be gone for a week. He'd already charged Zax with the task of *personally* ensuring nothing happened to her in his absence—a task Zax had accepted without demur—but leaving the country now was unfortunate timing. If Juliana were planning to come to him tomorrow night, or the night after, he wouldn't be there. He had hoped—prayed—she would come to him tonight.

He touched his arousal, settling himself into a more comfortable position, cursing under his breath that he couldn't control his reaction when he thought of her, couldn't prevent the throbbing pulse of sexual desire that invaded his body...and his dreams. Now that Juliana was here...in Zakhar...in Drago...in his own palace, seeking release without her wasn't an option. He would just have to suffer...and wait.

*Come to me, Juliana,* his heart pleaded as sleep finally claimed him. *Come to me.*

"Cut! And that's a wrap, everybody. Especially you, Dirk. I think that's it for you." The director looked at his assistant, who nodded, confirming this was Dirk's last scene on-site. There might be a few scenes back at the studio, and some voice work, but Dirk was free to leave Zakhar.

Juliana collapsed into a chair, for once not worrying about her costume. She wouldn't be wearing this one again, so it didn't matter. She watched as Dirk made the rounds of cameramen, lighting technicians, grips, makeup crew, wardrobe, supporting cast, extras, gofers, assistants and everyone else, shaking hands and sincerely thanking them all for doing such an excellent job on this movie. This wasn't new for Dirk—he'd been doing it on every movie Juliana had made with him, another lesson he'd taught her about professionalism. *I might be the star,* he seemed to be saying, *but this is a team effort and I couldn't do it without you.*

Dirk came back to Juliana last, holding out his arms to her. She stood and walked into his embrace, clinging to him tightly, little pinpricks at the back of her eyes. She didn't know when she would see him again, but she knew without a doubt they would never do another movie together. *And that's the only thing I'll miss about acting,* she realized with a shock. In *Jetsam* and *King's Ransom*—the start of her film career and the end—she'd starred opposite Dirk.

"Thank you," she whispered. "For everything. For believing in me, for believing I could play Tessa better than anyone else."

Dirk loosened his embrace and stepped back from Juliana. They'd always been very careful not to give rise to any gossip about their relationship, knowing their on-screen chemistry would always make people wonder. "You would have become a star without me, babe," he told her with a smile. "It might have taken a little longer, but the writing was on the wall."

"Thanks. But it's not just that you gave me my first break—you also taught me about being a professional. And that's not a little thing." She cleared her throat and changed the subject. "So when are you and Bree heading out? When's your flight?"

Dirk made a face. "We leave just after seven tomorrow morning. Come by and say goodbye to Bree tonight, okay? But not too late. I want her to have an early night and be rested before the flight." He gave her a considering look. "You're not coming back to Hollywood, are you? Not permanently. You're staying here with *him*."

"You know me too well," Juliana murmured.

One corner of his mouth quirked up in a smile. "It won't be easy, you know, not for either of you. But I will say this. He seems like a decent man, even if he is a king." He hesitated, then asked enigmatically, "Does he know the truth?"

She shook her head, her smile sad. "I told him, but he doesn't believe me."

Dirk whistled tunelessly. "And he still loves you?" He reached over and flicked her cheek. "Babe, that's a powerful love. Don't let him get away."

A week later Juliana toweled herself off after a long, luxurious bath. *I needed that,* she told herself. Another long day of filming had left her exhausted, but the bath had revived her. Rejuvenated her. Not to mention it had left her smelling sweet and clean the way a woman wanted to smell when she intended to entice a man. And not just any man, the man she loved.

She was careful not to rub her hip where she'd applied the patch five days ago, and instead just patted it dry. She turned so she could see her hip in the mirror, checking anxiously to make sure the patch was still adhering securely to her skin. It was, and she was protected.

*Tonight.* She smiled to herself. It had been a long, long week, made even longer by the fact that Andre hadn't even been in residence in the palace for most of that time—she'd found out by chance he'd left the country, something Zax had confirmed when she ran into him on the set. So even if she'd gone to Andre without waiting for her birth control to be effective, it wouldn't have mattered, since he wasn't there.

But he hadn't told her he was leaving. He'd sent her a formal thank-you card for filming the Red Cross appeal for donations—handwritten by one of his secretaries on thick cream-colored stationery with the royal seal of Zakhar on the cover and personally signed by Andre—but that was all.

That lack of communication would have to change. Not just about relatively minor things like schedules, obligations and commitments, but about important things. About what they were thinking. Feeling. About their long-term goals. Dreams. Desires.

Andre had arrived home today. Juliana knew that, even though he hadn't even come to watch the filming as he used to do. Hadn't sought her out. So tonight she would go to him. Tell him everything. Ask him the questions she'd wanted to ask for eleven years, and finally hear his explanations. And she would make love with him…the way she'd longed to do since their one and only night together.

She stepped into her silk-and-lace undies—one of the few luxuries she allowed herself—then pulled a clean, oversize T-shirt from the dresser, making a little face as she did so. Wishing for the first time she had something more…sexy. More…seductive to wear for Andre. A T-shirt seemed so prosaic. Certainly not romantic. And she wanted to be romantic tonight of all nights. *Too bad,* she told herself with a rueful smile. *Should have thought of that earlier.* She wasn't going to wait another night just so she could set the stage. Andre would just have to take her as she was. She was pulling the T-shirt over her head when the phone by her bed rang.

The palace operator spoke in her ear when she answered the phone. "I have a Mr. Marty Devens from Los Angeles on the phone, Miss Richardson," she said in her pretty, accented English. "Would you like to take the call?"

"Of course." Juliana wondered what Marty could be calling her about, and then, with Marty's first words, shock and disbelief settled in.

# Chapter 15

Juliana put the phone down, tears oozing from her eyes. She'd managed to hold off until she hung up the phone, but now…now she could cry for Sabrina. Sabrina, who was dead on a hospital operating table. And the twin daughters she'd tried so desperately to stay alive long enough to give her beloved husband were in neonatal intensive care—prognosis guarded but not optimistic.

Dirk was crazy with grief, Marty had just told her. Inconsolable. *Oh, Bree. Bree,* Juliana mourned, catching her breath on a sob. *What will Dirk do without you? Oh, Dirk, I'm so sorry. I wish I could be with you now. I wish I could say something to comfort you.*

But there were no words. Nothing anyone could say to bring Sabrina back, and that was the only thing that would comfort Dirk in the first wildness of his grief. How tragically she remembered that kind of grief, when it seemed as if Andre was dead to her all those years ago.

Heartsick, she crawled under the covers and huddled there, shivering, but not from the cold. Thinking that she couldn't go to Andre…not now. Not when her heart was breaking over Sabrina and Dirk.

*Bree's dead and Dirk might not survive.* That was all she could think of. *Bree's dead and Dirk might not survive.* She couldn't possibly sleep, couldn't possibly turn her emotions off enough to fall asleep, because the phrase kept repeating in her head. *Bree's dead and Dirk might not survive.*

On that thought she fell asleep, but it was a fitful sleep as she tossed and turned. When she woke hours later, unrefreshed, her first thought was for Dirk. She picked up her cell phone and placed a call to Marty. "How is he, Marty?" she asked as soon as the phone was answered.

"Not good. I wouldn't tell anyone except you, but I'm afraid for him. I don't think he's…rational. I tried to talk to him about the…the arrangements. About Sabrina's funeral. But it's as if he can't even hear me. He's in some other world. He keeps talking about how this is God's punishment."

"Oh, Marty…"

"Yeah. I always thought Dirk was so strong. But now I see a lot of his strength came from Sabrina. She was always there, standing by him, believing in him. Helping him believe in himself."

She took a deep breath. "So what are you going to do?"

"Whatever I have to do, with Dirk the way he is. Thank God I've got power of attorney from him. Otherwise…"

"I want to be there for the funeral," she told him. "Please hold off long enough for that. We're almost done here. Today's the last scheduled day, so if we can wrap things up I'll take the first plane out of here…probably this weekend. But I can't be sure exactly when I can get back, so…"

"Don't worry. I know Dirk would want you there. I'll make sure the funeral's at least a week from now. And maybe the additional time will give Dirk a chance to come to his senses, too."

"What's the word on the babies?" *Please, God,* she prayed. *Let them be all right.*

"I've been to the hospital, and as Dirk's attorney I'm getting regular updates. The babies are holding their own, that's about all I can tell you at this point. But they're so tiny, Juliana." He cleared his throat and she knew emotion was getting to him, too. "You've never seen anything so tiny as Dirk's little girls."

Juliana's heart squeezed as if a hand had invaded her chest. "Thank you for letting me know, Marty," she said. "Please keep me posted." She managed to keep her voice steady, but inside she was crying again. *Oh, Dirk! I'm so sorry.*

The mood on the set that morning was somber, sub-dued. Everyone had heard the news about Dirk's wife, and everyone was shocked. The story had been plas-tered across the internet, and though many of the details were luridly wrong, the basic fact was true—Sabrina was dead. Many of the people on the set had known Sa-brina, if only casually, but they all knew Dirk. Liked him. Respected him. Some even loved him—he was that kind of man. So no one was in the mood to film the last scenes on a movie that bore Dirk's stamp until Juliana made a speech.

"I know we're all in shock right now," she said when everyone was assembled. "And I for one don't want to be here. But until this movie wraps I'm stuck here. We're all stuck here. I think we owe it to Dirk to be professionals, the same as he is. Let's finish this movie for him. So we can all go back and give him our moral support as soon as possible."

She looked around the room, taking in the tearstains on some faces, including Maddie's face as well as that of Neil Grantham, the actor who was playing Dirk's grown son Raoul in the movie. Dirk had taken the young man under his wing, patiently coaching him the same way he'd done with Juliana on *Jetsam*. Working with him one-on-one to get the best performance out of him, but not just for the movie. Because he wanted to help others be the best they could be, just as he always tried to do his best, too. One of the scenes today was between Eleonora and Raoul, an intensely emotional moment between mother and son. If they could get through that scene, they could get through the rest. "Can we do that for Dirk?" she asked the group, but her eyes never left Neil's face.

She swallowed the sudden lump in her throat when Neil's expression changed, resolution replacing the shock and sadness. "I can do it," Neil said, his eyes steely, looking more like the Raoul of the history books than he ever had before. Then everyone else chimed in—the cast, the crew, even the director, a longtime friend of Dirk's.

Juliana had already changed costumes and had her makeup refreshed in a break between scenes when she looked up and saw Andre—ever-present bodyguard at his side—standing a short distance away, watching her.

She walked over to him, taking in the slight strain in his expression. Maybe most people wouldn't have seen it, but she did because she loved him.

"I was sorry to hear about your friend," Andre said softly before Juliana could say anything to him. "You and she were very close, yes?"

She nodded mutely, then said in a voice as soft as his, "She was like the older sister I never had, and in some ways like the mother I hardly remember. I could tell her things I could never tell anyone else." She blinked rapidly to hold back the tears that would ruin her makeup. "That's why it hurt so much when you accused me…" She didn't have to finish. She knew Andre understood what she was referring to.

"I am sorry, little one. I did not understand. Not then."

Juliana glanced at Andre's bodyguard, wanting to say more but unable to speak what was in her heart in front of him. She knew all Andre's bodyguards had to be discreet—he wouldn't tolerate one who wasn't. But she still couldn't talk freely in front of them. Andre understood that, too.

"Damon," he said, not turning his face away from Juliana's. "Please give us privacy."

"Yes, Sire," the bodyguard replied promptly, moving far enough away so they wouldn't be overheard, but close enough to still guard Andre…should it be necessary. And his gaze continually swept the room.

"You are returning to Los Angeles for the funeral," Andre said before she could. "My private plane could take you…and anyone else who wishes to go."

Touched by his offer, Juliana thanked him but shook her head and said, "The funeral won't be for at least a week. Marty—Dirk's agent and mine—is arranging everything, so I don't have to rush back. But I do have to go." She didn't want to leave Andre, not now, but she had to attend the funeral. Not only for Dirk, but for Sabrina, too. And for herself. To grieve…and to accept her friend was never coming back.

"And then…?"

She took a deep breath. "I want to return to Zakhar," she said on a rush. "If…if you want me to."

He went very still, almost as if he were afraid to breathe. "Come to me, Juliana," he whispered. "I have been waiting forever. If you come to me I will know—"

"Juliana?" Maddie's voice interrupted them. "They're waiting for you on the set."

Juliana turned. She wanted to tell Maddie to tell the director he'd just have to wait. But that would be unprofessional, would fly in the face of everything Dirk had taught her. "I'll be right there," she told Maddie. She waited for her assistant to leave before saying, "I have to go. They're waiting." Regret colored her words, and she prayed he would understand.

His faint smile told her he did. "Go," he said, touching her cheek with one finger, but careful not to mar her makeup. "Duty comes first. Did you think I would not understand?" He laughed softly. "You wrong me, little one. Duty I have understood from the beginning. Just… come to me when you can. That is all I ask."

Juliana had just laid her head on her pillow when the phone by her bed rang, startling her. Reminding her of last night's devastating news delivered via a phone call. *Please don't let it be Marty,* she prayed. *Please don't let it be more bad news.*

"Yes?" she answered cautiously.

The palace operator said, "I have Princess Mara on the phone for you, Miss Richardson. Would you like to talk to her?"

Her heart had jumped when the phone rang, but now it jumped again. Mara was calling her. Juliana had not spoken to her onetime best friend in eleven years. But the reason she'd cut off all contact with Mara was no longer valid, and now Mara was reaching out to her.

"Of course," she said swiftly as emotion swamped her, making it difficult to get the next words out. "Of course I'll take the call." A click sounded in her ear, then...

"Juliana? Is that you?"

"Mara?" Tears sprang to her eyes and her throat closed. "Oh, Mara, it's *so* good to hear your voice. You have no idea..."

"I was sorry to hear about your friend, Juliana," Mara said in her soft, pretty voice, with its faintly accented English. "I know what it is like to lose a friend." She hesitated, then added in Zakharan, "It is one of the hardest things in the world." Her voice broke on the last words, and suddenly both women were crying. Healing tears for both of them.

*Love is too precious to waste.*

Juliana woke in the middle of the night with that one thought in her mind. Her heart was pounding from the nightmare that had possessed her sleeping self until she woke, clinging to that phrase like a lifeline. A nightmare where Andre lay dead as Sabrina was dead. A nightmare where she wept bitter, futile tears over lost chances.

Earlier tonight, what had Mara said on the phone

about her husband? *"I almost lost Trace because he was afraid to believe in our love. Second chances come so seldom, Juliana, but I was blessed to have that opportunity. I grabbed it with both hands and will never regret it."*

Second chances.

Weeks ago when Dirk had told her he was quitting acting for Sabrina, what had he said? *"I don't know how much time I have left with her, but I want every minute, every second. She's mine until God takes her away from me, and I'm not going to waste a moment..."*

Sabrina was dead. There was no going back for Dirk, no chance to make different choices. But Andre was alive. Alive...and sleeping just a short distance away. And despite her grief, she wasn't going to wait until she returned from Hollywood as she had first thought. "I'm not going to waste a moment, either," Juliana whispered to herself as she threw off the covers and climbed out of bed with sudden determination. "Not a single moment."

She walked toward the tapestry concealing the doorway to the passageway between her bedroom and Andre's and dragged it to one side. She turned the key in the lock and pushed the door open, then hesitated. The entrance was pitch-black, and she didn't have a flashlight. She had no idea how far it was, and she really didn't relish the idea of feeling her way in the darkness. But there couldn't be anything to frighten her. Could there? Hadn't Andre said he'd had the passageway cleaned out? Still...

Then she remembered the scented candles in the bathroom, and she ran there, quickly lighting one. She shielded the flame with her left hand as she walked carefully back into her bedroom carrying the candle in her right, then slid behind the wall hanging and started down the passageway. The candle flickered, casting shadows this way and that, and she thought about Eleonora making her way through this same corridor more than five hundred years ago. Eleonora, who'd suffered years of torture and abuse at the hands of her captors, but who never gave up hope that someday Andre Alexei would ransom her. Eleonora, who believed in immortal love. *As I do,* she realized suddenly. *As I do.*

Moonlight bathed Andre's bedroom in an eerie, blue-white light when Juliana pulled open the unlocked door at the other end of the passageway. She blew out the candle and placed it on a small side table near the entrance, then stood with her back to the wall, her heart pounding so that she could barely breathe. Across the room she could see the vast bed with its satin coverlet askew, as if the bed's occupant had tossed and turned restlessly until he threw it impatiently aside. As if he couldn't sleep any more than she could. As if his memories of her matched hers of him…and one magical night.

Andre lay beneath a single sheet. At first she thought he was asleep—he lay so still and motionless. Then he moved so swiftly she was shocked. And when the sheet was wrenched aside she saw he was naked. A panic reflex forced her to turn toward the passageway, fumbling to move the heavy tapestry aside. She had just managed to get it open when Andre was behind her.

His arms reached around and pulled her back, then plastered her against the wall, and she could feel him hard and male everywhere his naked body touched hers. "No," he breathed against her ear. But it wasn't a demand. It was a plea. "No, Juliana. Do not run." His hands moved to her shoulders…down, down, until he touched her bare arms. She shivered. And knew she was lost when his lips found the sensitive place behind her ear. "Please," he whispered.

Eleven years ago this man had taught her everything she knew of love. Everything she knew of passion. And everything she knew of despair. But life was too short—how tragically short she knew now, and she no longer cared about the despair. Not even if he broke her heart again as he'd done so long ago. She would risk that… and so much more.

With a wild cry she twisted lithely in his arms, sliding her arms around his waist, her hands brushing against corded steel muscles. Then he was kissing her, desire blazing to life between them the way it always had. The way it always would. Eleven years had taught her that no other man could rouse her passion for one simple reason—no other man was Andre.

His arms were iron bands encircling her as he plundered her mouth. He whispered her name in between kisses that sapped the strength from her knees and made her tremble like a leaf. As if her name was the most precious thing in the world to him. As if she was. Her body responded to the flames he ignited with his words, his touch, his taste, and her womanhood throbbed…then melted at the knowledge of what was to come. So long. It had been so long since she'd let herself respond to a man—not just her body, but her mind—and she was momentarily confused. Then afraid. And then no longer afraid.

"Andre." Just one word, but all her yearning was embodied in it. All the pent-up longing to know again the physical release only he could give her. All the aching need only he could arouse…and assuage. And even more, the desire for his love her wounded heart cried out for. The devastating wound created by him. The wound no one could heal…except him.

The world shifted dizzyingly as he released her lips then caught her behind her knees and swung her into his arms. She curled trustingly in his embrace; one hand clasping his neck, feeling the controlled power there as he carried her across the room to his bed and sat her gently on the edge.

Her eyes widened and she couldn't help the small sound of panic when he drew back from her momentarily and she saw him naked in the moonlight, his body very hard. Very male. His erection rose from its thatch of golden-brown hair and she couldn't tear her eyes away. Somehow she'd forgotten how very big he was…in every way.

He sat next to her and drew her into his arms, his vivid green eyes alight with passion held firmly in an iron grip. "No need to be afraid, little one. Perhaps I am more man than you are used to now, but we fit together once before…perfectly."

Juliana shook her head, mutely denying there had ever been another man, but he misunderstood. "Perfectly, Juliana," he insisted. "Do not lie to yourself, to me." He soothed her gently with words and kisses until her desire returned. Then with exquisite tenderness that brought tears to her eyes, he slipped the oversize T-shirt from her body, drawing it away until she was naked except for the scrap of lace and silk.

He closed his eyes for a moment, as if he were remembering another night, and her body bathed in moonlight then as now. Then his eyes opened and the expression in them told her more than words that his memories, beautiful as they were to him, paled in comparison to the reality of the vision she created now. It was a heady feeling.

Juliana knew her body had changed. She had been eighteen then; she was twenty-nine now. Her breasts were fuller, her hips more womanly. But his body had changed, too. She had responded to his vibrant masculinity eleven years ago, but now she realized he had just been coming into full maturity as a man.

Andre was definitely a man now, in every sense of the word. He was taller, and his shoulders were impossibly wide, the muscles there and through his chest even more developed, corded power rippling beneath his skin. But his hips were still lean and taut. He was a physical force to be reckoned with, now more than ever. But when her fingers touched his manhood a spark transferred itself from him to her—that hadn't changed; their response to each other was as elemental now as it had been then.

"Trust me, Juliana," he said now. Nothing more. He waited, refusing to touch her, refusing to let his hands, his body convince her. *Naked and trembling,* his eyes had told her at the reception, and she'd called it arrogance on his part. But now she saw the tensed muscles of his forearms, and when she looked down at his hands she saw they had formed fists, as if it was taking every ounce of his willpower to keep from touching her. Her eyes slid upward, lingering on his arousal, then encompassing his hips, the taut muscles of his stomach, his chest. She saw the faint tremors that shook him as that iron will was threatened...but held. And she knew. *Naked and trembling.*

He hadn't just been talking about *her*, about making

her want him. He'd been talking about *himself*, as well. *"You will come to me because you want me the same way I want you."* In her mind she heard the rest of his statement, but now it took on a whole new meaning. Now she understood. *"You* will *want me again, Juliana. That is a promise, not a threat. And when I take you, you will understand why."*

Juliana looked up into Andre's face, saw the yearning there that matched what was in her heart, and her hands moved of their own volition. She slipped her thumbs beneath the delicate fabric and pushed it down, revealing herself to him completely. No barriers. No defenses.

Naked and trembling.

He moved then, shifting her body backward, pressing her against the pillows, his body covering hers with the same urgency she remembered from eleven years ago. Then memory blurred when he parted her legs and slid two strong fingers inside her, drawing a moan she couldn't repress. She was already damp, her body ready for him, and his fingers moved slowly...deep, deeper. Stretching her sweetly in a promise of things to come.

She shivered with anticipation, closing her eyes as she remembered the feel of him so long ago but so vivid in her mind—hot, hard, filling her so tightly, so completely, she hadn't known where she ended and he began.

"Perfect?" he whispered in a question that wasn't really a question because he already knew the answer, the husky sound of his voice making her shiver the way his hand did, his fingers sliding in and out, his thumb coaxing the tiny nub from its hiding place.

Then she was clinging to him, crying his name as he wove his dark, magical spell, the same way he'd done the first time he'd made love to her. She couldn't control her reaction to him now any more than she'd been able to do then. She loved him. She always had. She always would. She knew it, and she wanted him to know it, too. Wanted him to believe it. "Andre..." She arched against his hand. "Please...oh, please..."

"Yes," he breathed against her throat. "Come to me, Juliana. Come to me." Then he was whispering to her in Zakharan, the language she loved for its musical cadence. The language she loved because it was *his*. Whispered words that lured her ever higher as her body followed inevitably where he led.

She couldn't breathe. Couldn't bear his voice, his fingers, his body hard and insistent against hers for another minute. Not another second. She moaned and thrashed, wanting to escape but needing the feeling to go on endlessly. And then it was too late. His name was torn from her as her body simply exploded into a thousand pieces, each piece a glittering shard of ecstasy.

# *Chapter 16*

Juliana wasn't even aware Andre had moved. Wasn't even aware that he was sliding inexorably into her soft depths until he was buried deep inside her. She gasped and opened her eyes. His breathing wasn't quite steady and his eyes were hooded as he watched her, but there was an expression on his face she'd seen once before.

He pressed even deeper, making her shiver and burn. "Perfect, little one," he said, though she could see it was an effort to get the words out. Then he was driving into her, riding her hard, his big body controlling hers with what seemed to be practiced ease. She didn't care. She just wanted him, wanted everything he could give her. Her knees rose and grasped his thighs, opening herself more fully to him. He groaned deep in his throat and took full advantage, driving even harder, deeper, both their bodies shuddering with each heavy thrust.

His mouth found her breasts, teasing the nipples into tight little buds until she begged him to stop. But he didn't stop the torment until she was weeping from the unbearable pleasure, until she was clinging to him and crying out in ecstasy. Then he pulled her knees even higher, changing the angle, and pounded into her until he exploded, too.

Juliana was crying, her chest shaking with repressed sobs as her body trembled in the aftermath of pleasure so great she could have died from it. *Eleven years.* The words kept running through her mind like a filmstrip on an endless loop. *Eleven years I've waited to feel this way again. Only with Andre. No one else. Only with him.*

Andre was still embedded within her, and he was shaking, too. Only his shaking was from the breath rasping in his throat as he tried to breathe deeply enough to replenish his depleted muscles. But there was no softening of his flesh. He was still hard, rock hard. And when her tearstained eyes met his, she saw he knew it. He rolled over, bringing her with him and retaining his place inside her.

"Please…" she begged breathlessly, not sure if she was begging him to stop or to keep going.

"Yes," he said in his deep voice. "I will please you until we both burn, until we melt into one flesh, until you forget every man but me."

Words of denial trembled on her lips, but he thrust upward at the moment, impaling her, driving every thought out of her head but the feel of his body so deep he couldn't go deeper. She rocked against him wordlessly, matching his rhythm, and his fingers found her through the dark, silky curls. Then she was flying again, soaring high above the earth. The only thing anchoring her in place was his magician's voice whispering words of love in Zakharan.

Three times through the endless night Juliana dozed. Three times she awakened with Andre caressing her, his hard, urgent body drawing a response from hers she thought she was too exhausted to give. But each time her body quickened beneath his sure touch. Each time he brought her to a shattering climax. And each time he made her weep from the beauty of his lovemaking… and then held her close until her tears subsided.

She fell asleep after the last time as if she were drugged. At some point she felt him raising her up, dressing her with such tender, gentle hands her heart broke. Then he was lifting her in his arms as if she were weightless, carrying her through the dark passageway to her bedroom before anyone else in the palace was stirring.

She woke fully when he laid her down on her bed and drew the silk coverlet around her. She gazed up into his face and caught her breath at the love shining in his beautiful green eyes as he bent over her. "Andre… I…"

He took both her hands and raised them to his lips. "No, Juliana," he told her firmly. "Do not tell me. I do not want to know. All that matters is you are here now. All that matters is finally…*finally*…you came to me again after I have waited so long. All that matters is your body telling me no other man has given you what I have given you—no other man has made you weep with ecstasy."

That faint, tantalizing smile crept into his eyes. "You were mine eleven years ago, little one. You are mine again. That is all. It is enough. But this time I will never let you go." His lips claimed hers with urgency—a demand and a question rolled into one.

"I love you, Andre," she said in a voice as soft as a sigh when he finally raised his head, knowing she needed to tell him this if nothing else. "And you're right. No other man has ever given me what you've given me." *No other man ever will.*

When Juliana woke again she was alone. She could tell from the angle of the sunbeams shining through her windows the sun was high in the sky. Her body ached in secret places and she desperately needed a bath, not only to wash but to soothe. Andre would come to her that night—she knew it. And she wanted to be physically ready for whatever he had in mind. Not only for herself, but for him. No sacrifice was too great for the man who had entrusted his heart to her the way Andre had.

She ran a bath in the huge bathtub, generously adding perfumed bubbles from one of the expensive flagons that lined the surround. She submerged herself and lay back against the smooth marble, trying to make sense of everything that had happened. Not just last night, but eleven years ago. She tried to reconcile the Andre who had made her believe in eternal love, then and now, with the Andre who had sent her money for an abortion…just in case. She couldn't. Her father had been right—Andre wasn't that kind of man.

The Andre of last night was like the Andre who had made love to her all those years ago. The Andre who had treated her innocence as a precious gift. The Andre who had given her such aching beauty she had wept with joy. The Andre she would have trusted with her life as she trusted him with her heart.

Neither man was the man who had coldly sent Zakharian agents to an eighteen-year-old to tell her to forget any dreams she had of a handsome prince. Neither man was the man who wanted her to destroy the child they might have created.

Why had she believed those two agents when they said Andre had sent them? Because she'd been young and unsure of herself, unsure of Andre. Because he hadn't said he loved her during their incredible night together...not even once. Because he hadn't called her, hadn't written—not even an email—in the two months since she'd left Zakhar, not even in answer to her love letters and emails. And because at the time she'd asked herself who else but Andre could have known about that night.

Now she was asking the same question, but from a different perspective. It *couldn't* have been Andre—mind and heart were telling her she *must* have been wrong all these years. But if not Andre, then who? Who else had known? And why had he never responded when she'd tried to contact him?

A knock at the door to her suite startled Juliana out of her contemplative state. She dried herself quickly, making sure she didn't rub off the birth control patch on her hip. "Just a minute," she called out, frantically drawing on her underwear and wrapping her bathrobe tightly around her. "Who is it?" she asked when she finally reached the door.

"It is I, Miss Richardson. Daphne," the palace maid assigned to her called from the other side of the door. When Juliana unbolted the door and opened it, the young woman bobbed a little curtsy, smiled and handed her a sealed envelope bearing the Zakharian royal crest. "His Majesty regrets the intrusion, but requests I give you this as soon as possible."

"Thank you," Juliana said, staring at the envelope but slightly bemused by the curtsy. Daphne had done her best to wait on her hand and foot the entire time she was here, but she'd never curtsied before, and Juliana wasn't sure what to make of it.

Daphne's cheeks were very pink when she said, "Is there anything I can do for you, Miss Richardson? May I lay out your clothes for you? Bring you breakfast? I know you told me in the past you did not wish for breakfast to be brought to you, but…"

"No. Oh no, I'm fine, thanks." Juliana was consumed with curiosity about the envelope, but good manners dictated she wait until she was alone. If only Daphne would go…but it seemed the maid was disinclined to leave.

Another blush suffused Daphne's cheeks. "Please do not hesitate to call for me if you need anything," the maid insisted. "Remember, two rings on the buzzer, and I will be here directly."

"Thank you," Juliana repeated, starting to be amused at the young woman's overeagerness to serve. When she finally closed the door a thought occurred to her. *It's almost as if she were auditioning,* she told herself with a little smile. Then the smile faded as she asked, *Auditioning for what?* The answer, when it came, seemed almost impossible. *Auditioning to be my personal maid.* Not just now, during the making of *King's Ransom.* But for the future. Her future with Andre.

She broke open the seal with fingers that trembled

and pulled out the crisp notepaper, scanning the few
sentences in Andre's incisive handwriting that slashed
boldly across the paper. Then read them again. Slowly.

*Juliana,* the note said. *I trust you slept well. I watched
you sleep until I could no longer bear not being in the
bed next to you. Until I could no longer bear not holding you as you slept. Until I could no longer bear not
holding you as I have dreamed of doing since that first
night. But you needed sleep, little one, and I could not
deny you that. When you wake...whenever you wake,
I will be waiting for you in the little library, where it
all began for me so many years ago. Come to me, Juliana. Please come to me there. I will be waiting. Andre.*

Andre was waiting for her. That's all Juliana could
think of. She dressed hurriedly, choosing one of her
comfortable, lightweight summer dresses with a floating skirt that made her feel deliciously feminine. This
one was in her favorite lavender blue. She brushed her
hair and thought about pinning it up for coolness, but
decided against it as a memory from the night before
came to her. Andre twining her long hair around his
throat, his eyes closed against the feel of it heavy against
his skin. As if he had dreamed of doing that, too. As
if he had dreamed of so many things where she was
concerned.

She hurried toward the little library on the second
floor, so lighthearted her feet barely touched the ground.
When she reached her destination she recognized Lukas
on duty today, standing guard by the door. As he'd done
the first time she'd met Andre in the little library, Lukas
opened the door for her, then quietly closed it behind
her.

Andre was sitting in the same easy chair he'd been

sitting in before, reading and marking comments on a document he held in his hand. The stack of documents on the table beside him that he'd already reviewed was substantial, and Juliana felt a little stab of guilt that he'd been waiting so long while she slept. The skin around his eyes looked a little weary, too, when he glanced up at her entrance. Weary, as if he hadn't slept at all, although his eyes blazed bright green when he saw her. And Juliana couldn't help but blurt out the question. "Did you get any sleep?"

Andre placed the document on the table, stood and held out his arms to her. She walked into them as if it was the most natural thing in the world, and they closed tightly around her. She tilted her face, mutely asking, and he kissed her. Long. Slow. Savoring.

Eventually he raised his head and smiled down at her, answering her earlier question. "We have plans to make, little one. How could I sleep?"

"What plans?"

"I realize you must return to Los Angeles for your friend's funeral. And you must finish filming *King's Ransom*, but the producer assures me a few more weeks back in Hollywood should suffice to wrap things up. Will you wish to continue your acting career after we are married? It would be difficult, but not impossible. Your royal duties will have to take precedence, of course, but—"

"Married?" Juliana stared at him in shock, barely able to get the word out.

The smile faded from his face and he went very still. "I told you earlier I would never let you go. What did you think I meant?"

"I… It never occurred to me that you…that we…" she fumbled.

"You thought I would just take you…until I tired of you? Is that it?" he asked tightly, harshly. "Is that what you thought of me?"

The pain in his eyes coursed through her. "No," she said, shaking her head. "I knew you loved me, but I…I honestly didn't think beyond that. I just knew I wanted to be with you, too…in any way I could." Her eyes pleaded for understanding. "Andre, please. *Please* don't look like that. I *love* you!"

"Yes, you love me," he said in an emotionless voice. "But it is like before. You still see me as a man who could take you and then walk away. You still see me as the prince who took your virginity and never promised you anything."

He clenched his jaw as if other words wanted to escape, bitter accusations he refused to let himself voice. Then he turned sharply away and headed for the door. "How long?" she heard him whisper to himself in Zakharan in utter despair and realized she wasn't meant to hear. "Must I pay forever for one mistake?"

Juliana flew across the room and caught him before he could leave. "No," she said, throwing her arms around him from behind, pressing her body against his, holding him fiercely. "I don't think of you that way," she told him. "Not anymore." His body was rigid beneath her grasp but she could hear his rapid heartbeat beneath her ear, and she knew he wasn't as indifferent to her as he tried to appear. "Please," she whispered. "Please look at me."

He peeled her hands from his chest and turned, setting her away from him. "If not that, then what, Juliana?" he asked coolly, and she saw he had retreated behind defenses she would have to fight to tear down. He smiled cynically. "Or perhaps I am asking too much of you. To sacrifice the love and adulation of millions… in exchange for what one man has to offer."

"How can you think I give a damn about that?" she began angrily. Her acting career had always been her second choice, the only viable option left to her after Andre had brutally rejected her love. "That's not—" Then his words from early this morning came back to her. *"All that matters is finally…finally…you came to me again after I have waited so long."* What had he meant? If he'd been waiting for her to come to him, he couldn't possibly have sent those men to drive her away. He couldn't possibly…

Other words from earlier crowded into her memory. *"You were mine eleven years ago, little one. You are mine again. That is all. It is enough. But this time I will never let you go."* And suddenly she *knew.* The answer to all the questions she'd never gotten to ask him, including the latest—why hadn't he answered when she'd tried to contact him? "My father was right. You didn't send those men to me eleven years ago, did you?"

"What men?" Even though she already knew the answer, the honest perplexity in his face was the last piece of evidence she needed.

"You never answered any of the letters or emails I sent you those first two months," she said slowly. "But you never got them, did you?" He shook his head wonderingly. She covered her eyes with her hand for a moment as emotions bubbled to the surface, then looked at him again. "I wrote to you," she said in a low voice, "many times. Words from my heart. Letters. Emails.

Almost every day. But you never responded. I even tried to call you, but you never answered your cell phone. I knew you were busy. But I...I had begged you for only one night. And I started to wonder if your silence was your way of telling me that's all it would ever be."

Her lips trembled and she pressed them together tightly until she was able to control her emotions. "Then two months after I left Zakhar two Zakharian agents came to the university. They told me you had sent them." She ignored his sharply indrawn breath. "They said... They said..." She swallowed hard. "They handed me an envelope...with money. A lot of money. They said I could take the money and have an abortion if I was pregnant, or if I wasn't I should consider it a farewell gift. From you."

Andre's eyes went hard and cold and his lips formed a thin line. He clenched his right hand so tightly his fist was bloodless. "My father," he grated with repressed anger bordering on hatred. "My father has a lot to answer for...in hell."

"I threw the money back in their faces," Juliana told him. "I wasn't pregnant, but even if I had been, I would never—" Her voice broke. "I loved you. Even thinking you had sent those men, I loved you, and I would never have destroyed your child. *Our* child."

An earthy Zakharan curse issued from Andre's lips. "I *did* send an agent to America...in December, not earlier. But not to you. Only to check on you because you did not answer your cell phone when *I* called *you*. And you did not respond to the emails I sent, either."

Her eyes grew huge in her face. "You called me?"

He nodded. Then his eyes took on a puzzled expression. "It did not occur to me at the time, but now I realize my unanswered calls never went to voice mail." He shook that thought off. "Since you did not answer, I emailed you. The first one…it was just a few lines. I tried not to overwhelm you with the depth of my love, but I had to tell you what that night meant to me." He drew a deep breath. "I bared my soul to you, Juliana, but you did not answer, and that hurt me. Angered me. And yes, cut my pride to the bone. But eventually I sent a second email…"

He trailed off, an arrested expression on his face, and she prompted, "The second email…?"

"That is how he knew," Andre whispered to himself. "That is how my father knew to send those men to you." As she had done, he covered his eyes with one hand.

"What…what was in that email?"

Andre lowered his hand and gazed down at her, anger at his father and self-recrimination combined in the troubled face he showed her. "When I did not hear back from you after my first email I wondered if you had changed your mind once you started college. You were free, free to seek new experiences away from your father's sheltering influence for the first time in your life. Free of me. What if you no longer loved me? What if you regretted what we had done?"

Juliana shook her head in denial. "How could you think that?"

"When a man is feeling guilty, little one, many thoughts go through his mind. I had sworn to myself I would not touch you, so guilt over that night was my constant companion." He breathed deeply. "In the first flush of wounded pride I told myself I was not going to chase after a woman who did not care enough to at least acknowledge she had received my love letter." His lips curved into a rueful smile. "Arrogant. Proud. Stupid."

"Not stupid."

"Yes, stupid. It did not occur to me until several weeks later there might be another reason why you had not replied. What if there were something you were afraid to tell me? What if you were left dealing with the unintended consequences of that night, and thought you were on your own?"

He made a sound of self-derision. "Strange as it may seem, that only fueled my anger. That you would think me such an ogre you could not tell me. I almost picked up the phone to call you again, but the question I needed to ask…I did not want to confront you, and I feared you might hear the anger and hurt in my voice. So instead I wrote to ask if you were carrying our child." Juliana caught her breath. "When you never responded to my second email I agonized for two days, then went to your father to inquire about you."

"You told my father we…?" *Is that how he knew?* she wondered.

"No, of course not. I merely asked if he had heard from you. If he knew how you were doing. I pretended I was asking on Mara's behalf. He said you had told him you were very busy with school, too busy to write or call often."

Pain and guilt chased across Juliana's face. "I did tell him that," she admitted. "I was so wrapped up in thoughts of you that I…I really didn't want to focus on anything else just then. Not my classes. Not even my father. I spent most of my time waiting to hear from you." She started to tell Andre her father had known all along anyway, but he spoke before she could.

"After my conversation with your father I tried to call you, but again you did not pick up." Regret over lost chances was obvious in his expression. "So I wrote to you a third time, just before my unit shipped out to begin serving with the UN peacekeeping force in Afghanistan. Desperate to hear from you by then. Putting my pride aside, begging you to tell me if I had somehow offended you by asking if you were pregnant, even though that had never been my intention. Then I received an email reply saying you were not pregnant. Just that. One sentence."

She shook her head vociferously. "I didn't!"

"I know that now. But at the time? And yet, it did not sound like you. Part of me was sure you would tell me if… But just in case…I had to know. I could not go to Virginia myself—I was already serving in a combat zone in defiance of my father's wishes by that time, and I could not desert my post. I could not even request temporary leave—so I sent a trusted agent from Zakhar to check on you. When I knew you were not pregnant I was both relieved and disappointed."

"I don't understand."

He smiled sadly and raised a hand to caress her cheek once before letting it drop back to his side. "Relieved for your sake, little one. I wanted you to attend college, to see something of the world before…" His eyes held hers. "Disappointed…that was for me. I *wanted* you to be carrying our child. It would have been all the excuse I needed to bring you back to Zakhar and marry you out of hand, even though you were too young."

"Why didn't you? You knew I loved you, so why…?"

"I was twenty-two. You were eighteen. You had led a sheltered life, and I…I had already known for two years I loved you. Had already denied my own desires waiting for you to grow up." His eyes were bleak. "I needed you to be sure of your love. I needed you to understand how it was for me.

"But then you came to me that night. All soft and yielding, even more than my dreams. Offering me your love so sweetly I had no power to resist. I should never have taken what you offered that night—I know that. But I was too arrogant to know then that wanting is not enough. Even loving is not enough, not if there is no pledge for the future. And to my everlasting shame I did not give you that. There are some things a man does not do, Juliana. Not if he is to live with himself. But I have paid for that night." He laughed without humor and said under his breath, "I have paid bitterly."

She was barely able to get the word out. "How?"

His face contracted, and his lips tightened. "The tabloids love nothing better than to print scandal, especially about European royalty. If they cannot find a true story, they will make one up. They have been making up stories about me for years, about the latest woman in my life. I merely had to look at a woman and the world was told we were lovers. But there is a reason the tabloids must make up stories—there *is* no woman in my life…and has not been for eleven years."

At her amazed and wondering expression, he added drily, "No man, either. And yes, those rumors have been whispered in some circles because I do not use women for pleasure." He smiled in self-mockery. "No one wants to believe a man can remain faithful to the memory of a woman despite the many temptations crossing his path.

No one wants to believe he can remain celibate…for the sake of a woman and one precious night."

"For…me?" Juliana asked in a hushed voice.

"Only for you."

## Chapter 17

Juliana's eyes squeezed shut in pain as she comprehended the enormity of what Andre was saying. For any heterosexual man to voluntarily forgo female companionship completely for such a length of time was unbelievable, unheard of. And for a reigning monarch whose word was law in his country, wealthy beyond most men's dreams, virile and in the prime of his life—just how virile she had ample proof—it was beyond comprehension. And yet she knew he was telling the truth.

*"King's Ransom,"* she whispered under her breath. "You loved me...like he loved Eleonora."

He nodded slowly. "At first I remained faithful because I thought you were faithful to me." He hesitated. "I must tell you. I knew you were dating in college. My agent reported he had seen you—more than once—in the company of other men."

Juliana's gaze fell before his, remembering. Then she looked up at Andre again, determined to be honest with him. "I was so hurt…and yes, angry…at what I thought was your rejection that I did accept dates with other men. That's true. I won't lie to you. I told myself you weren't the only man in the world—that if you didn't want me, other men did. But none of them was you, and I…"

A self-deprecating smile touched his lips. "I had wanted you to spread your wings, little one, just not that way. I had not expected it of you. I will not lie either—I was jealous. And hurt. But I was still arrogant enough to believe you loved me in your heart of hearts."

"Andre—"

"No, let me finish, little one. I did not call again because by that time I knew if I heard your voice I would not be able to wait—your voice was a fire in my blood, and if I heard it I would have to have you with me. It was that simple. Yet how could I have you with me in a battle zone? In Afghanistan? I could not put you in danger that way. It was easier not to risk hearing your voice.

"I did not write again because the only words that occurred to me were demands for you to admit you loved me and pleas for you to return to Zakhar immediately and marry me, both things I swore to myself I would not do. Not until you had finished college. Not until you were a woman grown. And of course, I was not even in Zakhar at that time. Returning before my tour of duty was up would have been a shameful thing. I could not do that…unless you were carrying our child. And by that time I knew you were not.

"Then, too, I had not heard from you except for that

one cold sentence." His lips tightened. "My father's agents must have blocked my outgoing calls, intercepted my emails to you and every one of your attempts to contact me, so I did not know…"

She touched his arm in empathy for the pain his father's machinations and his own self-denial had brought him. "A soldier's lot is a lonely one," he continued. "His personal life is on hold. Often the only thing sustaining him is his belief in the importance of his mission. And that his loved ones will be there when he returns. Each day that passed without you was harder than the one before. Even though my days in Afghanistan demanded my full attention, the thought of you kept me going. But the nights…" He paused and his jaw tightened.

"And yet I told myself I could survive because I would see you once school was over for the year," he continued finally, "that of course you would spend the summer in Zakhar, and you would be there waiting for me when I returned from my tour of duty. I would have the chance to woo you in person as I should have done from the first. I would have you to myself for a few precious weeks, and you would know you were mine before I was forced to let you go again. But the end of the school year came and went, and you did not return. Not to Zakhar, not to me. Instead you went to Hollywood…and took a lover."

His nostrils flared as he breathed deeply. "My first reaction was betrayal…and blinding rage." The expression in his eyes frightened her for a moment. "I almost went after you then. After *him*. I could have killed him, and I told myself I could have taken you, forced you— No, Juliana." He held her firmly, refusing to let her look away. "I *must* tell you and then we will never speak of it again. I told myself I could force you to take me, whether you wanted me or not. You *belonged* to me, and you had dared to give another man what was mine alone."

Andre stared down at Juliana for endless seconds, until his frightening expression faded into something else. "But then I knew I could not. I could not take you in anger. I could never take you except in love—*but you did not love me!* My arrogance was humbled, and I knew somehow I did not deserve your love."

"I didn't," she began, wanting to deny that she'd taken a lover, but she knew she had no proof. Nothing to convince him. "What would have been the point of returning to Zakhar?" she said in a small voice. "I thought you didn't want me anymore. I thought you had forgotten me."

He smiled that faint smile. "That I could never do. But even though you did not return, even though you were not faithful to me, I remained faithful to you. I cannot really explain why. I did not start out saying, 'There will never be another woman for me,' especially after I learned what you had done. But you were there whenever I looked at another woman, and I could not…"

He drew another deep breath and expelled it harshly. "Time did not stand still—I had a job to do, which I did. I could not forget you, but I could focus on the task I had set myself to accomplish—bringing the best of the twenty-first century to Zakhar and its people. And I could change myself into a man worthy of your love."

"You were *always* worthy of my love," she told him, fighting back tears. "And I never forgot you, either. I just didn't know you loved me…" She trailed off, wish-

ing she could tell him the truth as she'd tried to tell him
once before…and have him believe her.

"The years passed," he continued when she stopped.
"My father pressured me to marry into one of the royal
houses of Europe—to father sons to inherit the throne
after me. He was obsessed with it." He laughed bitterly.
"He must have regretted then that he had driven you
away, but he never said anything, and I did not know.
I only knew I could never marry another, could never
father children with a woman I did not love—a woman
who was not you. Not even for Zakhar."

"Why didn't you…" she began, and when he looked
a question at her she tried to put into words what she
needed to know, needed to understand. "Why didn't
you come to me years ago? Why did you wait so long?"

"I did not know you loved me. How could I? Your
name was linked with one man after another." His face
was carved in stone, as if he could hide his pain behind
a marble wall. "I watched your career from afar, waiting for you to realize the difference between what those
other men offered you and what I did. Dreaming of a
day when you would return to me because you could
not stay away. Then my father died and I ascended the
throne."

A muscle twitched in his cheek. "There were other
things I had to deal with then. Mara was one of them.
That is another thing my father has to answer for. Someday I will tell you about her, but not today." His eyes
burned into hers. "And still I waited. Paying the price
for that night. Wondering if I would ever pay enough."

"You weren't the only one who paid for that night,"
she whispered. His brows drew together in a questioning frown. "You ruined me for other men."

A shaft of pain slashed across his face, and Juliana realized he'd misunderstood. "No, not that way. But every man I met I subconsciously measured against you. Every man who touched me, who kissed me…I remembered your touch, your kiss." Her voice dropped to a whisper as she confessed, "I remembered the feel of you deep inside me." She shivered, her body responding to then and now. "I could never find a man who erased that memory, who made me *want* to forget you. And so I could never let them touch me…that way."

He took a step closer. "What are you saying, Juliana? Are you telling me…?"

She knew he wouldn't ask. Didn't feel he had the right to ask. He loved her even believing she had not led a chaste life as he had. And in some elemental way that was as it should be. But she didn't want those lies about her to hurt him the way they'd hurt him for years. She had to try one more time. If he didn't believe her, at least she would have told him the truth.

"Yes," she said. "You're not the only one the press lies about. The first time one of those magazines claimed I had taken a lover, I protested. I even went to my lawyer, thinking to demand a retraction, and if I didn't get one I would sue. I wanted to proclaim my innocence to the entire world, most especially to you. Even though I believed you didn't want me anymore, your opinion of me still *mattered*. But my lawyer made me see I could never prove it in court. The man…" She swallowed. "I *had* dated him. I just refused to sleep with him. His pride couldn't bear being rejected. So he lied. He was the 'unnamed source' of the story. A trial would have come down to my word against his, with no guarantee anyone would believe me. And I was terrified that somehow you would be dragged into it…

"After that I knew there was no going back. I could never *prove* my innocence to anyone, much less you, so what did it matter?" She caught her breath on a sob, but forced it down. "I just closed my eyes and ears to the lies and continued acting. Only with acting could I escape the pain of losing you. Only when I was pretending to be someone else could I forget you."

She swallowed again. "At least my family and close friends knew the truth. No one who really knew me believed the lies, and no one who believed the lies really knew me." She looked away, remembering. "Then I returned to Zakhar to film *King's Ransom* and met you again."

"The only reason for *King's Ransom* was to bring you here."

Her brow wrinkled in puzzlement. "I don't understand."

"I knew that love story had always fascinated you. I found a good screenwriter, paid her, gave her access to private historical records from the palace library to research the story. Then I contacted the studio and offered to underwrite the film, but gave them two conditions— anonymity…and you. No one was to know of my involvement, especially you. And no other actress could play Eleonora. Then when they signed you I granted them permission to film on location."

"You…planned it?" she asked in wonder. "All of it?" When he nodded, she said, "I…I don't know what to say." Amazed. Trying to calculate what it must have cost him—the financing alone on a movie like this would have been…

*A king's ransom,* she acknowledged, stunned speechless by the realization. *Andre paid a king's ransom to bring me back to him. Just like...*

"I had waited too long for you to return on your own, but you never did. I had to find a way to bring you back to Zakhar. To me." He drew a deep breath. "I knew there was no other man in your life, and had not been for years. So I knew I still had a chance to win your love."

"How did you know that?" She shook her head. "The stories in the magazines...on the internet..."

He hesitated, as if he didn't want to confess something, then he said, "I had men watching you. Guarding you."

"What?" She didn't know if she should be angry, hurt or...touched. Touched that he'd wanted to win her back despite thinking the worst of her. Then she thought of something. "Do you have men guarding me here in Zakhar, too?"

"Of course," he said simply. "You are precious to me. I would do anything to keep you safe, even if it means protecting you against your will."

"That was one of your men? The man who saved my life when the car almost ran me down by accident?"

"Of course," he said again. "Lieutenant Marek Zale, a good man. He headed up the team guarding you in Hollywood, the team that followed you here and kept you safe. But once he saved your life he had to be pulled off the protective detail surrounding you. I did not want you to know you were being guarded, and if you saw him again you might have become suspicious." Then he added, "But was it an accident? I do not believe so, and neither does Lieutenant Zale. And there was the incident with the light that fell on the set." He started to say something else, but Juliana interrupted.

"They had to be accidents," she averred dismissively. "Who would want to kill me?"

He didn't answer and she was silent for a moment, putting aside that question and digesting his earlier statement about setting men to watch over her in Hollywood. Fitting this new aspect of him into what she'd thought she'd known. "When I met you again I didn't know what to think. You wanted me. You told me in no uncertain terms, but you thought I was…easy."

"Never that," he insisted fiercely. One arm wrapped around her like an iron band, drawing her flush against his body, and she could feel his desire. "Last night when you came to me…could you not tell? I thought it was painfully obvious the only reason I wanted you was because I loved you. Because I have always loved you."

His face wrinkled in pain. "The other men in your life…I told myself they did not matter—they were part of the price I paid for taking your innocence and then letting you go without a word." She closed her eyes at the harshness in his voice, but now she knew it wasn't directed at her; it was directed at himself. "But, Juliana," he continued, "I could never take you except in love. That is what I meant that first night."

She opened her eyes and saw the truth written on his beloved face. "I didn't know," she told him softly. She brushed the fingers of one hand along the curve of his cheek and felt it harden beneath her touch. "I didn't understand. I thought you were just staking your claim as the next man to have me, even though you'd already had me years earlier."

She gazed into his green eyes, those eyes that had haunted her dreams for eleven years, willing him with her soul to believe her next words. "I have no proof to offer you other than my love. I've never slept with any man...except you."

He stared down at her for endless seconds, then drew a sharp breath. He caught her hand, lifted it and pressed a fervent kiss into her palm. "Thank you for that, little one. I do not deserve it—and I would have loved you even if it had not been true—but...thank you."

"You believe me? Without proof?"

"Your eyes are all the proof I need." He smiled down at her. "Eleven years ago when you offered me the sweetest gift any man had ever been offered, your eyes told me you were innocent. But they also told me something else. They told me you loved me. Not as a girl in the throes of a crush the way you had loved me for years, but as the woman you had become that summer."

He kissed her reverently. "Now your eyes tell me the same thing. They tell me you are innocent—and that you love me."

Two hours later Andre reluctantly parted from Juliana at the door to the Queen's Suite. He'd told her he had every intention of accompanying her back to Hollywood for Sabrina's funeral—he'd rearranged his entire schedule to go with her, although he couldn't stay longer than that, couldn't stay while she finished out her obligations to *King's Ransom*—but he would be there to help her through the emotional trauma of the funeral. And when he'd told her he'd already set things in motion for their departure that evening, she'd convinced him he needed a few hours of sleep before they embarked.

Andre's press secretary had announced their engagement to the whole world an hour earlier, complete with hastily taken pictures of the radiant couple and the impressive engagement ring. "The sooner, the better," Andre had insisted. Juliana had maintained they had to call her father before that happened—no way was she going to hurt her father by not telling him first. This time when Juliana called him she *had* woken him from a sound sleep, although he'd assured her he didn't mind for a reason like this. After she and Andre had both talked with her father and received his blessing, Juliana had laughingly explained to Andre about the last time she'd called her father.

Then Andre walked Juliana to her door…hand in hand. His bodyguard Lukas followed a discreet two steps behind them, and Juliana's bodyguards had made themselves temporarily scarce at the silent command in Andre's eyes, although Andre no longer cared who saw him with Juliana.

They paused at the doorway to the Queen's Suite. Lukas stood off to one side, his eyes scanning the corridor in either direction, ensuring their privacy. "Come to me through the passageway, little one," Andre coaxed in a soft undertone as he leaned close to her. "How can I sleep without you now?"

Her eyes met his. "How can you *sleep* with me there?" she teased gently, her expression conveying she knew exactly what he had in mind…and it wasn't sleep.

He chuckled softly. "You are right, of course." He held her gaze. "I will have to learn to sleep with you at my side…but not today." He raised her left hand to his lips and brushed kisses over each of her fingers, lingering on the one wearing his engagement ring. Then he opened the door for her and pushed her gently through it before closing the door firmly, hearing the old-fashioned latch click into place. He turned and headed for the King's Suite, Lukas by his side.

"Congratulations, Sire," Lukas said, his sincerity obvious.

Andre smiled. "Thank you, Lukas."

Lukas hesitated, then added, "She is a wonderful woman, and you are a lucky man. All Zakhar will rejoice."

"Not all," Andre disclaimed. "There will not be universal rejoicing. But I do not care about that. It is her or no one." The two men shared a look of male understanding.

When they turned the corner into the corridor that would take them to Andre's suite, Lukas's hand quickly slid inside his unbuttoned jacket, then withdrew when he recognized the three men who stood in front of Andre's private office. Waiting. One was Damon Kostya, who wasn't supposed to be on duty that day. The second was the helicopter pilot who'd flown Andre to Taryna both days, the one who'd managed to land the chopper safely on only one engine. And the third was the man who'd saved Juliana's life the first time, Marek Zale.

Juliana thought about ringing for Daphne before dragging out a suitcase from the wardrobe where it had been stashed, tossing it onto her bed and flipping the lid open. *"Remember, two rings on the buzzer, and I will be here directly,"* the maid had told her earlier this morning, but Juliana decided to put off calling for Daphne until later. She didn't need help packing the one suitcase she would take to Hollywood, although she did want to discuss with the maid what she was leaving behind, the things she wanted Daphne to keep safe for her for when she returned to Zakhar.

"When I return," she whispered to herself, unable to hold in the thrill that accompanied the words. She went swiftly through the dresses hanging in the closet. She made a quick trip to the dresser for a handful of bras and panties, then another trip back to the closet for shoes.

She glanced down at the engagement ring on her finger, the ring Andre had given her just a little while ago that had featured prominently in their engagement photos—a large oval tanzanite gemstone of a peculiar saturated shade of blue with a purplish hue shimmering around it, surrounded by an impressive circle of diamonds.

"The original ring belonged to my grandmother," he'd told her as he'd slid it into place on her ring finger. "She had small hands, like you. But the central stone was a sapphire that paled in comparison to your eyes, so I replaced it with tanzanite." He'd smiled that faint smile she loved. "But even this stone does not do justice to your eyes, Juliana. Nothing could." After a deep breath he'd added, "I have been waiting eleven years to give this ring to you."

Hearing his words in her mind reminded her that second chances were granted to a very, very select few. She was going to grab at her second chance with both hands and never look back, just as Mara had done. "Now it begins," she said softly, then repeated the words in Zakharan, a smile wreathing her face.

A noise from the entrance to her bedroom made Juliana whirl around. Two men stood framed in the doorway. One man she recognized as one of the bodyguards assigned to guard her when she was outside her suite— Andre had introduced her less than an hour ago to the men on duty protecting her. The other was Andre's cousin, clutching a pistol in his right hand, his left arm wrapped around his hapless victim's throat. And the malevolent expression on his face was one she'd never imagined she would see there. Not in a million years.

## Chapter 18

Five men stood in Andre's private office. Four of them were absolutely convinced of Prince Xavier's guilt. The fifth, Andre, insisted on going over the evidence against his cousin, his lifelong *friend*—what little there was of it—one more time.

"A court would never convict Zax," he stated firmly. "Not without proof. Where is your proof?"

The other four men exchanged glances. Then Damon spoke. "No one else has a motive, Sire."

"Motive is not nearly enough."

Lukas added softly, "He is the head of the protection details, Sire. Yours as well as Miss Richardson's. He has knowledge of your movements *and* hers few other men possess."

"True, but knowledge alone is not proof."

Lieutenant Marek Zale stepped forward. After he'd been pulled off the contingent assigned to guard Juliana, he'd worked behind the scenes coordinating her protective detail, and Andre already had it in his mind to promote the man once Juliana became his queen. "The incident with the car was *not* an accident," Marek said now. "Of that we are sure. This brings us back to knowledge of Miss Richardson's movements, Sire, something Prince Xavier would have."

Lukas spoke up. "You know the light that fell was no accident. But I cannot see Prince Xavier having either the access or the time to accomplish this. A coconspirator would be necessary, most likely one of the crew who could be up there working on the lights and not be questioned. Someone who knew what scene was to be filmed, though, and who would be on that bed. There could only have been one target. And Prince Xavier has been on the set almost every day, 'checking out the security.' He would know the filming schedule."

"The helicopter's engine *was* tampered with," the military pilot insisted. "But whether the target was you, Sire, or Miss Richardson, we cannot be certain, but either way…the intent was murder. Could Prince Xavier have done it? Yes. He has access to that restricted area. Military access. And he is a trained helicopter pilot—he flew one in Afghanistan. Not a mechanic, that is true, but still…he has knowledge of helicopters and how they operate. It would take specialized knowledge to disable the engine in such a way that it would fail only after extended usage. If the helicopter had crashed, there would have been nothing showing it was anything but a tragic accident. But he did not necessarily have to do it himself."

"Each incident indicates someone with different skills," Andre argued. "While the man who sabotaged the light or tampered with the helicopter engine could also have driven the car, it is unlikely the same man did both the light *and* the engine. So yes, I believe there is a conspiracy. But it does not necessarily include Zax."

"But why make these attempts look like accidents?" Damon asked. "So much easier, so much more certain, to use a gun or a rifle to assassinate her or you if death was the only motive. Only someone who stood to *gain* by the death of either or both of you would want the deaths to appear accidental, so no suspicion would fall upon him. And should anything happen to Miss Richardson, Sire, or to you," Damon said reasonably, "it could only benefit Prince Xavier. No one else. He is your heir."

Lukas cleared his throat and jumped in. "Everyone who has seen you since Miss Richardson's arrival knows she is the one, Sire," he said softly. "Marianescus love once, then never again. All Zakhar knows this—it is not a secret. And you are a Marianescu. If Miss Richardson were to die…you would have no heir but Prince Xavier. Ever."

"My cousin has known of my plans regarding Miss Richardson for at least three years." Andre's tone was harsh. "Ever since I posted men to guard her in America."

"Yes, but she was in Hollywood then," Lukas said, "and no threat to the succession. Now she is here. Two attempts have already been made on her life since she arrived in Zakhar, and the attempt on your life—the helicopter—could also have resulted in her death."

*Damon and Lukas are right,* Andre told himself as he tried to put emotion aside and think logically. *Proof or no proof, only Zax stands to gain from these attempts. No one else.* And yet, he couldn't believe it of

Zax. Niko, yes. He could easily believe it of Niko. But not *Zax*. And he couldn't condemn his cousin to death without evidence merely because he had the only known motive. Could he?

Less than a year ago he'd sent Lukas and Damon to the United States with orders to shadow Trace McKinnon— the man who was now his brother-in-law—and kill him should it become necessary, in the name of protecting his sister. He hadn't hesitated then. Why was he hesitating now? Juliana was no less precious to him than Mara. He would kill to protect her, no question. But not in cold blood. Not like this. "I will not believe him guilty of seeking my death, or Miss Richardson's."

The other four men exchanged skeptical glances, but no one spoke until Damon said, "How many 'accidents' must occur before you believe what is plain to us, your men? Men who have sworn to keep you safe or die trying. There is not a man among us who would not give his life for yours, but would you ask us to throw away our lives merely because you do not want to accept the truth?"

Andre's face hardened at Damon's final argument. He still refused to believe in Zax's guilt, but he had to act—not just for Juliana or himself, but for the men risking their lives to protect them. *With great power comes great responsibility,* he reminded himself. He'd never shirked the difficult life-and-death decisions most men never even imagined making. He couldn't do so now. Not even when the man in question was his dearest friend, closer to him than the ties of blood that bound them.

*The ties of blood.*

A thought occurred to him, startling in its simplicity.

If Zax were arrested, tried and convicted of high treason, Niko would become Andre's heir until he had a son to supplant his cousin in the succession…assuming he and Juliana had a son. Was it possible this was *Niko's* doing? All of it? Not just the attacks on Juliana, but the assassination attempts by supposed traditionalists like Zax? Tampering with the royal helicopter? All designed to kill him and throw suspicion—if suspicion was aroused—on Zax? Niko's own brother?

And Juliana. Why try to kill Juliana now? As he'd told his men, Zax had known Andre's intentions regarding Juliana from the beginning. If Zax wanted to keep Juliana away from him, he could have killed her at any time, not waited until she arrived in Zakhar. And if Zax had wanted Juliana dead, she would be dead. *The same goes for me. If Zax truly wanted me dead, I would be dead already.*

But Niko hadn't known about Andre's plans in advance the way Zax had. *Not until Juliana arrived would anyone here other than Zax have known my intentions toward her. Including Niko.* Now everything made sense, including the slender evidence that pointed to Zax—evidence *arranged* to point to Zax. And Andre knew what he had to do.

Then he went cold all over. If Niko was behind the attempts on Juliana's life…then he'd just upped the ante. He'd just *increased* Niko's motive to kill her by announcing their engagement. *If anything happens to Juliana,* he thought with icy self-recrimination, *the blame is mine.*

He quickly dismissed the pilot with a brief word of thanks, then turned to Lukas and Damon. "Find Prince Xavier," he ordered them curtly. "Bring him to me. Do *not* kill him," he added in no uncertain terms. "But do not let him out of your sight. Understood?"

He waited until they left, then said softly to Marek, "Take as many men as you need and find Prince Nikolai. Arrest him. Then bring him to me."

"Arrest Prince *Nikolai*?" The surprise on Marek's face was apparent.

"Arrest him. He is the man behind these attempts to kill Miss Richardson…and me. Be very careful—he will be as dangerous as a cornered rat. But I want him alive. Understood?"

Juliana watched in horror as Niko reversed the pistol in his hand and with savage force clubbed the man he was holding just behind the right ear. The man crumpled. Niko then pointed the gun at Juliana. "Tie him up. Do it!" he added harshly as she hesitated. He turned the pistol until it was aimed at the other man's defenseless body. "Or I will kill him now."

Her automatic instinct was to run, to escape however she could, but Juliana knew she couldn't outrun a bullet. She also couldn't let Niko shoot a man in cold blood. She glanced desperately around the room, and her gaze lit on the belt to one of her dresses thrown across the bed. She grabbed it, and although her senses were screaming at her not to get any closer to Niko than she already was, she made short work of tying the man's hands. She didn't dare tie them loosely—Niko was watching her closely, and the barrel of the pistol had shifted until it was pointing directly at her.

Then she stood up and met Niko's eyes.

"You should never have returned to Zakhar," he told her, breaking the silence that was fraught with danger.

At first she was frozen by the threat confronting her, but then she retreated from him until she came up against the far wall. Niko followed her slowly, as if he knew she couldn't escape, then stopped two feet away. "You should never have agreed to marry Andre," he added, repressed anger in his voice. "Why did you? Was the humiliation of eleven years ago not enough to keep you away from him forever?"

Juliana didn't say anything. She couldn't. Her mind was working feverishly at the sudden revelation that Niko knew more than he should about what had happened eleven years ago, but whatever answer she gave could trigger violence. He was already primed to go off—his expression made that very clear.

Niko brought the gun up to caress her cheek with the barrel. "So beautiful," he said with regret. "I wanted you, did you know that? But it was always Andre with you despite my best efforts. You never looked at another man while he was around." His eyes narrowed until they were mere slits. "I plotted to have you anyway," he continued, his rapacious designs on her obvious. "But you were never alone. You were always with Mara or one of your other friends. I was never able to figure out a way to abduct you without risk to me."

"Andre would have killed you." The breathless words were out of her mouth before she could stop them.

His face contracted with anger and jealousy. "You are right. Even though he had not yet staked his own claim to you, he would have killed me if I touched you against your will." His hand clenched on the gun as he spewed out the hatred that had been building up for years. "Andre, the perfect prince. How I despised that about him. So *damned* perfect. He never put a foot wrong. Like a god. Even my own father wished I could be more like him. And the citizens of Zakhar adored him—why? Why him, and not me? Because he was the Crown Prince, that is why. He had everything. *Everything* that should have been mine save for an accident of birth."

"Aren't you forgetting something?" Juliana asked through stiff lips. "Aren't you forgetting Zax?"

"My brother?" Niko asked dismissively. "No, I had my own plans for Zax." He laughed softly, a sound of pure evil. "Whose gun do you think this is?" His smile told her he planned to kill her with one of Zax's guns and let his brother take the blame for her death. Since they shared the royal residence that had been their father's, Niko had access to everything that was Zax's. It also meant he had access to plant evidence against his brother. "I had plans for both of them," Niko continued. "But it was Andre I wanted to hurt most. And I made him pay. Oh yes, I made him pay in blood."

She managed one word. "How?"

"I followed you that night. You never knew, did you? You were so obvious in your attraction to Andre, it was easy to guess what you would try to do before you left. So I watched and waited. And you did not disappoint me. You were easy to follow, Juliana. For once you were alone, and I almost took you that night. But then I realized letting you go to Andre was better for my long-range plan." He laughed again. "You were so easy to manipulate after that. Almost as easy to manipulate as Andre's father." The barrel of the gun moved down her cheek, brushed her neck, then came to rest against one breast.

She suppressed a shiver of horror. "What did you do, Niko?"

"How do you think Andre's father found out about the two of you?" he asked. "I told him, of course," he said, answering his own question. "He was oblivious to the danger you represented until I brought it to his attention. But then he was determined to keep you apart. You were not of royal blood. You were not even of noble blood. And his obsession with the monarchy meant you were not good enough for his precious son." Niko sneered. "Andre's father was too obsessed to realize I had my own motives for keeping you away from Andre. He refused to believe it was you or no one where Andre was concerned, although I knew. He was pathetically easy to convince that Andre did not really love you—that you were merely a passing fancy—because he wanted to believe."

Inside Juliana was gasping as everything fell neatly into place, but she managed to keep it from her expression. "So it was all your doing?"

He snorted. "Hardly. Give credit where credit is due. I could not order the phone company to keep Andre's calls to you from going through, or yours to him. I could not control the postal service, email and internet in Zakhar. Only he could. And when Andre insisted—in defiance of his father—on serving with his unit when they went to Afghanistan, the king consoled himself with the thought that at least Andre could not go to you in America." His expression turned introspective for a moment. "Too bad Andre did not die in combat as I hoped he would."

He shook that divergent thought off. "No, Juliana, I

merely suggested what the king needed to do, and he did it. All of it. But I knew. Every step of the way, I knew."

He smiled a cold, cruel smile. "I thought the money was a nice touch," he said softly, menacingly. "And the message. That was the one thing you could not forgive, could you? It drove you away from Andre as it was intended to do."

She closed her eyes briefly as guilt washed through her, remembering how very nearly Niko had succeeded in separating her from Andre...permanently. Then she opened her eyes as Niko continued.

"But I had to be sure you would stay away. I could not let you marry Andre and give him heirs, heirs that would supplant Zax and me in the line of succession. So I had to make sure Andre would not pursue you when you did not return to Zakhar as he expected."

Even though she'd already been cold with terror, a chill ran through her as she grasped his meaning. "It was you? You were behind that lying story in the press?"

He laughed once more, and this time Juliana heard the insanity he'd kept hidden all this time. "Brilliant, was it not? I bribed that man to lie about being your lover. And I confirmed it. Confidentially, of course, but I knew I was fairly safe in doing so. The press shield laws in your country meant the reporter would keep his sources confidential. Zakhar's laws are different, but..." He shrugged.

The barrel of the gun moved once more, until it was pointing at Juliana's heart. "*That* is how I made Andre bleed," he gloated. "The only thing that would have made it more perfect was if I had been the man. My revenge would have been complete. But even without that it was bad enough for him. His precious Juliana sleeping with another man, taking a lover other than him. What a blow that was to his heart. And to his ego. He suffered," Niko said, taking a perverse pleasure in the fact. "Oh, how he suffered."

The insane light in his eyes faded for a moment. "I almost overplayed my hand there," he said thoughtfully. "It could have killed Andre's love for you, made him more amenable to his father's constant pressure to marry European royalty and beget heirs. But the temptation to make him bleed was too great to resist." Then he smiled again, and Juliana couldn't prevent the shiver that coursed through her. "But I was counting on the curse of the Marianescus. And I was right."

"Not a curse, Niko," said a stern voice from the other side of the room. "It is our greatest strength."

Niko jerked as if he'd been shot. He swung around to face Andre, who'd stepped out from behind the tapestry covering the secret passageway between his bedroom and Juliana's, and for a second the gun wasn't pointing at Juliana. But before she could escape Niko grabbed her around the waist and pulled her tight against his body, the gun pressed against her temple.

"Not one step closer," he warned.

"Or what?" Andre demanded. "Or you will shoot her?" He shook his head. "You will shoot her anyway. That was your intention the minute you walked into this room with a gun." He took a step toward them, then another.

Niko turned the pistol so it was facing Andre, and Juliana knew this was what Andre had intended, to get the gun away from her head by making himself the target instead. But seeing him in danger didn't make it any easier for her. And besides, Niko was still holding her captive.

"I will shoot you," Niko threatened. "Then her."

Andre shook his head again. "I think not. If you shoot me, you will never inherit the throne. And *that* is what this has all been about. You were very clever to try to throw suspicion on your brother—as my heir he had the best motive. But that will not work this time. Zax is already in custody."

"I do not believe you."

Andre smiled coldly. "Damon and Lukas will swear to it. So if I die here you will not escape." He paused a second. "You have tried three times to kill me, yes? Not just the helicopter, but the assassination attempts—supposedly by traditionalists like Zax—that was your doing."

The sudden stiffening in Niko's body betrayed him, and Andre nodded with certainty. "That was your plan all along. To kill me and have Zax blamed for it. You would have made sure there was evidence pointing to him, evidence that he had arranged my murder to look like an accident or a politically motivated assassination. Just as you tried to have Juliana killed and make it appear to be an accident—an accident that pointed to your brother as the only one with a motive. But you failed all across the board. You failed to kill me, just as you failed to kill Juliana."

"I did not fail!"

"Do not lie to yourself. You failed." Andre's assertion seemed to be deliberate provocation. "Juliana is still alive." He took another step forward. "And so am I." He shook his head a third time. "No, Niko, you will not shoot me. No matter what, you cannot afford to show your hand in my death."

"But you will be dead," Niko grated, and Juliana wondered how it was no one had ever heard the insanity in his voice before. "It would almost be worth it."

"Yes, I will be dead," Andre agreed, taking another step. "And your brother will sit on the throne in my place, not you. You will not even be his heir, because you will be dead, too, in the most gruesome way imaginable. Zakhar's laws have not moved with the times, not where high treason is concerned. You should know. You have blocked me on the Privy Council every time I have attempted to change that law. Do not forget," he said softly, "regicide—even attempted regicide—is high treason."

The gun wavered in Niko's hand, and Juliana wondered what Andre meant. She didn't have long to wait for an explanation. "Hanged. Drawn. Quartered." Andre's voice was cold and calm, sounding almost disinterested. "Not a pretty prospect, is it. Disemboweled while still alive. Emasculated. Watching parts of yourself burned before your eyes. Would you be dead before they cut your body into four parts, then beheaded you, I wonder? Or would you still be alive at that point?"

Juliana flinched at the description of the execution awaiting Niko should he succeed in killing Andre. She didn't want anyone to die like that, not even if Niko managed to kill both of them.

"No one has died that way in more than three hundred years!" But fear joined the note of insanity in Niko's voice.

"But no one committed high treason during that time," Andre explained reasonably. "So there was no need." The next step he took brought him almost within arm's reach of the gun aimed at his chest.

Cursing, Niko stepped backward, dragging Juliana with him, the gun still pointing at Andre. "Not another step. Or I *will* shoot you."

Niko's attention was distracted as the bound bodyguard staggered to his feet at that critical moment—blood trickling down the side of his neck—and tried to thrust himself between Andre and Niko's gun even as he fought the belt binding his hands. In that instant Juliana realized Niko's grasp had loosened. She knew he thought her of little consequence, just a pawn in his deadly sparring match with Andre. Like most men he believed her seemingly fragile appearance was all there was to her. But he was wrong. Dead wrong.

She twisted suddenly in Niko's hold, using a move Terry O'Dare had taught Tessa in *Jetsam*. A move Dirk had taught her. And as she twisted she knocked Niko's arm up just as he fired. But Andre had already moved lightning fast, hurtling himself at his cousin, taking both of them down.

The two men struggled on the ground for possession of the gun, but it was an uneven contest. Andre wrested the gun from Niko's hand, then skittered it across the floor as he pressed his right forearm against his cousin's throat. "I should kill you," Andre said in a deadly voice, not even breathing hard. Niko whimpered in fear, futilely clawing at the arm cutting off his oxygen. "Give me a reason why I should not."

Juliana raced across the room and picked up the gun, then turned to the two men on the floor, ignoring the bound bodyguard in her desire to prevent Andre from making a fatal mistake. "Don't, Andre. Please don't."

"You plead for his life?" he asked her, still in that same deadly voice, but without taking his eyes off his cousin. "When he would have taken yours without hesitation?"

"I don't care about him. I just don't want him to die at your hands. Not like this. Please," she added softly.

The decision hung in the balance for seconds, then Andre cursed under his breath. With a swift motion he jumped to his feet and jerked Niko to his, holding his cousin prisoner with a death grip on his shirt. A sudden pounding on the locked door to her suite made Juliana realize someone must have heard the gunshot and come running. Andre's bodyguard? One of the palace guards from the floor below? Or just someone from the palace staff? Whoever it was, they didn't know about the secret passageway. They only knew the entrance off the corridor.

Her eyes met Andre's. "Do I let them in?" she asked, her pulse beating so hard in her throat she almost couldn't get the words out. If Andre was going to kill Niko, there was no way she was going to open the door and let another witness enter the room, but... *Please, God,* she pleaded in her mind. *Please don't let him do this.*

Niko was still whimpering, begging for his life, and Andre spared him one contemptuous glance before turning his attention back to Juliana and nodding. "Let them in, little one. I will not kill him...since you ask it. I can deny you nothing."

# Chapter 19

They weren't able to leave Zakhar that night, after all. Niko's arrest meant both Andre and Juliana had to stay until they had given statements to the police, until Niko had been safely incarcerated and interrogated, and until his coconspirators had been disclosed and arrested.

Niko had talked. The threat of a trial for high treason with its gruesome punishment made him spill his guts in an effort to reach a plea agreement that would at least keep him alive. Prince Xavier, traditionalist that he was, had argued vociferously against leniency when he learned of the attempts his own brother had made on Andre's life, not to mention Juliana's. "High treason," he stated flatly to his cousin, "should only have one outcome—even for my brother."

But Andre, with Juliana's voice pleading with him to spare Niko's life ringing in his ears, agreed to leniency, providing his cousin confess everything and name the men involved.

The conspiracy had been small, according to Niko. Two of the men were already dead—the supposedly "politically motivated" assassination attempts had resulted in the deaths of the would-be assassins. Which left five men, all told, including him. And none of the conspirators were in it for anything other than money. No rebellion against Andre's rule or the policy changes he was implementing. No political agenda. Just money.

As Lukas had suspected, one of the five—the only American—was a lighting technician on the *King's Ransom* crew who'd been seduced into attempted murder by the money that had been waved under his nose. He confessed the minute he was arrested.

One of the conspirators was a member of the Zakharian National Forces with military clearance and access to the royal helicopter, lured into treason by his own greed. He, too, confessed when he was arrested and threw himself on the king's mercy.

The other two conspirators, one of whom was the driver of the Mercedes-Benz that had tried to run Juliana down, were Russians with lengthy criminal records and were members of the Russian Mafia, according to Interpol. Their participation in the conspiracy was no surprise given Niko's ability to pay handsomely. Andre's only question had been how his cousin had known these members of the underworld, but that had been explained with one word—*drugs*. The *Bratva* had been supplying Niko with drugs for years.

It was very late by the time Andre returned to the palace from the Drago prison where Niko had been taken to give his confession. There was still a massive amount of work to be accomplished nailing down what would eventually be a mountain of evidence, but all four of Niko's still-living coconspirators had been rounded up and were now safely incarcerated in the same prison. Andre had left only after Zax assured him there was nothing more either of them could do at that point.

The two cousins sat silently in the back of the limousine for the first part of the ride, with Damon, the king's bodyguard, sitting in front with the driver. Andre fought off a desire to close his eyes in exhaustion and instead murmured to Zax, "I am not quite convinced Niko was completely forthcoming in his confession."

Zax shot him a sharp look. "You felt that, too? I did not want to say it in front of the others, but there was a moment—just a moment—when I thought Niko was about to reveal another name. Then he changed his mind. And knowing my brother—coward that he is—I do not think anything short of torture will be successful in wringing further information from him at this point. Especially if he thinks you are satisfied with what he has already revealed."

Andre's lips tightened. "There are times when I could wish…"

"Yes, but you cannot. You would not be the man you are if you could. Let me deal with my brother—it is the least I can do for you. I will work on his fears—make him more afraid of me than he is of whoever he might be shielding. That might yield results."

Both men fell silent. Then Zax added quietly, for Andre's ears alone, "My resignation will be on your desk in the morning."

"Do not bother. I will refuse to accept it, and you will have wasted your time to no purpose."

"You cannot refuse to accept it. The scandal—"

"The scandal will be less of a scandal with you by my side," Andre insisted.

"There will always be those who say there is no smoke without fire. There will always be those who believe I had a hand in Niko's schemes." There was a bitter edge to Zax's voice. "*I* am the primary beneficiary should you die without sons, not Niko."

"Let them believe what they want to believe." Andre smiled wryly. "Is that not what you told me years ago? Those who wish to see evil will see evil. You cannot live your life based on what people believe of you. Only on what you believe of yourself."

"But—"

"You know your own innocence. As do I."

Silence stretched between them. Then Zax said in a low voice, "Thank you for that." Another long silence was broken when Zax asked, "Do me a favor?"

"Anything."

"Have sons. Soon."

Andre laughed, and Zax joined him. "That is my intention," Andre assured him when their laughter subsided. "Not to cut you out of the succession, but because Juliana has agreed to be my wife."

"Finally."

Andre breathed deeply, nodded and smiled with intense satisfaction. "Finally."

Quiet reigned for a moment before Andre said, "Tell me something."

"Of course."

"You have known my plans regarding Juliana from

the beginning. Yet never once since she arrived did you speak a word of encouragement. Never once did you express sympathy for my struggle. Why is that?"

A look of blank surprise spread over Zax's face. "Was the outcome ever in doubt? Surely you did not think…?"

"Not that you wished otherwise. But yes, I did wonder why you kept silent."

Zax made a sound of disbelief. "You have never failed in anything you set your mind to. This I have known since you were a small boy. How do you think I came to be called Zax?" When Andre lifted a questioning brow, Zax laughed softly. "You were two, I think. Yes, two. You could not pronounce Xavier, so you called me Zax and refused to call me by any other name. You called me Zax so often everyone in the family began to call me by that name, too."

Andre smiled his faint smile and shook his head. "Surely not."

"You were intrepid even then," Zax insisted. "You were no more than five when you set yourself up in opposition to your father. You were Mara's champion from the day she was born—did you think I could not see that? You would not bend then, and you have not changed since. Your strength of will is already legendary. It never occurred to me you could doubt yourself in this. It never occurred to me you would not succeed in winning Juliana's heart again. It was only a matter of time."

Andre laughed under his breath. "If you knew the thoughts running through my mind on occasion, you would not be so sure of me. I am not invincible."

Zax shook his head. "I know you better than you know yourself. I would never bet against you, for I would surely lose."

* * *

Back at the palace Andre immediately went in search of Juliana with Damon at his side. He was more than exhausted, running on reserves alone, having been awake for nearly thirty-six hours at this point. But he'd promised Juliana they would talk once everything was resolved, and he couldn't seek his own bed until he'd kept his word.

He found her in the little library, curled up on a sofa, fast asleep. Lukas was sitting in the chair across from her, doing nothing but watching her. Guarding her. Protecting her. Keeping him company was Marek Zale. Both men stood when Andre entered the room, but Marek reached him first.

"I failed you, Sire," Marek said. "My orders were to find Prince Nikolai and arrest him. Instead he almost killed both you and Miss Richardson."

Andre shook his head. "The failure was mine. I should have held off announcing my engagement to Miss Richardson until whoever was trying to kill her was caught. I knew better, but I—" *Wanted to shout my triumph to the world,* he thought but didn't say. "No, Marek," he insisted. "No blame attaches to you. If blame there is, it belongs to me and me alone for not realizing sooner the threat Prince Nikolai represented—the signs were there but I was blind to them."

"But, Sire, I—"

Andre held up a hand to interrupt him. "Do not argue, Marek. Learn from this experience as I have done, and put it to good use when planning the protection detail for Miss Richardson when she becomes my queen." He added softly, "I am relying on you."

Andre's words had the desired effect, and he watched

in silence as Marek left the room after he was dismissed. When he turned back he found Lukas and Damon standing shoulder to shoulder in front of him, at military attention, not saying a word. Puzzled, Andre asked, "What is this?"

"We failed you, too, Sire," Lukas said shortly.

Damon explained further, "We were convinced Prince Xavier was guilty based only on his obvious motive, not taking his character into account. We jumped to a false conclusion. We even did our best to convince you of his guilt. To pressure you to have him arrested. We failed you."

"Ahhh," Andre said, glad to have the riddle solved, but aware this posed a tricky dilemma. For the first time in forever he didn't know what to say to these men. Men who were not only the best of the best and who took what they saw as failure personally, but men for whom he felt friendship. Just as with Marek Zale, he had to find the words to let them know he understood their feelings of shame, but that no blame attached to them. None. Otherwise, their sense of failure would ruin them as fighting men because they would always second-guess themselves in the future, and that would dull their reaction time.

Then it came to him. "It took great courage for you to accuse your commanding officer, knowing that if you were wrong your careers could be destroyed. And yet you were willing to risk that, and more, to protect me. To protect Miss Richardson. Rest assured, though, you did not convince me of Zax's guilt." He smiled his faint smile. "Nothing could have done that."

Lukas started to speak, but Andre overrode him. "And by taking Zax into custody—by providing him with an ironclad alibi—you may have saved my life, and Miss Richardson's, too, because Niko could not afford to kill us unless he could blame it on his brother."

When he finally dismissed them to wait outside so he could talk with Juliana in private, Andre wanted nothing more than to sleep for the next twelve hours. But he couldn't do that. Not yet. He glanced in Juliana's direction and was surprised to find she was already awake. Awake, and aware of everything that had just taken place.

"You heard?"

She nodded, then held out her arms to him, arms that folded protectively around him when he went into her embrace. And as he lay there with her on the sofa, his head cradled against her breast, he realized he'd been wrong. There was one person who was closer to him than Zax. Closer even than his sister, Mara. One person he could trust enough to let his weakness show.

Juliana.

A woman strong enough to save herself and him. Strong enough to take a moral stand against him, to be his conscience. Strong enough to lend him her strength when his own wasn't enough. *My very own Eleonora,* Andre thought, just before sleep claimed him. He never knew Juliana lay awake through the night holding him, guarding him as he slept the sleep of the just.

The subsequent scandal caused by the arrests of the five conspirators couldn't be avoided. The news spread like wildfire, and the paparazzi had a field day. Rumor and speculation were rampant. There was scarcely a Zakharian who didn't condemn Prince Nikolai's actions as treasonous and clamor for his swift execution, the same way Prince Xavier had done. But when Andre announced he would commute any death sentence handed down to any of the five, all of Zakhar stoutly held that their king was well within his rights and praised him for his mercy.

"Mercy that should be credited to you," Andre told Juliana in private. She just shook her head and smiled.

It wasn't until two days later, after the initial furor had died down, that Andre and Juliana were free to leave Zakhar.

Juliana stood at Sabrina's grave with Andre, his strong arms around her, holding her as she cried. Shielding her from the paparazzi and their long-lens cameras. Pulling her face into the comforting shelter of his chest as she wept, not just for Sabrina lying so peacefully in her grave and for her twin daughters still in neonatal intensive care, but for Dirk, too. Dirk, who stood stoically at the graveside, his face displaying no emotion whatsoever, lost in a world grown dark and cold without Bree, a world where he blamed himself for her death.

*"This is my punishment,"* he'd told Juliana, his eyes wild with grief when she'd gone to see him the day before. "*God is punishing* me, *but* she *paid the price.*" And nothing Juliana said to him made the slightest difference. Nothing she said seemed to break through that impenetrable barrier. And now Dirk had shuttered himself against everyone and everything. Against friendship. Against every human emotion. Even against fatherhood—he'd only visited his tiny daughters twice in the neonatal ICU, both times for less than ten minutes.

Memories of Dirk and Sabrina came back to Juliana as she stood there. Good memories and painful ones.

Remembering with a pang of guilt how she'd been envious of her friends and the love they shared. Not that she'd wanted to take anything away from them; she'd just wanted what they had. Now she did…but now they didn't. *Now Bree's dead and Dirk might not survive.* She would carry that grief…and guilt…for a long time.

Later that night Juliana lay cradled in Andre's arms in her bedroom. Her little house in the gated community in the Los Angeles foothills—not far from the DeWinters' home—had been her solitary haven for years, and she'd made this bedroom and the large attached master bathroom with its whirlpool tub a place of refuge from the world. No man had ever been here with her…until Andre.

As they lay together in the aftermath of loving, they both realized they'd suffered for nothing. Nothing except the determination of a dead king and a covetous prince to keep them apart. Now they both knew they had remained faithful, not just to each other, but to their love. Forever and a day.

Andre's arms tightened around her. "It occurs to me I have never asked you, Juliana."

She nuzzled his shoulder dreamily. "Asked me what?"

"To marry me." She caught her breath, and he heard it. "Why did you not tell me I was still too arrogant, little one? Why did you not tell me I should not assume your consent when I placed that ring on your finger?" He laughed softly. "You should not let me be too sure of you, Juliana. Did no one ever tell you that?"

She chuckled and snuggled closer. "I didn't dare say no to you," she teased. "Not after you threatened I would have no other lover than you from that moment on. I was terrified." She kissed him as she said it, so he'd know she didn't really mean it.

He was silent for a moment. "I did not mean to make that threat. I swore to myself I would wait for you to come to me, and then I would know you loved me enough to take on the arduous job of being my wife. Being my queen." He sighed. "It will not be easy, little one. But then, I think you know something about the life I lead because in many ways you have led the same life. Very little privacy, and what little I have I guard fiercely. Beyond that, there will be times I must put duty to Zakhar above my love for you, as I have done before. Zakhar…but no other woman."

"I know." Her voice was little more than a whisper in the darkness.

"Most of the sacrifices will be yours. Your country. Your freedom. Your friends. Not that you will never see them again, but your royal duties will have to take precedence. Zakhar will have to become your first priority."

"No," she told him firmly. "Not my first priority. *You* will be that. Always. Then our children. Zakhar will have to take third place."

He lay very still beneath her. "You cannot know how I have longed to see you with our child," he said, obviously deeply moved by her assumption they would have children together. He shifted her so he could place a large hand on her stomach and caress her there. Tenderly. "That day on the set…seeing you as Eleonora about to give birth, I wanted that to be our child in your womb. And that night I realized I had been lying to myself thinking I could ever let you leave. I cannot."

His voice was harsh in the darkness. "I am no gentleman, little one. Know that. Believe it. I would have killed Niko in an instant merely for threatening you. Merely for putting the look of terror in your eyes I saw when I entered your bedroom."

"But you didn't kill him," she reminded him softly.

"Only at your request." He breathed sharply. "There is a savage side of me you have not seen until now. The civilized man the world sees is merely a veneer. Can you still love me knowing the truth? Knowing I am no gentleman?" He didn't give her a chance to respond before adding in a pain-racked voice it hurt her to hear, "The other day I told you I can deny you nothing, but that was a lie. There is one thing I *can* deny you—only one. Your freedom. Can you live with me knowing that now you are mine again I will never let you go?"

"Don't let me go," she whispered to him, soothing him with a gentle caress. "I know you're not a gentleman, but I don't care. Just love me, and don't ever let me go."

# *Epilogue*

With all the pomp and circumstance for which the fairy-tale kingdom was justly famous, Zakhar celebrated the royal wedding on the first day of December. The bride's distinguished father—the former US Ambassador—was there to lead her down the aisle. The groom's best man was his cousin Zax. And Princess Mara was the matron of honor—the word *matron* taking nearly everyone in Zakhar by surprise, since almost no one knew she had married the previous January. But her plebeian husband—a tall, handsome man who squired her everywhere with an unmistakably protective air—soon became a crowd favorite because of his obvious devotion to her.

While there had been some grumbling from certain older factions within the country that the king was marrying an actress and not a scion of European nobility, not to mention the short engagement period, the younger generation was almost universally thrilled. The fact that Juliana had spent her teen years in Zakhar and spoke Zakharan went a long way toward dissipating any criticism. And when the announcement was made that the new queen was retiring from acting to devote her time to her future subjects and her royal duties there was national jubilation.

National jubilation reached epic proportions ten months later when the official announcement went out on thick cream-colored stationery, hand-inscribed, and embossed in gold leaf with the royal seal of Zakhar. "Their Majesties, the King and Queen of Zakhar, are pleased to announce the birth of Crown Prince Raoul Theodore Alexei Stepan of the House of Marianescu."

The news bulletin stated, "Her Royal Majesty Queen Juliana was safely delivered of a son at 8:27 a.m. today. Her Royal Majesty and her son, the Crown Prince, are both doing well."

Juliana lay in her hospital bed gazing at the downy-haired baby boy in her arms, then at the man sprawled in the chair by the window, fast asleep. Maternal tenderness for both father and son made her smile. Andre had been terrified in the delivery room—determined not to betray it in front of her, but terrified all the same. Worried something would go wrong. Afraid deep down he'd lose her in childbirth the way his father had lost his mother giving birth to Mara. Not that he would say that to her. Oh no! He'd tried so hard to hide his fear, not wanting to alarm her in any way, but she knew him too well.

Her smile deepened. She'd wanted Andre with her, but it almost seemed as if she were giving *him* support rather than the other way around. And then, when their son was born relatively quickly and everything had gone so well, Andre had quietly fallen apart. His tears had been hot against her breast as he'd buried his head there, swearing he'd never put her through that ordeal again, his fingers desperately clutching her hands. *But he will,* Juliana told herself with another smile, a secret one this time. She was ecstatic over the birth of their first child—the son he needed to carry on the unbroken line of Marianescus ruling Zakhar—but she was also looking toward the future and the other children she would give him someday. Daughters as well as sons. Daughters he would love and cherish—unlike his own father—as much as his sons. *Someday soon.*

Andre had been ready with a list of names. He'd adamantly refused to let the doctors tell them if Juliana was carrying a boy or a girl ahead of time, but he had names for both already picked out. Raoul Theodore Alexei Stepan. Juliana had groggily listened to the string of names, understanding each choice and approving it until she came to the last one. Raoul—that was easy. Raoul was the firstborn son of the first Andre Alexei, and one of the greatest kings Zakhar had known. A good omen. Theodore—that was the masculine version of part of his beloved sister's name, Mara Theodora, and meant *divine gift*, another good omen. Alexei—that was easy, too, named after himself and the first Andre Alexei.

But Stepan?

Juliana had been puzzled until Andre had explained, and then her tears had come. "When he died in the landslide I held him in my arms and closed his eyes so he would appear to merely be sleeping," he'd confessed in a low voice. "But I could think of no words to comfort his mother other than to say Stepan was a good name for a son." With that she had loved him anew.

"I am blessed," she told her son quietly now. "I have you and your father. Nothing can top that, not even the success of *King's Ransom*." Her final movie had opened that summer—to a blockbuster box office and unbelievably glowing reviews—and was still going strong in the fall despite the fact that neither she nor Dirk had done any promotion for the movie at all. Of course, all the fairy-tale publicity surrounding her wedding to Andre—which had been broadcast to nearly five hundred million viewers around the world—and her subsequent pregnancy hadn't hurt ticket sales. There was already insider buzz of Academy Award nominations.

She'd finally convinced Andre to screen *King's Ransom* with her...but not until after the movie opened to the public. Not until she was about to deliver his child. As if the on-screen intimacy between Juliana and Dirk made him uncomfortable...until he could believe without a shadow of a doubt that nothing would ever separate them again.

Thoughts of Dirk and *King's Ransom* reminded Juliana of her friend Sabrina and the baby daughters she'd given her husband before she died. Against all odds Linden and Laurel had not only survived, but thrived—God had answered her prayers with a resounding "Yes!" where the babies were concerned. But not with Dirk, and Juliana's heart still ached for him.

The sacrifices she'd had to make in her life had not been as bad as Andre had feared when he'd asked her to marry him. Juliana had thrown herself into her new role as Zakhar's queen with the same wholehearted enthusiasm she'd always shown with any role, although this was real and not make-believe.

She hadn't been content with merely the figurehead position taken by previous queens in their charitable endeavors, either. No, she'd been an active participant, especially with those things near and dear to her heart—such as anything to do with children. Pregnancy hadn't slowed her down in the slightest, except at the very end.

And through it all she'd had Mara's friendship to sustain her. Mara's example as a royal princess to guide her. Not to mention Mara's advice on her pregnancy. Mara's twins—a healthy boy and a girl—had been born only three months ahead of Raoul.

Juliana glanced over at Andre again and saw he was finally awake. Awake and staring at her and their son, love for them both lending a radiance to his tired face. She held her hand out to him, and he came to sit on the edge of the bed. "Meet your son," she told him with a soft smile, turning the baby to face him. She took their son's tiny fist and placed it in her husband's hand, amused at how tentatively he stared at it, as if afraid something so small would break if he breathed. "Look, Andre," she said tenderly, inserting a finger to open the tiny fist. "Raoul has your fingers."

His eyes met hers, a shadow in their green depths. "Did you think I needed that proof?"

She shook her head slowly. "No more than the first Andre Alexei needed proof when he acknowledged Eleonora's son was his before it was confirmed." Her smile faded and she gazed at him with a solemn expression. "When I was eighteen I wondered if my children would inherit that endearing genetic defect from their father. Then later I knew they wouldn't…because I would never have children."

He glanced down at the baby in her arms. "But you did."

"Only with you." Her sudden radiant smile coaxed a smile from him in return. "Only because you paid a king's ransom to bring me back to you." She cupped his cheek with one hand, love welling up in her as she quoted softly, "'Two hearts as one…'"

He turned his face to kiss her palm, his warm, firm lips sending a thrill coursing through her body the way they always had. The way they always would. "'…Forever and a day,'" he finished for her in the deep voice she loved. "'Forever and a day.'"

* * * * *

*Niko's allies have not yet been discovered—*

*Don't miss the next thrilling installment in the* MAN ON A MISSION *miniseries,*
*ALEC'S ROYAL ASSIGNMENT,*
*coming in August!*

*And don't forget the previous titles in the miniseries:*
*REILLY'S RETURN*
*CODY WALKER'S WOMAN*
*McKINNON'S ROYAL MISSION*

Available July 7, 2015

### #1855 HOW TO SEDUCE A CAVANAUGH

*Cavanaugh Justice* • by Marie Ferrarella

Kelly Cavanaugh and Kane Durant could barely be friends, much less partners, and never in a million years lovers. But while working together to solve a series of seemingly random home invasions, whatever chill existed between them transforms into a sizzling passion...

### #1856 COLTON'S COWBOY CODE

*The Coltons of Oklahoma* • by Melissa Cutler

Pregnant and desperate, Hannah Grayson never expects to face the baby's father at a job interview! Cowboy Brett Colton gives her the position and vows to protect her and their unborn baby, but when long-buried secrets turn deadly, no one on the ranch is safe.

### #1857 UNDERCOVER WITH A SEAL

*Code: Warrior SEALs* • by Cindy Dees

Eve Hankova demanded answers from the Russian mob about her missing brother, thereby adding herself to their list of enemies. Her only shot at answers—and survival—lies with her reluctant rescuer, a burned-out and far-too-appealing navy SEAL.

### #1858 TEMPTING TARGET

*Dangerous in Dallas* • by Addison Fox

After priceless jewels are discovered in the floor of a prominent Dallas bridal boutique, a detective and the alluring wedding caterer he's protecting race to find the villain plotting to recover the gems...and perhaps they'll give in to a simmering attraction, which might necessitate a walk down the aisle!

---

**YOU CAN FIND MORE INFORMATION ON UPCOMING HARLEQUIN® TITLES, FREE EXCERPTS AND MORE AT WWW.HARLEQUIN.COM.**

# REQUEST YOUR FREE BOOKS!
## 2 FREE NOVELS PLUS 2 FREE GIFTS!

**⊕ HARLEQUIN®**

## ROMANTIC suspense

### *Sparked by danger, fueled by passion*

**YES!** Please send me 2 FREE Harlequin® Romantic Suspense novels and my 2 FREE gifts (gifts are worth about $10). After receiving them, if I don't wish to receive any more books, I can return the shipping statement marked "cancel." If I don't cancel, I will receive 4 brand-new novels every month and be billed just $4.74 per book in the U.S. or $5.49 per book in Canada. That's a savings of at least 12% off the cover price! It's quite a bargain! Shipping and handling is just 50¢ per book in the U.S. and 75¢ per book in Canada.* I understand that accepting the 2 free books and gifts places me under no obligation to buy anything. I can always return a shipment and cancel at any time. Even if I never buy another book, the two free books and gifts are mine to keep forever.

240/340 HDN GH3P

| Name | (PLEASE PRINT) | |
|------|----------------|--|
| Address | | Apt. # |
| City | State/Prov. | Zip/Postal Code |

Signature (if under 18, a parent or guardian must sign)

### Mail to the **Reader Service:**
**IN U.S.A.:** P.O. Box 1867, Buffalo, NY 14240-1867
**IN CANADA:** P.O. Box 609, Fort Erie, Ontario L2A 5X3

**Want to try two free books from another line?**
**Call 1-800-873-8635 or visit www.ReaderService.com.**

* Terms and prices subject to change without notice. Prices do not include applicable taxes. Sales tax applicable in N.Y. Canadian residents will be charged applicable taxes. Offer not valid in Quebec. This offer is limited to one order per household. Not valid for current subscribers to Harlequin Romantic Suspense books. All orders subject to credit approval. Credit or debit balances in a customer's account(s) may be offset by any other outstanding balance owed by or to the customer. Please allow 4 to 6 weeks for delivery. Offer available while quantities last.

**Your Privacy**—The Reader Service is committed to protecting your privacy. Our Privacy Policy is available online at www.ReaderService.com or upon request from the Reader Service.

We make a portion of our mailing list available to reputable third parties that offer products we believe may interest you. If you prefer that we not exchange your name with third parties, or if you wish to clarify or modify your communication preferences, please visit us at www.ReaderService.com/consumerschoice or write to us at Reader Service Preference Service, P.O. Box 9062, Buffalo, NY 14240-9062. Include your complete name and address.

SPECIAL EXCERPT FROM

 **HARLEQUIN**

## ROMANTIC suspense

*Pregnant and desperate, Hannah Grayson never
expects to face the baby's father at a job interview!
Cowboy Brett Colton vows to protect them, but someone
dangerous is stalking the ranch...*

*Read on for a sneak peek at*
*COLTON'S COWBOY CODE by Melissa Cutler,*
*the latest in Harlequin® Romantic Suspense's*
**THE COLTONS OF OKLAHOMA series.**

"You, Brett Colton, are as slippery as a snake-oil salesman."

"I prefer to think of myself as stubborn and single-minded. Not so different from you."

The suspicion on Hannah's face melted away a little bit more and she closed her lips around the fork in a way that gave Brett some ideas too filthy for his own good.

He cleared his throat, snapping his focus back to the task at hand. "When my parents remodeled the big house, they designed separate wings for each of their six children, but I'm the only one of the six who lives there full-time. You would have your own wing, your own bathroom with a big old tub and plenty of privacy."

For the first time, she seemed to be seriously considering his offer. Time to go for broke. He handed her another slice of bacon, which she accepted without a word.

"Where are you living now?" he said. "Can you look me in the eye and tell me it's a good, long-term situation for you and the baby?"

She snapped a tiny bit of bacon off and popped it into her mouth. "It's not like I'm living in some abandoned building. I'm staying with my best friend, Lori, and her boyfriend, Drew. It's not ideal, but with the money from this job, I'll be able to afford my own place."

"And until that first paycheck, you'll live at the ranch." He pressed his lips together. That had come out a smidge more demanding than he'd wanted it to.

Their gazes met and held. "Are you mandating that? Will the job offer depend on me accepting the temporary housing?"

Oh, how he wanted to say yes to that. "No. But you should agree to it anyway. Your own bed, regular meals made by a top-rated personal chef, and your commute would be five minutes to the ranch office. The only traffic would be some overly excitable ranch dogs."

"I know why you're doing all this, but I really am grateful for all you're offering—the job and the accommodations. In all honesty, this went a lot better than I thought it would."

"The job interview?"

"No, telling you about the baby. I thought you'd either hate me or propose to me."

Brett didn't miss a beat. "I still might."

*Don't miss COLTON'S COWBOY CODE*
*by Melissa Cutler, part of*
**THE COLTONS OF OKLAHOMA** *series:*

*COLTON COWBOY PROTECTOR by Beth Cornelison*
*COLTON'S COWBOY CODE by Melissa Cutler*
*THE TEMPTATION OF DR. COLTON by Karen Whiddon*
*PROTECTING THE COLTON BRIDE by Elle James*
*SECOND CHANCE COLTON by Marie Ferrarella*
*THE COLTON BODYGUARD by Carla Cassidy*

*Available wherever Harlequin® Romantic Suspense*
*books and ebooks are sold.*
www.Harlequin.com

HRSEXP0615R2

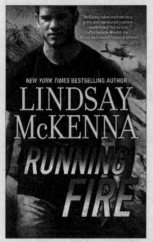